THE FAVORED QUEEN

Also by Carolly Erickson

the
FAVORED
QUEEN

A Novel of Henry VIII's Third Wife

Carolly Erickson

ST. MARTIN'S GRIFFIN

NEW YORK

THE FAVORED QUEEN. Copyright © 2011 by Carolly Erickson. All rights reserved. Printed in the United States of America. For information, address St. Martin's Press, 175 Fifth Avenue, New York, N.Y. 10010.

www.stmartins.com

The Library of Congress has cataloged the hardcover edition as follows:

Erickson, Carolly, 1943–
    The favored queen : a novel of Henry VIII's third wife / Carolly Erickson. — 1st ed.
        p. cm.
    ISBN 978-0-312-59690-3
    1. Jane Seymour, Queen, consort of Henry VIII, King of England, 1509?–1537—Fiction. 2. Queens—Great Britain—Fiction. 3. Great Britain—History—Henry VIII, 1509–1547—Fiction. 4. England—Fiction. I. Title. II. Title: Henry VIII's third wife.
    PS3605.R53F38 2011
    813'.6—dc22

                                                                              2011024757

ISBN 978-1-250-00719-3 (trade paperback)

First St. Martin's Griffin Edition: August 2012

10 9 8 7 6 5 4 3 2 1

ONE

H AS she lost her baby?"

My question hung in the air, unanswered.

The three Spanish midwives, brought from Legrogno especially to attend Queen Catherine at this, her tenth delivery, did not meet my steady gaze but looked down at the thick carpet at their feet. The queen's closest friend and principal lady in waiting, Maria de Salinas, her expression somber and her shoulders rounded in defeat, stood loyally beside her mistress's bed but said nothing. The surgeons who had been summoned by King Henry to attend the queen were nowhere to be seen.

Queen Catherine lay asleep in her high carved wooden bed, mouth agape, her sparse greying auburn hair spread out over her lace-trimmed pillow, the pillow sweat-stained and rumpled as were the bedclothes. Her face was haggard, weary. As those of us who served her knew well, she had been struggling to give birth ever since the previous evening, and it was clear to me now, as I looked down at her, that the effort had taken all her strength. She looked like a woman nearer in age to sixty than forty, though her fortieth birthday had been celebrated by her entire household not long before.

As I watched, she began to murmur in her sleep, as if troubled by disturbing dreams. Her small white wrinkled hands, the fingers bent and swollen, clutched convulsively at the satin counterpane.

I glanced around the darkened bedchamber, taking in the closely drawn thick curtains of purple damask, the heavy, old-fashioned furnishings the queen had brought from Spain many years earlier when she came to the English court as a bride, the religious pictures and crucifixes on the paneled walls, the elaborately embroidered prie-dieu, embroidered by the queen herself, where I had so often seen her kneeling in prayer, the implements of torture (as I thought of them) used by the midwives and laid out on a table beside the bed. Knives, probes, metal clamps and pincers. Bowls and towels, powders and flasks full of medicines. Cruel tongs used, I knew, to reach in and grasp a resistant infant trapped inside a diseased womb. I shuddered at the sight of them, and looked away.

Another sight also made me shudder. A plain wooden chest stood against one wall of the room, its lid not quite closed. Protruding from one corner was a bloody cloth. A sheet, I thought. Hearing me approach, the midwives must have tucked the bloodstained sheets hastily into the chest, and left one corner out.

The pungent odor of lavender filled the room. Lavender, given to women after childbirth to induce a restful calm and sleep. And there was another odor as well. The sharp, unpleasant odor of opium. I had smelled it often, for my father's physician prescribed it for him to ease the pains of his gout.

So the queen had been given opium to assuage her labor and

to induce the sweat trance believed to lessen the fever that carried off so many women after giving birth. Opium, that helped the mother but often (so I had heard it said) cost the child's life.

I was still waiting for an answer to my question. There had been a delivery, of that I was certain. But what of the child? We had not heard the cry of the newborn, the joyous shouts of welcome and triumph from the midwives and physicians when the newborn was a boy.

All was quiet in the room, except for the sound of the queen's ragged breathing. Then I heard a stifled sob. One of the midwives had tears rolling down her olive-tinted cheeks.

"Will no one tell me plainly?" I demanded. "Has she lost her baby?"

After a pause, Maria de Salinas looked at me and gave the slightest nod.

"He lived for an hour," she said. "Only an hour. He was baptized." At these words Maria and the other women crossed themselves. "We prayed," Maria went on. "But it was the Lord's will to take him."

My heart sank. Once more, I thought. Once more, to hope month after long month for a living child, and then to be so cruelly disappointed. I could only imagine the queen's deep sorrow and dismay.

"Has the king been informed?"

"No, Mistress Seymour," Maria answered in her heavily accented English. "It was the queen's wish that he not be informed for a little while yet."

But I had my orders. King Henry had insisted before leaving for the hunt that should the queen's child be born while he was away, a messenger would be sent to him at once. It was my responsibility to follow the royal order.

I left the bedchamber and sought out Queen Catherine's gentleman usher Griffith Richards, giving him the sad news and instructing him to send word to the king.

"I will go myself, Mistress Seymour," he said. "I know where the huntsmen are today."

"Ride slowly then," I said softly. "The queen is in no hurry to let her husband know what has happened."

He sighed and nodded. "Yet again," he said. "Yet again." He turned and left the room, and I noticed that he did not make haste.

Several hours later Maria de Salinas came to me.

"Mistress Seymour, Her Highness is asking for you."

I followed her at once into the royal bedchamber where Queen Catherine, out of bed and dressed in a becoming, loose-fitting gown of fine magenta wool trimmed in miniver, was seated before her pier glass.

"Ah, Jane," she said as I entered, "gentle, kind Jane. Soothe me. Brush out my hair."

"Yes, Your Majesty."

I took the soft brush from the dressing table and began to gently run it through the thin strands. I saw the queen's eyes close in pleasure as I did so.

"I must not let the king see me in my tired state. I must try to be pleasant to look at when he comes, when I greet him. After all, he will be tired from his hunt, and in need of refreshment and rest. He will not be in a mood to hear bad news about our child."

"May the Lord bless the little one and take him to His bosom," I said.

"Amen," was the queen's soft reply. Her thin lips were curved into a wan smile.

"Another small shrine to be added," she remarked, indicating a cabinet above the prie-dieu where were kept eight miniature portraits, one for each of the children she had lost. Above each portrait was a silver crucifix, below each a tablet with the name of the baby. "We had planned to name this one Edward—or Isabel, had she been a girl. After my sainted mother."

Her voice, normally low and pleasant, trembled slightly and she was speaking so softly that it was hard for me to hear her. I felt as though I were listening to someone in a trance. I thought of the opium, the sweat trance . . . was the queen still under the influence of the strong medicine? She did not seem like herself. Though she often honored me with her confidences, the way she was talking to me now was more open and free than in the past. Almost as if I were her confessor, Fray Diego, and not her maid of honor, Jane Seymour.

She went on talking, as I brushed the long thin strands of hair and gathered them into my hand. I could not help but notice that the brush was filling with hair; there were thin patches where the queen's scalp all but shone through. What did it mean, that her hair was falling out?

I looked into the pier glass and saw a slight frown pass across her features. "I was so certain that this time . . . this time . . . the Lord would give me a strong boy. I made a pilgrimage to Our Lady at her shrine at Walsingham. Afterwards I felt so certain that she would grant my wish."

I knew well that the queen had made a pilgrimage to the shrine, for I had gone with her. Had she forgotten? Had the opium made her forgetful?

"Perhaps she will, Your Majesty. Next time," I said.

She shook her head. "No. I cannot go through such a terrible labor again. No, this was the last time." She made a small sound. I realized that she was laughing quietly to herself.

"My old duenna, Dona Elvira, used to tell me when I was a little girl that I never knew when to give up. I kept on doing the same thing over and over, she said, even though I never got the result I wanted. I guess she was right."

"Your Majesty has been granted a beautiful, intelligent daughter, Princess Mary. Your jewel and delight, as you always say."

"Yes. But she is not a prince. And England needs a prince."

I had nothing to say to that, so was silent. Everyone knew the situation, the problem—many called it a crisis—over the succession. King Henry needed a son to inherit his throne. But he had only a daughter, only Princess Mary, who had been given the title Princess of Wales, the title traditionally given to the officially designated heir, but who could not be expected to reign. No woman could govern the unruly English, that was evident to all. The chronicles told of a queen in the distant past, Queen Maud, who attempted to rule but was overthrown. No woman had tried since. Better the throne should pass to the king's natural son, the boy known as Henry Fitzroy. But should he be the one to inherit, there would be challenges to his rulership. There would be chaos, possibly civil war, as in the time of King Henry's grandfather.

So the king's loyal subjects prayed that the queen, despite her many failures in the past, would at last give birth to a healthy boy. But those prayers—including my own—had gone unanswered.

Presently I said, "Shall I bind Your Majesty's hair?"

"Yes, Jane. And put on my hood, the cheerful rose-colored one with the pearls."

"That one is very becoming."

"It brings a little color to these pale cheeks. Henry complains that I am too sallow. And then, Jane, it will be time to bring in the other ladies and the maids of honor. I must tell them my news myself."

I did my best to complete the queen's coiffure—normally the task of her hairdressers—and to put her hood in place. Together we regarded her image in the pier glass. She smiled. She had come out of her trance. Once again she was the serene, gracious royal wife, head of her extensive household. The signs of her recent ordeal were there to be seen, in her drawn features and the dark circles under her eyes, but her manner was more confident.

"Please tell Maria that I am ready. And send Fray Diego to me, to hear my confession."

Her confession, I thought. What had she to confess? Surely bearing another stillborn child after undergoing many hours of heroic labor was no sin? Or did she imagine that the death of her child was a divine punishment?

I went out through the antechamber and into the room where the ladies in waiting and maids of honor were assembled.

"She is ready," I told Maria de Salinas. "She asks for Fray Diego, to make her confession, and then she will speak to us all."

I remember so well what happened later that afternoon. We had all taken our places in a reverent circle around the queen's chair, where she sat in benevolent calm. There were her Spanish ladies, Maria de Salinas, Ines de Venegas, Francesca de Lima and others whose names I barely knew, not having occasion to speak with them or perform tasks alongside them. And there were the chief officers of her household, and her chaplains and confessor. And then there were the women I knew best, the ladies in waiting and, especially, the other maids of honor.

There were nine of us, as I remember, and we were a widely

varied lot. First came Anne Cavecant, Lord Cavecant's daughter and the oldest among us, ashamed of her looks (she was rather homely, with a long sharp nose and pockmarked skin and a shy, almost furtive expression) and even more ashamed that, at twenty-seven, she was still without a husband. It was said that she had once been chosen by an elderly knight to become his fourth wife, but he had died before the wedding ceremony could take place. Since then she had waited in vain for another man to choose her.

Lavinia Terling was sly and pretty with hair that fell in long blond waves and innocent-looking blue eyes, a well-behaved girl but with only one thought in her head: how soon would she marry, and how rich and highborn would her husband be? The Belgian among us, Jane Popyngcort, insisted upon dressing in the foreign style rather than wearing English gowns and hoods. She was said to have been King Henry's mistress when both were young, and this gave her a certain air of mystery. ("Though she didn't last," the other maids said behind Jane's back. "She couldn't have mattered very much to him.")

Of the remaining maids, the ones who stood out most were Bridget Wiltshire, small and feral and as lean as a greyhound, and with a sharp tongue and a quick wit, who had just become engaged to Lord Wingfield, and her close friend Anne Boleyn, the temperamental dark-haired, dark-eyed sister of the king's mistress Mary Boleyn Carey whose name we were not allowed to mention in the queen's presence. Anne, so it was said, was well beyond the age when a gentleman's daughter (and the niece of the powerful Duke of Norfolk) ought to be married, and although she had had at least three chances for a match, none of them had resulted in a betrothal.

I was the youngest of the maids of honor, but—I am not being immodest, merely telling the truth—I believe that, among the English women in Queen Catherine's household, I was the most favored by her. She liked having me near her, especially when upsetting events were challenging her usual calm and self-possession. There were many such challenges in those years, when I first came to court. Naturally her Spanish ladies resented the favoritism she showed me, believing that since they shared her native speech and customs, they should be the ones to be kept nearest her person. I was well aware of this resentment and did what I could to lower it. But I knew that Maria de Salinas and the others regarded me as a presumptuous intruder in their midst, and imagined that I had risen to favor with the queen through trickery or by slandering them, whereas in fact I had merely been myself.

The queen was preparing to speak. There was quiet in the room; even Bridget and Anne, whose giggles and titters were forever interrupting solemn occasions, were silent for the moment.

All eyes were on Catherine. Then, with a sweet and gracious smile, she addressed us.

"By now you all know that the Lord has not seen fit to bless this kingdom with a male heir to the throne. My son, Edward, did not live to take his first breath."

Polite murmurs of consolation greeted these words. The queen acknowledged them with a small nod, then went on.

"Our prayers are not always answered as we would wish, as Fray Diego reminds me. The Lord's purposes are not ours. But then, it is not our bodies, or their fruits, that matter, it is our eternal souls. As we read in the gospel, they should not be feared which have the power of the body, but Him only, that hath power over the soul.

"I have been shriven," the queen went on, "and will be churched in due course. Until then I will keep my chamber, and will expect you all to say little of what has passed here in recent days. If you should be asked, 'What news of the queen?' you ought simply to say, 'The Lord's will has been done.'"

Maria de Salinas stepped forward to indicate that all present should take their leave, and we did so, each of us passing in front of Her Highness and bowing. "I am grateful for your loyal service," she said to each of us, or "Thank you for your continual prayers."

We had not gone far in this small ceremony when we heard heavy footfalls outside the queen's apartments. Boots thundered along the corridor outside, and almost before we could react, or even draw back in alarm, the heavy double doors burst open with a loud crack of splintering wood and King Henry came into the room. I almost wrote that he exploded into the room, such was the force of his vital presence. His angry presence.

He wore his green hunting jerkin and a cap with a feather such as huntsmen wear. Leaves and twigs stuck to his jerkin and were caught in his long blond hair. He has ridden here in great haste, I thought. He has not taken the time to make himself presentable. His muddy boots left ugly dark tracks on the immaculate carpet, and the long knife that hung from his belt, its blade glinting in the firelit room, was still red with the gore of his kills.

He strode up to the seated Catherine.

"Why was this news kept from me, madam?" he barked. "Why was I not told at once?" His rich, resonant voice filled the room. We all stood still, in awe of his royal anger, of the sheer force of his presence. Would he blame us for withholding word of the stillborn prince? I felt myself shrink, as if, by making myself smaller, I could avoid his wrath.

He glared down at Catherine, who looked up at him with her usual mildness.

"I believe a messenger was sent to you, sire. Had I been able, I would have brought you the news myself. But I was quite ill, indeed very ill—"

"Ill! Ill! You are always ill! You are useless! The one thing I ask of you, the only thing I have ever asked of you, ever since I married you—out of pity—and you have not been able to do it!"

He fairly spat out the words, his sharp, assaultive tone far more bruising than the words themselves. Catherine continued to look at him mildly. He began to pace, scattering the women in the room as he neared them, swerving back and forth. I could see that he was sweating.

"I bring physicians to examine you," he was saying, "apothecaries to give you drugs to make you fertile, we pray together, you go to every shrine in Christendom—and this is the result! Another dead boy! How many is it now? Ten? Twenty?"

The king paused in his diatribe, and seeing my opportunity, I slowly moved toward the door. The others too began filing slowly out of the room.

Catherine reached out toward me.

"Stay, Jane," she said quietly.

"Go!" the king shouted. I knew I had to do as he asked, and I quickly and quietly exited. But once I was in the corridor beyond the queen's bedchamber I stopped, and listened to the quarrel that erupted—a quarrel far more venomous than any I had ever heard, either in the palace or outside of it.

I was not the only one listening. The queen's Spanish ladies lingered there in the corridor, as I did, as did Jane Popyngcort and Bridget Wiltshire and Anne Boleyn and a few of the ladies in waiting. The Spanish ladies crossed themselves from time to time, and exclaimed to one another in their own tongue. I was feeling worried. What would the king do to Catherine? Clearly she had foreseen how angry he would be, that was why she had asked Maria de Salinas to delay sending word to him of the stillborn child. How extreme could his anger become?

"Enough!" the king kept saying, this one word trumpeting out again and again amid the torrent of his harsh words.

"Enough indeed," I heard Anne say to Bridget. "All this is just wearisome. What does he expect, married to an old woman like that, with a dried-up womb—" Only Anne didn't say "womb," she used a much more rude and disrespectful word.

"Hush!" I heard myself say. "Have you no sense of duty to your mistress? Surely the poor queen deserves civility, after all she has been through!"

Anne turned toward me and looked at me, a frosty look.

"And who are you, Mistress Seymour, to tell me how to act? Your father is a landed knight, I believe, while my uncle Norfolk is the greatest noble in England!"

I stood my ground. Anne might be among the most attractive of the maids of honor (though far less attractive than the beautiful Lavinia Terling), with an allure that was difficult to define but unmistakable—I could see the lust in the men's eyes when they looked at her—but that did not excuse her rudeness.

"I have often heard the queen say that charity and kindness have no regard for birth or rank. Our Lord and exemplar was not a nobleman, if I remember my gospels correctly." I knew my words sounded sanctimonious, yet I went on, keeping my voice low.

"I believe your father is no more exalted than my own, despite his wife's family connections," I began. "And how is it that you are not yet wed, though you must be at least twenty-five?"

I could tell that my question stung. Anne's black eyes grew

narrower, and before she turned away she said to Bridget, "Listen to the stunted little nobody! I've heard—" But what she had heard, and was confiding in Bridget's ear, was drowned out by the king's voice rising to a new level of vengeful accusation.

"Enough!" he was saying yet again. "There will be no more dead sons—or dead daughters either! You may enjoy your bed in peace—and solitude! I will announce this afternoon that my son Henry Fitzroy will be named Duke of Richmond. Once he receives that title he will be the highest-ranking noble in the land. Higher than your daughter, madam, higher even than the pompous Norfolk! Henry Fitzroy will be the next King of England, and there's an end to it!"

And hearing the king's footsteps approaching, those of us in the corridor scattered, like sheep before the wolf, and sought the shelter of less troubled quarters.

TWO

"WILL! Oh Will! The baby was born dead. The poor little thing! I'm afraid they gave her opium and it killed the baby! And the king is angry and shouted at her!"

Amid the quiet and solitude of the privy garden, behind the dovecote and to the right of the ale house, I poured out my heart to Will, who opened his arms and enfolded me in them. Strong arms. Arms that had always been there to comfort me, ever since we were children and I fell and scratched my leg or I had a fight with Ned or one of my cousins or my father ordered me to be locked in my room without food for a day and a night.

Will, laughing, good-natured, blond, blue-eyed Will Dormer, who I would soon marry. Who would be the father of our children when we moved to the country, far from the sorrows and turmoil of the court. To some rural oasis with sheltering copses and a narrow rippling stream running down to a wide flowing river. Where deer came to feed and rabbits and hares chased one another through the underbrush and where, in the spring, a carpet of bluebells—no, an ocean of bluebells—would spread themselves out beneath old oaks and pale birches. Where there were no dead babies, and no tears.

"Jane! Dear!"

Will was trying to bring me out of my reverie, but I resisted. I clung to him. I had had very little sleep in the past two days and the queen's trauma, and her terrible quarrel with the king, had unnerved me.

I took pride in my ability to retain my composure, and as a rule, I did. It was one of the reasons the queen liked to keep me near her. I was sympathetic, but I did not allow my feelings to overwhelm me. She once told me, in what I knew was meant to be a high compliment, that I was blessed with gravity, and was almost as self-possessed as a Spaniard.

But now, worn down and alarmed, I felt no gravity at all. I felt only the need for comfort.

"You should have seen her, Will, with the little coffin for the baby. A tiny little thing all covered in purple cloth . . . it was so pathetic. She buries all the stillborn babies they say, though the king takes no notice of their small graves and never visits them—"

"Jane! You must listen!"

Unwillingly, I unwound myself from him and pulled back.

"I know you are distressed about the queen but I must talk to you about another matter—even more urgent—and I have not much time. I am ordered to the Maidens' Bower and Master Woodshaw is angry when I am late."

At the mention of Edward Woodshaw I bristled. Will had served in the king's household for two years, but his most recent court appointment was deeply distasteful to me.

"I hate that you have Edward Woodshaw as your master! The master of bawdry, I call him. The king's procurer!"

"The post was not of my choosing, as you know, Jane. I make the best of it."

"But the Maidens' Bower! The shame of the court."

The notorious Maidens' Bower was the king's most private chamber, where the young women he kept for his secret amusement were housed. Secret—yet not secret, for the entire court was aware that the royal den of pleasure existed and that Edward Woodshaw presided over it.

Because my Will was a handsome young man, barely twenty-one, with strong muscles and broad shoulders and a great deal of charm, he had been taken from his original post in the stables—where he had enjoyed being a groom, he loved horses—and placed among the king's chamber gentlemen, where he served in the Maidens' Bower under the tutelage of Master Woodshaw.

The new post was considered a sign that Will was looked on with favor by the senior officials of the court; if he acquitted himself well, he could expect to be given a higher office soon, and more responsibility.

"You should be proud of Will," my brother Ned told me. Ned, despite his youth (he was four years older than I was), had been taken into the household of the great and powerful Cardinal Wolsey, and was advancing, though never rapidly enough to satisfy himself, for he was very ambitious, and very able—and, it had to be admitted, more than a little ruthless.

"When you and Will marry, you will both be highly placed at court."

"I hope we will marry very soon," I had told Ned. "I hope the wedding will be within a few months." I did not add that I looked forward to my marriage and my departure from the court, not my advancement. I was eager to escape the tense atmosphere in the queen's apartments; although I felt a great deal of sympathy for Queen Catherine, and was honored that she singled me out as a favorite and liked having me near her, in truth I did not like being needed so much, or called on so often to give her companionship. I could not help absorbing her sadness, and felt a sense of desolation, being near her; I admired her bravery and envied her faith, but I yearned for lighter company and happier hours. Hours I planned to spend with Will.

And I was eager to escape the constant irritant of the queen's Spanish gentlewomen, whose needling and prodding vexed me. As I had tried to tell Will, women can convey a lot without using words; the Spaniards said a great deal with their eyes, their inadvertent shoves that were really quite intentional, their murmured barbed remarks to one another. They knew how to show disrespect in a thousand hidden ways. I had no doubt they wanted me gone—

"Jane!" It was Will's voice again, more insistent this time. "You must listen, you really must."

I looked at him, and saw the dismay that clouded his usually clear blue eyes.

"Jane, I have some unhappy news."

"What is it?"

"I went to my parents, as we agreed I would. I told them you and I had plans to marry soon, and that we asked for their blessings."

"And?"

"They told me to forget any plans we might have made. That a marriage between us would be impossible."

For a moment I was too surprised to speak. I had been warmly welcomed into the Dormer household since childhood, indeed the Dormers had smiled on me and embraced me as if I were one of their own. That Will and I would marry one day was understood. Or so I had always thought.

"But they love me!" I said at length. "I'm sure they do."

"Yes."

"Then why?"

Will looked very uncomfortable.

"At first they said, 'We have always hoped that you would marry well, and you have a chance now to marry into the Sidney family. That is the future we intend for you.'

"I said I didn't care about that. That I wanted to marry you, Jane, and no one but you.

"We quarreled. They accused me of not caring about the family honor, the family fortunes. I said that your family was every bit as honorable as the Sidneys—which we all know isn't true, the Sidneys are more exalted in rank, I was merely speaking out of loyalty—but it was no use. They were not angry, merely firm. They said I had to marry the Sidney heiress. But then—"

"Yes?"

"This is the terrible part, Jane. Are you certain you want to hear it?"

"Of course. I must know why they are suddenly so opposed to me, after all their years of kindness and welcome."

Will hung his head.

"Your father and my sister Margery—" he said, his voice low.

"Yes?"

"My father surprised them. They were—your father was—"

I knew what he meant at once, but could barely say the words, much less believe them. I stared at Will, confused and dumbfounded.

"Are you telling me," I managed to say at length, "that my father and your sister were in bed together? Naked? Acting—as if they were man and wife?"

"It was a storage room," Will blurted out, "and they were standing up, my father says—and they were only half naked."

"No! It can't be true!"

Will put his head in his hands, then ran his hands through his hair.

"My father would not lie about such a shameful, sinful thing," he said. "I believe him. And if I ever see your father anywhere near my sister, I'll thrash him. If it weren't for you, and my love for you, I would gladly kill him."

I sat still, stunned.

"I must go, Jane. We can talk later." He kissed me swiftly on the cheek and strode off.

Half an hour later I was still sitting in the same place, still in a state of disbelief. My father, John Seymour, was fifty years old, Will's sister Margery was barely fourteen. The weight of shame—assuming what I had heard was true—was too heavy to be measured. How would I ever be able to comprehend it, let alone overcome it?

And yet, what Will had told me brought back a shadowy memory. A most unwelcome memory, one that I had never allowed myself to think about very much or try to understand.

When I was a child, there had been a serving girl at our family estate, Wulf Hall. A very young girl, dark-haired and smiling, agreeable and eager to please. I had liked her, and had often gone down into the kitchens to find her because she gave me drippings from the joints of meat that turned on the spits and bits of crust from the freshly baked loaves as they sat cooling in their baskets. Even when she was very busy with her assigned tasks she stopped to greet me and hand me a tidbit.

One day I was startled by a sudden outburst of shouting. The household was in turmoil, the steward flustered, the serving girl in tears. I felt sorry for her distress, and started to go toward her, but then I saw my father, an odd look on his face, his fists clenched at his sides. I stopped where I was. The girl ran swiftly out of the house and did not return. My mother was in tears for days, and would not speak to my father or even look at him.

I had been far too young to understand what had happened at the time, but now—was it possible that my father had seduced other young girls? Or had it not been seduction, but mutual passion? Passion gone wrong, ending in tears and banishment from the house?

A serving girl was one thing, Will Dormer's sister quite another.

I wanted to know the truth—yet part of me held back. Questions arose, I could not help them. Had Margery been a willing partner? And if not, why hadn't she screamed for help? A dreadful thought: would she become pregnant? The highborn men of the court were prone to taking mistresses—just as the king had—and having children by them. Not only King Henry, but the Duke of Norfolk and lesser nobles. They were brazen in their adulteries. They brought their mistresses to court at times. They flaunted them. The king's close friend and brother-in-law Charles Brandon, Duke of Suffolk, though married to the king's beautiful sister, Princess Mary, with whom he had at one time been deeply in love, had taken a young girl as his mistress. And not just any pretty young girl, but one related to Queen Catherine's lady in waiting. Or so it was said in the royal apartments.

It would seem that my father was allowing himself to imitate the example set by others. It was a curse of our times. A canker spreading through the court. And it had shattered my dream of love and ruined my hopes.

THREE

THE only sound in the spacious, wide-aisled, torchlit hall at Bridewell Palace, with its high hammerbeam ceiling and its tapestry-covered walls, was the sound of a small boy's coughing.

All the chief notables of the court had been summoned to the hall to witness a solemn and significant event: the creation of the king's natural son as Duke of Richmond and Somerset, Lord High Admiral of England, Duke of Normandy and Aquitaine, Lord of Ardres, Guines and Calais (though the French king Francis would dispute these claims), Lord of the Marches, Seneschal of Gascony and Garter Knight.

On this day the boy, Henry Fitzroy, would be exalted above every other noble at the court, though he was only in his sixth year and was not, it had to be admitted, in the best of health.

His coughing continued, a small sound in the large room, and the longer it went on, I noticed, the more the king tried in vain to hide his irritation. King Henry stood, a tall, broad-shouldered, massive figure splendidly arrayed in robes of cloth of gold, at one end of the long room, watching his son's approach and looking more and more dissatisfied.

It was not just that little Fitzroy was ill, it was that he was so very small for a boy nearly six years old, and pale, and that he did not stand erect but slumped; his legs in their silken hose were thin and crooked, and when he reached out for the hand of Charles Brandon, who stood at his left, and looked up at the tall, strongly built Brandon there was a touching look of entreaty on his pallid features.

Brandon, who I always thought of as warm-hearted and helpful, seized the small white hand in his much larger, sun-reddened one and smiled encouragingly. The sour, hawk-faced man who stood at the boy's right, the Duke of Norfolk, considerably shorter than Brandon and lacking Brandon's lithe, muscular athleticism, did not offer his hand and looked away.

Now there were two dukes beginning to walk down the length of the room, toward the king. Soon there would be three, though I found it hard to imagine little Fitzroy as a great nobleman— indeed the greatest nobleman in the realm. I knew, however, that his future was already being mapped out; the estates where he would live, his newly appointed household of a hundred and thirty-two servants, his tutors and riding master and chaplains, even his future wife. It was said that he would soon be betrothed to Mary Howard, Norfolk's daughter, and that in time the blood of the Tudors and the blood of the Howards would run in the veins of a new line of kings.

From where I sat, with the other maids of honor, I was well positioned to view the ceremony, and also the others who were present. At the king's insistence, Queen Catherine was there, composed and dignified, her black lace mantilla draped over her English-style hood in a way that shielded her face from observation. Her daughter Princess Mary, a pretty blond girl of nine, with a delicate frame but a clumsiness of movement that marred her regal standing, sat upright and looked offended. She ignored Henry Fitzroy, and fixed her gaze instead on her father.

Mary understood full well that the elevation of Henry Fitzroy made it plain that he was the king's choice to be the next ruler of the realm. Mary was being shunted aside, dishonored, her place taken by the boy of illegitimate birth. And not only that: it was said she had been abandoned by the Emperor Charles, the young ruler of the vast Hapsburg lands, who was to have been her husband. Her betrothal had been broken off not long before, leaving her with neither the prospect of the throne nor of marriage. It was no wonder, I thought, that she did not look at little Henry Fitzroy as he made his way slowly down the room.

Cardinal Wolsey, the wealthiest and most powerful of the dignitaries and certainly the largest in girth and bulk, stood near the king, his flowing crimson damask robes, heavy gold cross and jeweled rings gleaming. And not far from the cardinal I noticed Thomas Boleyn, Anne's father, who was much whispered about because he was said to be rising in influence and wealth and getting above himself. He was only a gentleman, not a nobleman, but he was married to the Duke of Norfolk's sister Elizabeth, and with the duke's aid and influence behind him, was doing his best to make himself indispensable to the king.

All this interested me, I confess. My brother Ned was always eager to hear from me what was being said—often in low tones—in the queen's chamber and he in turn passed on to me what he was hearing and what he was told by his servants.

Oh, the court was full of gossip just then! There was so much uncertainty about the future, and an unsettled feeling about the times we were living in. The court was a seething hive of rumor and talebearing, and the elevation of Henry Fitzroy only made the rumors and tales increase.

Would the diminutive, unhealthy Henry Fitzroy live to become king? And if he did not, would the king contrive to set his queen aside and marry a woman who was fertile? What did the astrologers and fortunetellers have to say? What women did the king prefer to have near him, either in his apartments or in the Maidens' Bower, that chamber of delights? Would Henry Fitzroy's mother become the royal mistress once again?

On and on, back and forth, the gossip flew, so much of it swirling around the small boy who was about to become Duke of Richmond and Somerset.

Trumpets blew a fanfare, and the choir began to sing. I guessed that the king, who was a gifted composer, had written this anthem in celebration of his son's creation as duke. As the voices rang out, the boy and his two supporters reached the platform where the king stood, and went up the few steps to reach it. Then the men moved aside, leaving only the boy and his father.

The ducal coronet was produced, and King Henry placed it carefully on his son's head. A mantle of purple velvet furred with ermine was placed around Henry Fitzroy's slender shoulders, and fastened with a golden pin. Prayers were said, oaths repeated. Then came a shout of acclamation, and a final flourish of trumpets, the new Duke of Richmond and Somerset was hailed and reverenced by all present, and the king impulsively reached down and picked up his small son, swinging him up in his arms as if he had been no heavier than a puppy and striding down into the crowd to show him off. In the commotion, the boy's coronet fell to the floor and Thomas Boleyn, alert to the emergency, dove down amid the mass of skirts and shoes and retrieved it.

He handed it, smiling, to the king who snatched it and replaced it on little Fitzroy's head.

But the noise, the crowd, the king's exuberant tossing and swinging of his son were upsetting the boy. I was near enough to see that his face was crumpling and he was starting to sniffle, then to cough.

The king's expression darkened. Abruptly he handed his son to the nearest woman—the boy's hovering mother, Elizabeth Blount—and strode off toward the banqueting hall, where a feast had been prepared. As he walked he burst into song—one of his own songs, "To the greenwood go"—and soon the spacious hall was all but empty. Yet I saw that Elizabeth Blount still lingered, sitting quietly in a recessed window-seat with her son beside her, talking to him softly and wiping the tears from his face. As I went to join the other maids of honor at the banquet I could hear him coughing.

I had already ordered my wedding gown from Mr. Skut the queen's dressmaker. It was to have been the loveliest gown I had ever worn, the bodice and sleeves of a pale watery blue—the blue of the spring sky—and the wide skirt and petticoats of cream satin. Mr. Skut had smiled when he held the blue cloth up to me and nodded approvingly.

"Yes, this will suit," he said in his usual understated way— but I could tell that he was very pleased with the effect.

That had been a happy afternoon. Now, with a heavy heart, I had to tell Mr. Skut I would not be needing the gown after all.

I had sent a message to him, asking him to come to the queen's apartments. He arrived, bringing two assistants and a seamstress. They were loaded down with baskets of cloth and lace and trimmings.

"Ah, Mr. Skut," I said when he arrived, "I'm afraid I must ask you not to go any further in making my lovely wedding dress. You see, there is not going to be a wedding after all."

He looked very surprised. "No wedding? But your plans were all made. I do hope there has not been a dreadful accident of some sort—"

"No, nothing like that."

"Not a death in the family I trust?"

I shook my head. I did not want to have to account for my change in plans, even to think of it made me both sad and angry.

He looked at me gravely.

"But you, Mistress Seymour, such a fine young lady, of high breeding and pleasant in manner, entirely satisfactory—indeed superior—in every way?" He paused. "Ah, pardon me. It must be the gentleman who was unsatisfactory. Forgive me."

The conversation was proving to be more painful than I expected. I swallowed. I felt my face growing hot.

"The gentleman is certainly not unsatisfactory. He is Will Dormer—"

"Of the Maidens' Bower?" Mr. Skut lifted one eyelid quizzically. I knew what he was thinking: Will had found another woman he liked better than me. And he had found her among the fallen women (as my late grandmother would have called them) in the Maidens' Bower.

"My Will is the best and most loving of men," I said staunchly.

"Then why—"

"The cause is not important," I said, rather too brusquely, wishing Mr. Skut would leave.

But he lingered, looking uncomfortable.

"I assure you, the gown will be paid for," I added—and was immediately aware that I had said the wrong thing. For he was lingering, not because he was worried about his pay, but because he was concerned for me.

"As you say, the cause is not important, only the wellbeing of the bride," the dressmaker said gently. "We will put the gown away for now. It can always be completed at another time, when a happier betrothal is announced."

His kindliness affected me deeply. I thought I might start to cry. I shook my head, thinking there will be no other time, no happier betrothal. But before I could say what I was thinking, the assistants had lifted the elaborate blue bodice and pair of slashed sleeves and one silken petticoat out of their baskets and were shaking them out and displaying them to full advantage.

Seeing them, I felt more forlorn than ever.

Just then Bridget Wiltshire came into the room.

"Mr. Skut! I thought I heard your voice." She looked quickly from the dressmaker to me—in my distress—and then at the elaborate bodice and sleeves and petticoat.

"How beautiful!" she exclaimed. "And I thought you were making your most pleasing gown for me!"

Bridget's wedding to Lord Wingfield was to take place in a month's time, and Mr. Skut was making her gown.

"Jane?" She looked at me once again, a quizzical expression on her narrow face. It was all I could do to remain self-possessed enough to say, somewhat haltingly, "Mr. Skut has been sewing this gown for me, and may complete it later on." With that I took my leave, doing my best to keep my composure.

But Bridget was too clever not to realize that something was wrong. She had a nose for trouble, the queen liked to say of her, partly in admiration, partly in distaste. I sensed that Queen Catherine had never found Bridget Wiltshire ladylike enough to satisfy her, or to be truly worthy of membership in her household.

"Jane! Wait!" She followed me into another antechamber. "That beautiful gown—is it to be for your wedding? Are you secretly betrothed?"

"I am not," I answered irritably. "If I was, my family would announce it." I had not spoken to any of the other maids of honor about Will, or of the plans we had made together.

Bridget looked fully into my eyes, and when I met her steady gaze I was surprised to see there, not only curiosity and interest, but a measure of friendly concern. I had always thought of Bridget as lightminded and frivolous, self-regarding and oblivious of the needs of others. Anne Boleyn had these qualities, and Bridget was her closest friend; I assumed Bridget had them too.

"If it is a question of a payment to Mr. Skut," she said now, "I will loan you what you need."

Her generosity unnerved me. I shook my head, unable to speak. Once again I was near tears.

"Jane?" Bridget's voice was soft. All of a sudden I felt something give way within me. I felt the full weight of my sorrow, bearing down with merciless force. I gave in. My tears flowed freely.

Bridget produced a handkerchief at once, and led me to a cushioned bench.

"Tell me all," she said, her voice as practical in tone as it was sympathetic. "And then I will tell you what has happened to me."

"To you?"

"Go ahead. Tell me." She did not say, "Hurry up and get on with it," but she might as well have. Knowing that she was eager to share something with me—and that she had trouble too—lifted my sorrow a little.

"Where to begin?" I mumbled.

"Who is the man?"

"How did you know—"

She shrugged.

"I—we—" I was rarely at a loss for words, but I was now. I cleared my throat and wiped my nose.

"Will Dormer and I want to marry, and have wanted it for a long time," I managed to say. "But Will's parents want him to marry Mary Sidney instead. They have refused their permission."

"And you imagine that you could never love anyone but Will—and that you could not bring yourself to marry for any reason other than love, as Lavinia will probably do. All Lavinia cares about is having a rich husband."

"I love Will," was all I said.

"What if you marry him without his family's blessing?"

I shook my head. "The disgrace would be terrible." Even as I said this I was thinking, there will be disgrace in any event, once my father's behavior with Will's sister becomes known. But at least Will won't be harmed by it.

"Tell me what has happened to you," I said to Bridget, relieved to be shifting my thoughts from my own difficulties to hers.

Hearing my words a hard, grim expression came over her face, her mouth firm and her eyes unsparing.

"My friend Anne," she said, "tried to take Richard—Lord Wingfield—from me. She laid her plans with care. She went to her brother George (George will do anything she asks, they say he has been that way since they were children) and told him she wanted him to take Richard hunting. Richard loves to hunt, of course he agreed. Then she said she wanted to go along, and she promised Richard she would bring me along as well. But of course that was a lie. She never invited me—never even told me the three of them were going."

Listening, I shook my head. "Deception," I said, and Bridget nodded.

"Well," she resumed, "they got to the hunting lodge, a place deep in the forest, where there was no one to observe them, and no family to restrain them. Anne had her maidservant with her, but according to Richard she tripped the girl, injuring her but making it look like an accident, and then sent her back to London. For the next few days they were alone—except for the huntsmen and grooms."

"And you didn't know anything of this?" I asked.

Bridget shook her head.

"Anne chose her time carefully. She knew I would be in the West Country with my uncle and aunt, preparing for my cousin's wedding, during George's hunting trip. She was clever— she is clever. And devious." Bridget smiled. "It is her nature."

"What happened there in the forest?"

"She went to Richard, and boldly offered herself to him—if he would promise to marry her. He refused."

"Yet you are still friends. You stood with her this morning, in the queen's bedchamber, laughing and talking as always. How could you do that?"

"I wasn't completely surprised by what she did. I know her nature. She is wayward, and has been since we were young girls. We were in Brabant together, in the household of the Archduchess Margaret, and Anne tried to seduce our chaperone, Seigneur Bouton. She was barely fourteen then. She did it because she knew her sister had slept with him. She was always trying to outdo her sister, you know. When we moved on to France, a few years later, she and her sister Mary were always competing over men. They were quite notorious."

I had heard it said of Anne that she was a wanton girl, like her sister, whose liaison with the king we were forbidden to mention in Queen Catherine's apartments. But until then I had never heard anyone confirm this gossip as true, or talk of any sisterly competition between them.

"If anyone tried to take my Will from me, I'd kill her," I said impetuously.

"Not if you had seen her attempt to do the same thing many times before—with any number of men—and fail. I watched Anne once at a banquet in Paris. The entire French court was there, from King Francis and Queen Claude to the king's very pious, very moral mother Louise of Savoy. The hour grew late, the guests began to be sodden with wine. We English girls were dressed in gowns of the newest Italian style, brought from Venice—the women in Venice are very bold, as you may know, and very sensual. The bodices of our gowns were daringly low. Anne and Mary both pulled theirs down as low as they could, flaunting themselves quite shamelessly. Watching them, I began to giggle. I couldn't help it, they were so amusing. I wasn't the only one to laugh.

"Finally, at about midnight, when many of the older people, including Louise of Savoy, had left the table and gone to bed, Mary and Anne began displaying themselves more suggestively, walking among the men and bending down so that the youngest and most handsome of the diners could feed them morsels of sweet cakes and lumps of sugar. They put on quite a spectacle, bending ever lower, taking down their hair and sweeping it from side to side, then tossing it back. When the last of the courses had been served and removed both Anne and Mary began to dance. Anne is a very graceful dancer, and she outshone her sister."

I had often witnessed Anne's skill at dancing, not only in the English courtly dances but the French ones, with their intricate steps and difficult hops and leaps. Anne's dancing put my own leaden-footed efforts to shame.

"By this time it was very, very late," Bridget was saying, "getting on towards morning, and many of the banqueters had gone off to bed or were asleep, snoring, with their heads on the tables. Mary and Anne both began whispering in the ears of the men who were still awake. Mary left the room with one of the men right away, but Anne went from one groggy man to another, whispering in each one's ear, without success.

"I had seen it happen before," she went on. "Mary, being the prettier of the two, was quickly chosen, while her dark, less attractive sister was passed over. I knew that this infuriated Anne, who was very competitive and determined to win, at all costs."

"And did she eventually find a partner for the night?"

"I don't know. I fell asleep myself. But I do know that she went up to Richard, knowing that Richard and I were betrothed, and that I loved him, and whispered in his ear. He was amused. I saw him smile, then shake his head in a friendly way. She soon gave up."

I thought over what I had been hearing.

"All I know is, she'd better stay away from my Will."

"I thought you said he wasn't going to be your Will."

I frowned at Bridget then. She was too abrupt, too blunt.

"In any case," she was saying, "you needn't worry. Your Will is far from rich enough or highly placed enough for Anne to want him."

Now I was really offended. I drew myself up to my full height (which is not very high, I am a rather small person) and said, "If Anne Boleyn doesn't know that a loving heart and a true nature are worth far more than wealth and status, then she is foolish and does not deserve to be happy."

Bridget smiled indulgently.

"A pretty speech, and a loyal one. You are young, you do not yet know how harsh a place the world can be."

"I'm learning," was all I said. And I was. I was being taught, just then, about betrayal. How a lecherous, wanton man of fifty could betray his daughter by wrecking her hopes for marriage. How a loose, reckless girl could betray her closest friend by trying to steal her fiancé. And how a pitiless, tyrannical king could betray the loyalty of his suffering wife by berating and blaming her for a tragedy that was not her fault.

Harsh lessons, I thought, unsought and repugnant. I had no desire to learn any more.

FOUR

WILL came to me after matins, putting his fingers to his lips and quietly taking my arm and leading me into the privy garden, our accustomed meeting place. I could see the excitement in his eyes even before he spoke.

There had been a heavy dew the night before and the skirt of my gown was wet as Will drew me across the lawn. Several gardeners were at work but they did not appear to be taking any notice of us.

"Jane! I've done it! It's all arranged!"

I caught his excitement at once. My heart began to pound in my chest. Had he somehow convinced his parents to change their minds and allow us to marry after all? Was it possible? I took his hands in mine.

"Are we to be married then?"

"No—better than that. I have arranged our escape!"

"What?"

"Our escape—from the court, from my parents, from everything!" Gleefully he went on. "Your friend Bridget has a cousin who is sailing to the Spice Islands and will let us go with him! From there we can go where we like, do what we like. We'll find some far place—so far and so rare it has no name. We'll find a deserted island and name it after you!"

I was too stunned to speak. Will had found a way out of our dilemma!

Or had he? Questions arose in my mind.

"Is this cousin of Bridget's a man who can be trusted?" I asked Will.

"She assures me that he is. He has gone on many ventures, and returned enriched."

"Pirates get rich."

"I don't believe this venturer is a pirate, Jane."

"How sturdy is his ship?" was my next question.

"She is called the *Eglantine*. She has weathered several voyages."

I knew nothing whatever about ships, nor did Will. I did not even know what questions to ask. However, Will convinced me that he had already thought of everything that might go wrong, and had satisfied himself that we would be in safe, trustworthy hands on our journey. The *Eglantine* would leave us in the Spice Islands, take on a precious cargo of cloves and cinnamon and then return to England, to sell the spices at a large profit.

"I have arranged to pay our way by becoming an investor in the coming voyage," he explained.

"And how much will it cost?" I wanted to know, imagining that Will would have to pay a great deal for his share in the venture.

"The cost is small," he said after a moment's pause, "compared to the likely gain." He sounded more mature, in that moment, than I had ever heard him sound before.

"And besides, we will have each other," he added, taking me in his arms and giving me a lingering kiss.

"Tell no one about our plans, Jane," he cautioned me as we parted. "No one at all. Gather your things in secret and pack them in a small trunk. We sail in six days' time. Be ready!"

I nodded eagerly, my thoughts racing. How could I fit all that was precious to me into one small trunk? How could I leave my family and friends without saying goodbye? I loved Will, of that I was certain. Perhaps that was all that mattered. Perhaps one day, when Will and I had been married for years and living on our faraway island, when we had children and wanted them to know their relations, we might return.

Careful not to reveal the enormous change in my future plans, and hiding the smile that crept over my lips every time I thought about sailing away and leaving all my cares and worries behind, I got on with the secret task of packing and preparing for our departure.

From the storerooms at Baynard's Castle I unearthed a trunk so long unused that the gilt initials *MP* beneath the old lock were nearly worn away. Into it I placed the missal I had had since childhood, a miniature of my mother and another of my grandmother, my sturdiest cloak, petticoats and riding boots, some blankets for the babies I hoped to have—one of the blankets had warmed me in my cradle—and a small pouch of silver coins, all the money I had in the world. Though in truth I wondered what use silver coins might be in a place so far away it had no name. I entrusted the trunk to a Thames waterman who promised to take it to the *Eglantine* the night before she sailed.

Then I tried to settle myself to wait for the six days to pass. It was hard to sleep, I was so eager. When, after a long night of wakefulness, I did manage to lose myself in dreams, I dreamed of the ocean, blue and deep and benign, and of Will saying "we will have each other" in his reassuring voice.

On the fourth day of my vigil a letter came. It took me by surprise, for it was brought to the queen's apartments by a servant from the convent of St. Agnes's, a house of nuns not far from the capital. I wanted to read it when I was alone, so I put it in the pocket of my skirt and waited until the end of the day to open it.

"Jane, please help me!" I read, the letters formed with a shaky hand, and in a downward-slanting slope. I recognized the writing. The letter was from my sister-in-law Cat, brother Ned's wife. "Everyone in the family has turned against me," she wrote. "Come to St. Agnes's as soon as you can and I will tell you all. Your sister, Catherine Fillol Seymour."

I did not know what to make of the brief letter but could not ignore it. Ned's wife was so much older than I was—by some seven years—that we had never really been friends, though always on terms of family warmth and welcome. Ned's marriage to Cat had been arranged between the two families, he did not choose her. She was a tall, plain woman whose posture and manner made it clear that she saw herself for what she was, and was only too aware that she lacked beauty and charm. She dressed in gowns of costly cloth but in dark, drab colors; she took no pains to find a dressmaker with the skill to flatter her spare figure or suggest more becoming shades. I mentioned Mr. Skut to her more than once, and offered to send him to her, but she had no interest in employing him, though she thanked me for thinking of her and wanting to help.

In truth Cat held herself to be of low worth as a woman, I suspected. In her mind, all her worth lay in the value of her inheritance, which was large and growing larger under Ned's skillful management. Without that inheritance, Ned would never have married Cat, for he certainly felt no love for her. But then, I had never known Ned to love any woman. Love, he said, was a snare and a hindrance to good judgment. It passed swiftly and usually left bitterness behind. Whenever I heard him say this I felt very sorry for Cat. Yet I imagined she understood that as an heiress she would be desired for her wealth. It was accepted by all at court that marriage was in most cases a matter of money, lands, and the influence and high standing that went with them. To believe otherwise was to be naive—or a dreamer.

As I read Cat's urgent, worrying plea for help, with its dreadful assertion that everyone in the family had turned against her, I felt regret that I had not spent more time with her in the past, or gotten to know her better. I rarely saw her; she stayed in the country on Ned's estate most of the time while Ned devoted himself to his duties at court. She lived a quiet, retired life. One that suited her, or so I had always supposed.

I did not hesitate to respond to Cat's cry for help. I rode to the convent and arrived just as the nuns were singing compline, and found Cat waiting for me inside the convent gates. She was under guard. Her two small sons, Henry and John, were asleep on a pile of blankets in one corner of the sparely furnished, candlelit room.

Cat fairly ran toward me, eager to tell me all about her difficulties. I had never seen her in such distress.

"What is it? Why are you here?" I asked. "Let me take you home."

"I can't go home!" she burst out. "Ned won't let me. He sent me here and paid the nuns to promise to shut me away and never let me out while I live."

"But what could have possessed him to do something so cruel?"

"He believes that I have destroyed the honor of the Seymours—that I am the devil's pathway, as he put it."

I shook my head in disbelief.

"Jane, I beg you, listen to the truth! God strike me dead if I am lying! Your father has made me his mistress—against my will, I swear. He threatened to take my boys and never let me see them again unless I agreed to bed him. I had to agree. I assure you I had no will to do so!"

I felt something obdurate growing within me, a force as hard as granite. I wanted with all my strength to resist what my father was doing—preying on young women. First Will's sister, and now my sister-in-law. How many others had there been? How many would there be, unless he was stopped?

"Ned found us out," Cat was saying. "He was furious. Your father lied to him and told him I was no better than a tavern wench, offering myself to any man who would take me. He said I was not worthy to be Ned's wife or to be the mother of our sons."

I looked over at the sleeping boys, my nephews, so very young and vulnerable.

Cat had begun to cry. "Ned says the boys are not his. Now that he knows the truth about me, he has no idea who their father is. But he's wrong, Jane. Our sons were born long before your father made his demands on me. And I have always been a faithful wife."

"I will talk to Ned," I said.

Cat hung her head. "He won't listen."

"I will do what I can."

"Jane, don't let anything happen to my children. I love them more than anything in the world."

"I know you do. You are the best of mothers."

She walked over to the low pile of blankets where the boys lay, and put out her hand to softly stroke their hair.

"They are disowned by their father—yet they are Seymours. I swear it."

"Can they stay here with you?"

Cat shook her head. "Only for a few more days."

My plans with Will, my hopes for marriage had begun to dissolve before my eyes. Unless I could persuade Ned to soften his harsh attitude, or find someone else in the family to take the children in, I would have to become the protector of my young nephews. I sighed.

"I will take care of them, Cat," I said. "No matter what."

"I cannot spare the time to talk to you now, Jane," Ned said sharply as soon as he saw me enter his study and approach his vast desk strewn with documents and books, bits of paper and inkpots. He did not look at me but busied himself with examining the documents and writing on a large scroll held down with heavy seals. I knew he meant to warn me off. But he would not succeed.

"I have been to see Cat," I began. "What you are doing to her is unloving and unjust. I believe her to be the victim of our father's lust, and nothing more. She deserves pity and mercy, not punishment!"

"Oh? And what would you know of lust, my virgin sister?"

"I know that our father seduced Will Dormer's sister."

"The Dormers are trying to convince the world of that, so that they can hide the truth about the girl—that she is a Jezebel of lust herself."

"Ned! She was only fourteen years old! And our father is fifty!"

I saw his eyebrows rise slightly. Evidently he did not know how young Margery Dormer was. But he said nothing.

A messenger hurried into the room, handed a sealed document to Ned, saying "For the cardinal," and left. Ned broke the seal and perused the document—or pretended to. He frowned in concentration, reading the words before him, his lips moving.

I waited for him to finish, but after a moment or two I realized he was not going to finish. He was going to keep reading, keep concentrating on the document he held in his shaking hand, until I left him in peace.

But I had no intention of leaving him in peace.

"Does mother know that you have ordered your wife shut up at St. Agnes's?" I persisted.

I could tell by the set of Ned's jaw that I had asked an awkward question.

"Not now, Jane." As he spoke, another man entered the room. Ned gave him instructions and sent him out again.

"I must know. What am I to say to mother when I see her?"

"I said, not now." For the first time Ned looked at me—or rather, glared at me—and I could tell that his irritation was turning to anger.

"Can't you see that we are much preoccupied with the King's Great Matter? Have you no understanding at all?"

"My understanding is as ripe as yours, Ned, as well you know. And this is no trifling thing we are discussing. This is your wife. Your family. Your sons."

Ned threw down the document he was holding.

"They are not my sons! No one knows who their father—or fathers—are."

"You cannot disown your own children! You must not!"

"I cannot," Ned said between clenched teeth, "be responsible for my wife's transgressions."

"Henry and John are not transgressions, they are little boys. They resemble you—not in temperament, I hope, but certainly in looks. They are Seymours. And if you intend to abandon them, I do not."

"My wife's bastards are never to be brought within my sight again. Now I must take these papers to the cardinal."

With that Ned swept out of the room, his stride purposeful, his jaw firmly set against the onslaughts of reason, the claims of fatherhood, and the disillusionments of marriage. All I could do was watch him go, and curse his harshness. The fate of little Henry and John was in my hands.

I retrieved my trunk from the Thames waterman and prepared myself to disappoint Will by telling him I could not, after all, go through with the plans we had made. But as it turned out, there was no need. Will came to me, downcast and full of disappointment, on the night before we were to leave.

"We can't make our escape, Jane," he told me sadly. "The *Eglantine* was not as sound as I was told she was. She foundered off Shoebury Ness two days ago, in rough waters. She went down, and no one has seen so much as a timber of her since."

FIVE

OVERNIGHT, it seemed, Anne Boleyn became the talk of the court.

A rumor went around that the king's chief huntsman had told his grooms and his fewterers that while staying at a country house, King Henry had sent Anne a buck that he had killed that day. And with it he sent what the messenger said (in whispers of course) was a love letter.

Hardly had this news been spread than another rumor came to everyone's ears: the king had sent Anne more gifts, it was said, and more messages, and she had sent gifts and letters to him in return.

Soon it was being whispered that they met in secret, at a well guarded house, hidden in the forest, and that they exchanged kisses there—and more.

To these stories—confided in the greatest excitement—were added others: that King Henry was meeting with his legal advisers and requesting that the pope declare his marriage to

Queen Catherine no marriage at all. That he be declared a bachelor, free to marry any woman he chose.

This was the King's Great Matter, as I had heard my brother Ned call it. The greatest and most important issue at court.

There was only one conclusion to be drawn from all that we were hearing. Anne Boleyn was to be the king's new wife, once Queen Catherine was put aside. And all eyes were turned to Anne.

No one I knew had ever called her a beauty. Lavinia Terling, Bessie Blount, the king's sister Mary: these were the beauties of the palace. Nor was Anne pretty, like her soft-eyed, round-figured, gentle sister Mary or the voluptuous Bess Holland or Margaret Aylesford, who at one time had been Cardinal Wolsey's mistress and who lived at court, as her brother was one of Queen Catherine's confessors.

Fair-skinned, blue-eyed blondes were what men admired, fair women with sweet voices and retiring dispositions; Anne was as dark as a gypsy, with eyes like coals and thick black hair and the temperament (when angry, which was often) of a snarling vixen. What was more, she was said to be deformed, her swarthy complexion marred by moles. One of her fingers was cleft at the tip, so that it appeared to be two fingers and not one.

"The mark of the devil," said Maria de Salinas and the queen's other ladies nodded in agreement.

I remembered what Bridget had told me about Anne, especially about her rivalry with her sister. Mary Boleyn Carey had been the king's mistress for a number of years. Was Anne trying to seduce the king in order to compete with Mary? According to Bridget, she was brazen enough. Was she attractive enough? She was still unmarried at nearly twenty-five years old. (Uncharitable critics said she was older.) Why? Had her uncle, the powerful Duke of Norfolk, been planning for her to marry the king all along, just as he had planned for Henry Fitzroy to marry his daughter Mary? Had the duke assumed that Queen Catherine would die before long, her body worn out by her many childbirths, and that when she died, Anne would become the king's wife?

There was endless speculation, endless appraisals and reappraisals of Anne were made—many of them begrudging—and Anne herself, very conscious of all the attention she was receiving, became noticeably more aloof and superior. She wore a gold bracelet that the king had given her, engraved with two hearts entwined and a bow and arrow. She waved it around a good deal, making sure it was seen by everyone. When asked about it she said nothing, she merely smirked, her black eyes sparkling, then tossed her head and flounced off.

All the talk in those days was of Anne, but I continued to nurse my wounds and think of myself. I was in pain. I had lost Will. I was deeply disappointed and convinced that I had no future. More and more I felt aggrieved. I blamed my father. He was the one whose wanton passions, and lack of morality or restraint, had brought shame on our family and left me with only the bleakest of prospects.

I had never loved him, he had been too harsh and punitive a parent to nurture love. Now I hated him, as I had never before in my life hated anyone. Even to be in the same room with him was galling beyond measure. To see him—he was, I admit, a handsome man, though gruff and coarse—to hear his loud, strident voice, to accidentally brush past him aroused my fury, especially when he was shouting and laughing and throwing back his great head with its mane of grey-white hair. Everything about him revulsed me and filled me (God forgive me!) with murderous thoughts.

My grievances were many. My father's lust had prevented my marriage and blighted Ned's life and the lives of his children as well. His lies had ruined the reputations of at least two women—not to mention at least one servant girl, and I suspected there had been others. I believed in Cat's innocence and was much inclined to believe Will's sister innocent too; I thought her a victim of my father's demands.

My only consolation was that he was in constant pain from the gout, and that the pain was becoming worse. His cries of agony and his shouts of complaint were growing louder.

"Can you die from gout?" I asked his physician.

He hemmed and hawed. "I have never heard of it happening," he said at length, "but it is not impossible."

"Not impossible" was not at all a satisfactory answer. At least, I thought, if his gout is excruciating enough, he will be prevented from seducing any more women, or from forcing himself on them through threats.

When my mother came to court, which she rarely did, I could hardly bear to look at her. What did she know, or suspect, of my father's doings? No doubt he had lied to her, just as he had to Ned, and she had wanted to believe him. Yet I knew she had been fond of Cat, and was very fond indeed of her two young grandsons. She must miss them, I thought.

Yet I never heard her so much as utter their names.

My little nephews were living in the greatest secrecy at Croydon, in a house that belonged to the king's good friend and trusted chamber gentleman Thomas Tyringham. I had arranged for them to be sheltered there, their true identities hidden. The servants in the household were told only that the boys were the orphaned sons of a kitchen maid who had fallen ill and died; they were being cared for, so the story went, out of the king's charity.

I had hired a nurse and two maidservants to look after the boys, and I visited them as often as my duties in the queen's household allowed. Henry was barely three years old, and John only two, far too young to understand anything except that they missed their mother. They cried for her every night, the nurse told me. I was no real substitute for Cat, but the boys smiled when I visited and enjoyed the treats and toys I brought them. I hugged them and told them I loved them and tried to give them some motherly comfort.

I often asked myself what future they might have, and how and when they would ever be told the truth about who they were, but never arrived at any answers, only more questions. Like me, they seemed adrift, the course of their lives much in doubt. Disowned by their father, their mother taken from them, no one else in the family coming to their aid, they had no one but me. I vowed never to abandon them, or to reveal who or where they were to a hostile world.

"Where is my lady!"

King Henry's rich booming voice, more jovial than commanding, rang out through the queen's apartments.

"Where is my Lady Anne? My joy, my light?"

I winced.

He came bounding in to where Queen Catherine sat at her embroidery, her maids of honor seated in a semi-circle around her. Jane Popyngcort, her favorite reader, was reading aloud to us all as we sewed, from *The Lives of the Saints*.

At the sound of the king's voice the reading ceased, and we all knelt.

King Henry held out his hand to Anne, and she looked over quickly at the queen—who did not kneel, but went on with her embroidery, sitting where she was, taking no notice of her husband or Anne, though her wan cheeks flushed red.

Boldly Anne stood, and took the king's beringed hand. Henry motioned for the men waiting in the corridor outside to come in, and they obeyed, a dozen or so musicians, carrying drums and sackbuts and viols. They struck up a dance tune, and Henry led Anne in a lively dance, hopping and kicking with the energy of a man half his age and looking very pleased with himself as he grasped Anne and partnered her, smiling, through the twining, twisting steps.

"What a charming tune," I heard Queen Catherine say to her husband as she looked up briefly from her stitching. "Is it one of your own composition?" The king ignored her.

"She dances well, does she not, my joy, my little puffball?" Henry said to no one in particular.

"Like a tavern whore," I heard Maria de Salinas mutter under her breath.

King Henry dropped Anne's hand and moved deftly to stand in front of Maria.

"What was that?"

Maria de Salinas was no coward. She looked up at the king, her eyes venomous.

"I said nothing," she answered, her voice seething with resentment, her Spanish-accented English exaggerated, or so it seemed to me. "I just sneezed."

"Are you sneezing at my lady?" the king demanded, with sudden ferocity, at which the Spaniard took a deep breath and sneezed, loudly and insultingly, in Anne's direction.

"Out!" shouted the king, pointing to the door.

"But my lord—" Catherine began.

"Quiet, woman!"

Maria de Salinas got up slowly, and started to walk toward Catherine. But Catherine shook her head, ever so slightly. Maria stopped, cursed, and left the room.

"See that that woman leaves my court," the king snapped to Catherine's gentleman usher Griffith Richards, who bowed in acknowledgment.

Meanwhile Anne, knowing all eyes were on her, strolled to where the queen sat, still poking her needle into the cloth, held stiff in its frame, then drawing the needle out again.

"Another altar cloth?" Anne asked in her silkiest voice, moving to Catherine's side and plucking idly at the cloth-end that lay across Catherine's lap. "Or a new cover for your prie-dieu?" She smiled. I thought her expression closer to a sneer than a smile.

"The Lord loves fine embroidery!" Anne said with a flick of the cloth.

"The Lord loves virtue—and modesty," Catherine remarked, without looking up from her sewing.

"And fruitfulness," Anne retorted. "Fruitfulness above all, in a woman."

Catherine looked pointedly at Anne's belly, and smiled slightly. The look was not lost on Anne—or on the rest of us.

"A woman of twenty-five," Ines de Venegas said, "ought to be married so that she can prove herself fruitful. Unless, perhaps, she has some flaw." She held up her hand. "Such as too many fingers. No man would want a wife like that." And she sneezed, following which the rest of us sneezed, all together.

"Enough!" Henry called out and signaled to the musicians, who began to play the dance tune once again. He reached for Anne and held her closer to him than before as they dipped and swayed, deliberately altering the steps of the dance and substituting their own, more abandoned and suggestive chore-ography. Henry pulled Anne toward him, so tightly that her bodice was crushed against his doublet, then released her so that she practically fell back, half-laughing with the shock of his sudden release. He leaned over her and brushed his lips against her cheek, then murmured in her ear, then held her clasped hands behind her so that she was imprisoned in his embrace.

I turned away, I could not watch the embarrassing display—not because it was wanton and lewd, which it certainly was, but because the king and Anne were deliberately humiliating Catherine, flaunting their liaison (for how could anyone doubt that they were lovers after this display?) and challenging the queen to reprimand or insult them, as Maria de Salinas and the other Spaniard had done.

I was not prudish, Will and I knew each other's bodies well though we had not made love; we had been saving that ultimate delight for our wedding night. But all our intimacy went on in private, while the king and Anne were carrying on a public performance. And a performance intended to wound.

"Now, madam, what think you of our dancing?" Henry said, addressing his wife, when the tune ended. Despite his exertions he was not at all winded, though Anne, at his side, was panting and flushed, her black eyes bright with excitement.

Catherine's response was swift.

"The king does honor to my maidens when he takes them for his partners," she said equably. "And by honoring my maidens, he does honor to me!" She resumed her needlework, and the rest of us, having gotten up off our knees during the dancing, followed her example after King Henry threw up his hands and left the room, the musicians following at his heels.

Anne remained standing, her nose in the air, tapping her foot impatiently. Presently she whistled for her little dog, which jumped into her arms and began licking her face.

In the silence that followed, I sneezed. Soon others began sneezing, first Bridget, then the Spanish gentlewomen, then the other maids. Catherine could not help but smile at this sign of our loyalty. Anne stamped her foot.

And then, at a signal from the queen, Jane Popyngcort resumed her reading from *The Lives of the Saints,* telling the story of Saint Clothilde, a Christian among the pagan Franks in a long-ago age, who endured with miraculous patience and fortitude all the cruelties and humiliations of the barbarians, all the while smiling and forgiving her enemies and committing them to the mercies of the Lord.

"The prince! Make way for the prince!"

Dust rose in thick clouds as two horsemen galloped along the narrow roadway, shouting and waving their whips, scattering all the impediments in their path—heavily loaded carts and trudging peddlers, villagers on foot and pilgrims bound for the shrine of St. Hertha.

I was on my way to Thomas Tyringham's Croydon estate to visit my nephews when my journey was interrupted by the riders and their raucous shouting. I turned my horse toward the bushes that lined the roadside and let her crop the dry grass. Soon a small procession came into view as the dust began to clear.

First came a herald, bravely suited and mounted and wearing the king's livery. Then followed five mounted halbardiers, attempting to ride in phalanx though the road was too narrow and dipped sharply in the center. The halbardiers were escorting a gleaming silver litter, the metal worked into an elaborate design. Purple velvet curtains fringed in silver tissue hid the litter's occupant, though not for long. Presently the velvet curtains parted slightly, and I saw, peering out, the pale face of a small boy. I recognized Henry Fitzroy, who by order of the king was referred to as "the prince," though in fact he was only a duke in rank.

The costly litter was princely indeed, but there was nothing regal about the boy's white face; he looked frightened and ill. I imagined that the swaying and jouncing of the litter as it lurched along the rutted road had sickened him.

"Set me down!" he called out weakly.

At first he was not heard, the hubbub of squawking chickens and braying donkeys, loud voices and the rattle of carriage wheels drowned out his words. But after he had shouted several times the litter was at last set down.

He pushed the curtains aside and stumbled out. He closed his eyes and crouched in the dust of the roadway, heedless of his cream-colored silken hose and his shoes with their elaborate silver buckles, his shirt of fine white linen, so thin his skin could be clearly seen through it. His bejeweled hat with its colorful feathers fell off, his finery soon became smeared with the dirt of the road.

As I continued to watch, six men who had been farther back in the procession rode up, dismounted, and encircled the crouching boy. I could hear him coughing.

The entire procession came to a halt as the six men—I knew them to be royal physicians, who accompanied Henry Fitzroy wherever he went—examined their patient and conferred with one another. At length they remounted and the file of men and horses resumed their journey, at a slower pace. I fell into line not far from the silver litter, concerned that my own progress was likely to be slow, and that John and Henry, who had grown very attached to me, would be distressed and in tears when I did not arrive.

Before long the procession stopped again, and without waiting for the physicians to dismount and come to his aid, young

Fitzroy burst out of the litter and ran clumsily to the roadside where he was sick.

No one helped him.

Having rid his stomach of its contents, he rinsed off his face in a muddy stream and managed to climb back into the swaying vehicle.

Resigned to being late to meet my nephews, I touched my whip to my horse's flank and she jolted forward, shooting past the heralds who were resuming their loud demand for all in the road ahead to make way for the prince. I dug my heels into her sides and soon she was trotting along at a brisk pace toward Croydon.

SIX

FOLLOWING the sinking of the *Eglantine,* Will had said nothing more about our finding a way to escape together to some faraway place, but he had not lost all hope. He refused to yield to his parents' demand that he marry into the Sidney family, and told me often that he was waiting for me, and could never love anyone else. It moved me to tears to hear him say this, but even as I wept I shook my head, for my better judgment told me that all was against us. I was at war within myself; my despair over my future was all but unshakable, yet a flicker of hope remained, for I wanted so badly to believe, against all evidence, that there might still be a chance for us to make a life for ourselves far from the restrictions of the court and of our parents.

I was well aware that in choosing to care for my nephews I had taken on responsibilities that bound me and restricted me, yet when at my most sanguine I could see my way past them. Henry and John, against all odds, were thriving; though they missed their mother, they no longer cried for her every night, and as for their father, my brother Ned, he had always been a very remote figure to his sons, hardly ever seeing them as he was nearly always at court, constantly preoccupied with his duties for Cardinal Wolsey and with his own advancement. The boys had forgotten him, or so it seemed to me. At any rate they never said his name.

I thought that odd—and I thought it even more odd that though I was assured by their nurses that they often cried for their mother at night, they did not speak her name to me.

I had given up all thought of trying to convince Ned to restore his family, releasing his wife from her convent captivity and acknowledging her sons as his own. My poor sister-in-law Cat languished in isolation day after day, month after month, and I was not even allowed to visit her or write to her. No one in the family or among our servants ever mentioned her existence, and in fact Ned was talking of taking another wife. Like King Henry, he was seeking a way to have his first marriage declared no marriage at all (a "nullity," in the language of the lawyers, whose terms we were all growing accustomed to using as the King's Great Matter became more and more important). But I knew that Cat was no nullity, and I did not forget about her, or cease to think of her and her difficulties.

Meanwhile King Henry had laid siege to Catherine and was storming the walls of her impregnable dignity every day. We all heard him, demanding and arguing, attempting to wear down Catherine's resistance and shatter her pride.

"You must listen to reason, madam," he insisted. "You must remove yourself from our court and enter a convent. You have no place here! You are not a legal wife!"

We heard Catherine's low voice in reply, though it was often difficult to make out her words.

"You and I have been living in sin all these years!" he went on. "You must repent—within the walls of a nunnery, where you may pray for forgiveness and mend your life."

It was always the same. He argued, urged, persisted in his forceful tone, and she resisted, quietly adamant. She infuriated him, until he became shrill.

"Haven't I told you a hundred times that all the clergy of England have accused me of tempting the judgment of the Lord, by wrongfully taking my dead brother's wife? 'If a man taketh his brother's wife, it is an impurity,' he quoted. 'He hath uncovered his brother's nakedness; they shall be childless.' There it is, from the Book of Leviticus."

But Catherine, whose chaplains were quite adept at quoting Scripture, had been advised to answer this passage with another, and we heard her doing so in uncharacteristically loud tones.

"The Book of Deuteronomy is even more clear," she began. "'When brethren dwell together, and one of them dieth without children, the wife of the deceased shall not marry to another, but his brother shall take her.' You would have sinned, my lord, had you not married me after your brother Arthur died and left me a widow."

At this Henry cursed, and shouted, and demanded once again that Catherine retire to a convent. Had he been the Duke of Norfolk or my brother Ned, I thought, he would not have argued, he would simply have acted. He would have had his soldiers seize the queen and drag her off to a nun's cell. But he was not that kind of man. He was not a brute, or a churl. And he had lived, fairly amicably it was said, with Catherine for nearly twenty years.

More important, according to Ned—my source for all that was vital at court, especially where the King's Great Matter was concerned—was the fact that Queen Catherine's nephew was the most powerful man in Europe: Emperor Charles V. Ruler of a vast empire, commander of vast armies and possessor of untold treasure from the silver mines of the Americas. Emperor Charles, who was Queen Catherine's protector—or so she believed. King Henry would not dare imprison her or harm her without risking the wrath of the fearsome emperor and his armies—not while his own treasury was all but empty, according to Ned, and his fighting forces sadly weakened as a result.

King Henry did not harm his wife, at least not physically. But he wounded her all the same. He banished her favorite Spanish ladies from court, and sent many of them back to Spain. She wept for days. She mourned their loss, they had been her lifelong companions and dearest friends and confidantes (though I remained her confidante, and she trusted me). And, what was even more hurtful to her, the king sent Princess Mary away as well. Separating mother and daughter was indeed cruel, and the queen suffered. She suffered, not only because her beloved Mary, her jewel and delight, was kept from her but because she feared their separation would be permanent.

"He will never let me see her again," she said to me, shaking her head sadly. "Not even if I do everything he wants. And I will not. I cannot. My poor, dear child. What will become of her?"

Had Anne or had she not agreed to marry the king? That was the question, endlessly debated in the chambers where we maids of honor clustered in corners to share what we knew, or suspected. The queen was still queen, but might not be for much longer, if the king's lawyers and Cardinal Wolsey had their way. Was there a private agreement between the king and his new mistress? An agreement to wed? Would we soon be forced to bow to Anne as we now did to Queen Catherine, and to revere and serve her as we revered and served our present queen?

The thought was too strange. Queen Catherine was a royal princess by birth, as far above us in rank as it was possible for a woman to be. Anne was just a girl, like us, in the queen's court. The Boleyns were not royal. Anne's mother was a Howard, to be sure, and the sister of the highborn Duke of Norfolk. But the Howards were not Tudors. Anne certainly did not act the way a royal lady ought to act—gracious, kind, generous to her inferiors. Pious. Dignified. Anne was none of these things.

But she might, we maids whispered to one another, be fertile. Indeed, we whispered after glancing at Anne's waist, she might at that moment be carrying the king's son.

Bridget, who had become Lady Wingfield and was no longer a maid of honor but a higher-ranking lady in waiting, remained Anne's friend—her closest friend at court. She appeared to have forgiven Anne's treachery in attempting to seduce Lord Wingfield, and of all of us, she was the one most likely to be told Anne's secrets. Yet she claimed that Anne had told her nothing at all about her intimacy with the king or her expectations for the future.

This puzzled us. Anne was boastful, not secretive. She sought attention.

"The king must have told her to be silent," we said to each other. "It must have been a royal command."

Anne was silent, but her behavior spoke loudly. She treated Queen Catherine with increasing disdain, she smirked and snickered, she looked down on the rest of us as if from a lofty height—the height of a throne, perhaps, I was thinking.

She appeared laden with pearls the size of pigeon's eggs and rubies larger than I had ever seen any woman wear—rubies that could only have come from the royal treasure stored in the Tower.

Diamonds sparkled in Anne's thick black hair, and at her neck, and were sprinkled over the bodices of her gowns. Diamonds from the king, gifts made to the woman he meant to marry.

Yet Catherine was still our royal mistress, and most of us were still loyal to her. When Anne was disdainful toward the queen we sneezed—our private signal of disapproval and disgust—and when she flaunted her beautiful jewels we bumped against her and made her spill her wine on the skirts of her gowns. We were petty. We were mean. We told tales, and whispered together and laughed while looking directly at Anne, leaving no doubt that we were laughing at her expense. We staged wounding little collisions, banging into her or tripping the servants so that they fell across her path. We made certain this happened so often that she was covered in bruises, just as I had been when I first came to court and Queen Catherine's Spanish ladies had pushed and shoved and jostled me. We let the queen's lapdogs track their muddy feet across the embroidered counterpanes on Anne's bed, and attract the fleas from the rushes and leave them behind in the soiled satin folds.

Anne swore at us, and sulked, and complained, but we were too sly for her. We escaped punishment, for the most part. But we were all waiting, most impatiently, for the news we expected to hear any day, news that the king had found a way to put his wife aside and marry Anne Boleyn.

Then one day I noticed that Jane Popyngcort, the Belgian noblewoman among us rumored to have been the king's mistress in the long-ago days when he was a young man making war in France and feasting in Flanders, appeared wearing a startling ornament: a heavy gold pendant with a large ruby and garnet. A piece of jewelry to rival the costly gems Anne wore.

"You don't suppose he's gone back to her," Anne Cavecant

said to me as Jane entered the room. "Or perhaps he has two mistresses now, a young one and an old one, Anne and Jane." She giggled.

Jane sat down among us and took up her embroidery. I looked around for Anne, to watch her reaction, but she was nowhere nearby. I felt very curious about Jane and her fine piece of jewelry, and became even more curious when, the following day, Jane once again appeared lavishly adorned. This time she was wearing a large ornate gold cross on a thick gold chain—another rich gift, we all supposed.

"Are you to be married then, Jane?" Anne Cavecant asked. "Are your lovely ornaments gifts from your future husband? And is he in the lowlands across the sea, or here in England?"

"I am returning home," was all she said, her English distorted by her thick accent. "After I arrive, I do not know."

"You must have some plan in mind," Lavinia Terling put in. "Your parents, your family, must have a match arranged for you. And a large dowry perhaps?"

"I do not know. It is possible." She would not look at any of us when we questioned her. She was secretive, suspicious of our questions. Yet as the time for her departure drew nearer, she displayed more costly adornments. Gifts from a man who was already married? we asked one another, exchanging knowing glances. Or a sudden inheritance, perhaps?

Jane's newfound riches intrigued us, and her silence about them intrigued us even more. It was a mystery, a diversion from the endless talk and rumor and guesses about the king and Anne.

Before long the mystery deepened. Jane Popyngcort departed for the Flemish court, saying little to any of us but spending the final hour before her departure closeted with the queen. At the end of that hour I saw Ned come for Jane, with an escort of liveried grooms, to escort her to the river stairs where a wherry waited to take her to her ship.

My interest aroused, I went to stand before a barred window from which I could see the river and watch the small boats come and go. In a few minutes Ned and the grooms came into view, with Jane in her traveling cloak in their midst. Her trunks were put aboard the wherry, and with them, a smaller casket, so heavy it took two men to lift it.

Later I told Anne Cavecant and Lavinia Terling what I had seen.

"What do you suppose was in that heavy casket?" I wondered aloud.

"Those jewels and chains of hers," Lavinia said. "She must have had quite a few."

"It was coins," Bridget announced, coming up to the three of us. "I wormed the truth out of one of her little Flemish maidservants. The girl was terrified. She knew something she wasn't supposed to know. She overheard Jane talking, in English, and understood what she heard. Jane thought the maid knew no English. It was all about the king and Anne Boleyn's mother. How they had been lovers, long ago."

Bridget's eyes widened and she grinned. "Imagine the scandal!"

I thought about my own father and Cat. Yes, I could indeed imagine the scandal. But I had to know more.

"Did King Henry pay Jane to be quiet about his past relations with Anne's mother? Has he slept with Anne and Mary and their mother too?"

"That's what the girl heard. And Jane was paid all right, but not by the king."

"Who paid her then?"

"The girl doesn't know. Someone at court."

"The cardinal," Anne Cavecant said. "He's rich."

"Or Anne's father?" I speculated.

I was trying to puzzle it all out. Henry had seduced all the Boleyns (something I had never heard before), and Jane knew of it. She must have threatened to tell what she knew, and demanded payment to keep silent. But there had to be more to Jane's secret than the threat of scandal, it had to represent a threat to the success of the King's Great Matter. There had to be some way in which Jane, if she revealed the truth, could ruin the nullity suit, or prevent King Henry from marrying Anne once the suit was successful. If that was indeed his plan. I resolved to ask Ned about this.

In the meantime we watched, and waited, and told each other what we knew, or suspected. We heard of great events occurring in the world beyond England's borders: a terrifying victory by the armies of the pagan Turks over the Christians at a place called Mohacs; the destruction of Rome, heart and center of all Christendom, by the soldiers of Queen Catherine's nephew Emperor Charles, and the capture and imprisonment of the pope; and in the northern imperial lands, vast warfare with the peasants rising up to fight against their masters. Surely the end of the world was approaching, many thought, on hearing these things. Surely the biblical apocalypse was upon us.

But to us, in those tense days, the expected end of King Henry's marriage to Queen Catherine counted for more than anything. We were in dread that our own little world was about to end, there in the queen's apartments, and that all that was familiar and right and precious to us was about to be swept away.

It was Lavinia Terling who first began to shiver, and grow warm, and complain that she needed air and a drink of cool water.

The June sun burst down on us from a cloudless sky, we were all hot as we prepared to leave Greenwich to travel to Waltham Abbey in Essex, to begin our summer progress.

There was much confusion as the servants were packing all the bed linens and tapestries, plate and carpets, cooking pots and clothing and hunting gear into chests and baskets. Dogs were barking and the horses, impatient in the heat, were stamping and whinnying with impatience.

And Lavinia was shivering.

She was no longer hot, we realized. She was cold. She had a chill. Her blue eyes were clouded, her bow-shaped mouth twitched, her lips pursed unattractively. As we watched, her face began growing pink, then red. Her blond hair became damp beneath her cap, rivulets of perspiration were running down her neck and into the bodice of her gown.

"Jane!" I saw panic in her eyes. She reached out for me, calling my name, and I instinctively drew back.

"Help me, Jane! I'm so hot!"

All her clothes were damp.

Suddenly everyone did as I had, and moved back, away from Lavinia.

"The sweat! The death sweat! She has the sweat!"

"Get away! Get back! Get out!"

The sweat was a scourge that ravaged us, leaving many dead. It was far worse than the plague, though its visitations were less frequent. When the sweat appeared, it spread swiftly, leaving many dead. Everyone who came down with it died, or nearly everyone. They died horribly. Painfully. And quickly! Healthy at noon, dead by suppertime, went the saying we all learned as children. Healthy at supper, dead by midnight.

And now the sweat had made its appearance among us.

Instinct took over, and we began to run.

The king was shouting. "Fitzroy! Get Fitzroy to the north! Haste, haste!!"

Sparing barely a glance for the rest of us, he was swiftly mounted and galloping away.

Servants, guardsmen, grooms, everyone was running. Carts were overturned, the terrified horses trapped in their harnesses, screaming, struggling to right themselves. Flour poured from broken barrels, beer ran out in streams from splintered casks and sank into the thirsty ground. Squawking chickens fluttered, half flying, half running underfoot.

"The sweat is in the palace!" came voices all around me. "Abandon the palace!"

Amid the tumult I saw two men roughly snatching Lavinia and putting her on a horse, then whipping the poor beast until it ran, flanks red with blood, toward the open fields.

I went quickly in the opposite direction, toward the riverbank, thinking—though my mind was too dazed to think very clearly—that I might find a boatman who would take me away, anywhere, away from the threat of death.

Then all of a sudden Will was beside me.

"Thank heaven I found you," he said, grasping me by the shoulders, his eyes full of concern. He inspected me closely.

"Are you hot? Are you sweating?"

I shook my head.

He lifted my arms, heedless of the tightness of my sleeves, and ripped away the cloth that covered my armpits.

"Good," he said. "No sores." Victims of the sweat developed large painful blisters, often under their arms or in their groins.

"And you, Will? How are you?"

"Well."

"You were with Lavinia," Will said.

"Yes. We were all preparing to travel together, Lavinia and I, Anne and Bridget—"

"But Lavinia was the only one who became ill."

"As far as I could see."

"Listen to me, Jane," he said, grasping my shoulders more tightly, his voice more urgent than I had ever heard it. "Nowhere is safe. You must go back into the palace."

"But there is disease there!"

He shook his head. "You must go back inside, shut yourself in with the queen, in her apartments, and bar all the doors and windows. Do not let anyone in. No one. Do you understand?"

I nodded.

"Above all, do not let anyone in who has sweat on their foreheads, or whose clothes are damp, or who looks weak. There is food in the castle larders. Bring it up into the queen's rooms. And bring water. Lots of water. You may have to stay there for some time. If anyone in the queen's rooms comes down with the illness, be ruthless. Throw them out the window, into the moat. It is your only chance to survive, Jane."

"Into the moat?" A horrifying thought—and one I would never have expected to hear from Will. Surely he couldn't have meant it. Or could he? "But the queen has a physician—" I began.

"He may have deserted her. Besides, there is little physicians can do against the sweat."

A terrible thought came to me. What if Will got sick? What if he died?

"Dear Will, if anything should happen to you—I couldn't—I don't think I could—"

"Yes you could. Of course you could. You are strong. And that is why you will stay healthy, and safe, here with the queen." There was an edge in his voice, almost a hint of anger. He was being stubborn, challenging fate. He was saying that if he should die, I would find the toughness deep within me to go on without him. He was not allowing any thoughts of death, or defeat, to weaken him or frighten me. And it worked; I took heart from his stern, resolute optimism.

"I will go to Croydon now to make sure Henry and John are safe and well. I will send you word as soon as I know they are all right."

"And Cat?"

He nodded. "I will try to find out whether the nuns of St. Agnes's are affected."

We made our way back, through the chaos in the courtyard to the palace entrance. There was fighting, shouting. Amid the damage and disorder, men were assaulting one another, struggling over damaged carts, chasing terrified horses that plunged and reared and galloped this way and that. Amid the noise and confusion, the palace itself looked deserted, unprotected. There were no guardsmen to prevent us from entering through the series of gates, no grooms to bar our way upstairs to the threshold of the queen's apartments. After assuring himself that I would be all right, Will turned to me and enfolded me in his arms and kissed me. A deep, long kiss. I tried to suppress the thought that it might be our last.

Will hugged me fiercely and we wished each other luck and I tried to smile jauntily and bravely as I waved goodbye.

"Soon, Jane, soon," Will called out as he went. "Keep me in your heart."

"Always."

After he was gone, I slumped against the wall, closing my eyes and feeling the weight of my weariness descend. My legs were weak under me. I was dizzy. Were these signs that I was coming down with the sweat?

I did not feel hot. My face was not damp, and my clothing too was dry. I entered the queen's apartments, unchallenged. No guardsmen stood guarding her outer door, none of the ladies in waiting or maids of honor were present inside to welcome me. I found Queen Catherine kneeling on her prie-dieu in her bedchamber, praying in a low voice for mercy. Candles burned before the small portraits of her dead babies. A lifeless Christ hung limp on a large wooden crucifix fastened to the wall.

Help us, I prayed silently. Help us now.

"I hope you are not feeling ill, Your Majesty?"

"No, Jane. I am not."

The royal bedchamber, and adjacent rooms, were all but deserted save for Griffith Richards, the queen's faithful gentleman usher, who stood by the bedchamber door, a short sword at his waist. Guarding the queen—though neither he nor his sword could guard her from the terrible sickness. Beyond him, in a small antechamber, half a dozen trembling servants cowered. As I watched, I noticed that they were keeping a wary eye on one another. Anyone, any time, could show the telltale signs of the sweat, as Lavinia had. They were watching for even the slightest such sign. A shiver. A twitch. A stink. A dampness.

I went over to the gentleman usher. "We must be careful," I said softly. "We must not let in anyone we do not know, anyone who looks ill."

I checked to make sure all the doors and windows were barred, as Will had cautioned me to do. The few servants were sent down to the palace larders to fetch barrels of salt meat and oats, sugar and honey, beer and ale.

I remembered what Will had said about throwing anyone with the disease out the window into the moat. It had seemed too outlandish a suggestion to be thought of. But the more I considered the danger we were all in, the more seriously I took it. Most of the windows in the queen's apartments were small—too small for a body to squeeze through. I went to the largest of them and grasped the old iron bars that formed a protective grid over it. I tugged. Immediately I felt the stonework give way slightly. Under the more powerful tugging of a strong man like Griffith Richards, I thought, it would give way completely. It would be possible to pull the iron back so that a struggling, unwilling body could be pushed out. It was a long drop to the moat below.

A deadening silence filled the queen's rooms. The courtyard outside had grown still, except for the occasional muffled shout or gallop of horses' hooves. As if from a distance, we heard the first faint wails from the village beyond the palace walls, wails of lamentation for the dead.

Healthy at noon, dead by suppertime.

The long summer twilight grew dim. Servants brought in a meager supper and set it before the queen. She ate little. No one was hungry. We were all waiting, in a state of dread, for someone among us to begin to shiver, and then grow warm, and demand a drink of cool water. We watched each other apprehensively.

Finally, when it grew dark, I helped the queen prepare for bed.

She did not want to talk. She was preoccupied, made numb, it seemed, by the sudden crowded events of the day.

"Henry, Henry, Mary," she kept repeating in a whisper, her eyes intent on some unseen image. Presently she lay down to rest, with Griffith Richards standing guard just outside her door.

It was after midnight when there came a pounding at the outer entrance to the royal apartments, where two thick oaken doors separated the quarters of the king and queen from the wing where royal officials and visitors normally occupied their offices and chambers.

I peered out through the crack between the doors.

"Yes? What is it?"

A man stood before the entrance, out of breath and coughing. He was well dressed but his clothes were dusty. He removed his hat.

"I am Doctor Lawrence Barchwell," he said. "Of the cardinal's household."

"Is His Eminence well?"

"He is, thanks be to God. But many among his servants have died. Also one of his sons." I knew that Cardinal Wolsey had a mistress and children, somewhere to the north of the capital. "He sends me with word of the lady Lavinia Terling," the doctor said.

"Lavinia!" Poor frightened Lavinia, red-faced and reeking when last I saw her, sweat pouring from her, reaching out for me, imploring me to help her. I shuddered at the memory.

"She has been found. Dead in a wood near Clopsfield."

Healthy at noon, dead by suppertime.

"Was she alone?"

He nodded.

"Lord rest her soul," I said, and crossed myself.

"Are you ill?" I asked the doctor.

"No," he answered, and smiled wanly. "Not at present. If I were, I would be the first to know. And I would not have entered these precincts."

I did my best to scrutinize his face through the narrow crack in the door. I saw no signs of the sweat on his brow. I thought he was telling the truth. I took the risk of offering him some of our food and he entered the outer chamber.

"Will you rest here for the night?" I asked, but the doctor shook his head.

"Thank you but no," he said. "There are many who have need of me. I dare not rest until I have given what help I can." Then, thanking me once again, he took what we had to offer, and rode off toward the village, where lights burned dimly.

When the doctor had gone I lay down and tried to sleep. But the image of Lavinia's ravaged face would not leave me. The most beautiful of us, turned so ugly by the merciless disease, and then taken so cruelly, so quickly.

Would we survive?

I went to the queen's prie-dieu and knelt. The cushion was still warm from her body. It was a long time before at last I got up off my knees, went to my bed, and lay down in the darkness. Spare us, spare us, spare us, was all I could think. Let us live through this night. Spare us.

SEVEN

We awoke to the sounds of mourning.

Bells rang out ceaselessly, their funereal pealing reminding us constantly that we were surrounded by death—and menaced by it.

Carts piled high with corpses rattled through the palace courtyard, rolling slowly toward the uncultivated fields where, each year in plague season, a huge pit was dug to hold the bodies of the dead. The carts were followed by weeping mourners, some solemn, some near hysteria and frantic with grief.

I stayed within the queen's apartments, just as Will had said I must, but from the windows I could see, within the palace grounds and along the riverbank, villagers trudging past, many carrying crying children in their arms. Some came to the palace and tried to force their way in, but we were barricaded securely. No one gained entrance.

No one, that is, until Anne Boleyn arrived.

Anne had not been with the rest of us when Lavinia Terling became ill and fear of the sweat began spreading. She had been with the king, having left early that morning to go riding with him. No one had seen her since then. She had not been with the king when he returned from his morning ride—just at the time word began to spread that Lavinia had the sweat. He had ridden into the courtyard of the palace in the midst of the spreading panic. And he had left again at once.

Now Anne had returned, and was demanding entrance to the palace.

"We must let her in, of course," Queen Catherine said when I brought her to a high window and she saw Anne and heard her shrill cries.

"But Your Highness, we cannot let anyone in with us. She might have the disease."

"And if she did have it, would she be able to pound so loudly with her fists and call out so fiercely?"

For Anne was indeed making a very loud racket and showing no sign of weakness.

"I will see to her," Griffith Richards said, patting the sword that hung from his waist. I knew that he had no love for Anne; he blamed her for enticing the king into adultery, even though he knew well enough, as we all did, that King Henry had had a long list of previous mistresses, including Anne's sister—and, if Jane Popyngcort was to be believed, Anne's mother.

"Where is the king? I know he is here, waiting for me. Let me in! I demand to see him! I demand that you let me in at once!"

At length, and only after Queen Catherine ordered him to do so, Griffith Richards admitted the furious Anne, who in her bedraggled state, her clothing and boots dirty from the road, her tangled black hair tumbling down her back, her face smudged and her eyes full of fury, resembled nothing so much as a spitting tomcat. When she stomped into the queen's apartments I saw several of the serving girls giggling at the sight of her, which only made her more infuriated.

"Where is he? Where is the king?"

I thought, if only the guards were here, they would never allow her to behave this way.

I followed Anne as she searched from room to room, sighing with exasperation, and coming at last to the queen's bedchamber. Catherine sat at her table, reading.

"Where is the king? What have you done with him?"

Catherine paused before replying, and fixed Anne with her level gaze.

"It is our habit—indeed it is our duty—to bow before the queen," I said to Anne, my tone sharp. "And as you know full well, we maids of honor do not speak to the queen unless addressed by her first. Have you forgotten?"

Anne glared at me briefly, then turned her eyes on Queen Catherine.

"My husband is not here," Catherine said quietly. "No doubt he is in seclusion, as he ought to be. To ensure that his precious life is spared in this season of danger."

"He ought to be with me!" Anne burst out. "He took me riding. Then he rode off on his own. He left me!" Her voice quivered, no longer the voice of a petulant woman, but an anxious child.

"He is the king," Catherine said mildly. "You are hardly his only concern."

Catherine's words had a bitter edge, which surprised me. But Anne barely seemed to hear her. She seemed to enter a state of reverie, her voice plangent.

"He didn't say anything to me, he just rode away. There was a farm, I went there but they said there was sickness. I thought he would come back for me. Why didn't he come back?"

She seemed genuinely bewildered. I thought, she must be very tired, to speak like this to the queen.

"Why didn't you ride to Hever?" I asked. Hever Castle was the principal dwelling of the Boleyns.

"I started to, but then I heard there was sickness in Kent, so much sickness—"

"But your family, weren't you concerned to find out whether they were afflicted?"

Anne turned and looked at me then, a look I could not fathom at first. A shadow passed over her face, her expression altered.

"My sister is ill, her husband is dead. My brother may be dying. I did not need to know any more than that." She sat down before going on.

"There is disease everywhere. Every rider I met said so. 'Do not go to Canterbury! Do not go to London!' they said. 'Do not go north.' I thought I might ride to Croydon, but then I learned that Thomas Tyringham was dying, and that many others in his household were dead and buried. So I came back here. I was sure the king would be waiting for me here! Where is he?"

"Thomas Tyringham? Dying of the sweat?"

Anne nodded. "What can it matter to you?"

My muscles were tense with fear. My nephews. Will. They were at Croydon, on Master Tyringham's estate. I had to know that they were not among those stricken.

"Are you certain of this?"

Anne shrugged. She looked weary, and passed her hand over

her forehead. "The roads are full of stories. Tavern gossip. Everyone is afraid." She paused, then said simply, "I need to lie down."

Though we had little enough water, Catherine insisted that Anne be allowed to wash, and told Griffith Richards to bring her a basin and ewer of water. He obeyed—with an ill grace. I led Anne, who was suddenly docile, with no trace of her former fury, into the room where the maids of honor usually slept and lent her some of my clean clothing. I knew that the clothes would be ill-fitting, as Anne was taller than I was, and more curvaceous.

Griffith Richards brought the water and we left Anne to cleanse herself in private.

"She is so frightened," I remarked to Richards as we waited together in an adjacent room.

"As well she ought to be," was his reply. "And not only of the sweat. She knows that everyone is against her."

"Everyone but the king."

"Ah, but the king is changeable. He cannot be relied on. And there is no one else for her to turn to. All who love our good queen Catherine must despise Anne. Even her uncle Norfolk criticizes her for being too proud."

Anne's uncle had begun to speak ill of her, and his words were repeated. She thought too highly of herself, he said. She wore too many jewels. She gave herself airs. She spoke too familiarly to the king. She imagined that one day she would be the most important woman at the court. What the duke wanted was quite different. In his plan his daughter Mary would be exalted to the highest rank, the loftiest position of power and influence among all the ladies of rank. She would marry Henry Fitzroy, and Henry Fitzroy would one day be king. By then Anne Boleyn would be forgotten, and Queen Catherine would be living in obscurity in a convent. Queen Mary would be supreme above all other women, her son by Henry Fitzroy would be the heir to the throne. And the Duke of Norfolk himself would be the true font of power.

"Her uncle accuses her of being too proud," I told the gentleman usher, "and yet she is guilty of nothing more than obeying the king's will. His royal command."

Richards was not convinced. "No matter what the king may say or do, we are all master of our souls. We must all answer to God for our sins. She could have said no to his wooing. She could have fled, run to the safety of her family."

I shook my head. "The family that tolerated—no, encouraged—her sister's pastime with the king? I hardly think so. The Boleyns have profited greatly by their daughters' sinning, as you put it. Thomas Boleyn seems very quick to seek his own advantage."

"All the worse for her then," Richards snapped. "A sinner from a lair of sinners."

I could not help smiling at him, as if to puncture his hauteur. "And are you so free from sin?"

He had no answer, but kept his expression of disdain.

I shrugged and let the moment pass. I was just as harsh in my judgment of my father as Griffith Richards was in his judgment against Anne. And was I, Jane Seymour, entirely free from sin?

Presently I went in to where Anne, having washed, had gone to bed and was sleeping, her mouth open, her thin lips twitching faintly as she dreamed.

I looked down at her, wondering why I had seemed to argue with Griffith Richards on her behalf. I had no more love for her, or regard for her, than he did; I thought her a self-obsessed, rude, irreverent girl whose cruelty to the admirable queen was hateful.

Yet I thought I had detected, in her childlike fear earlier that afternoon, something very vulnerable, something that tempered her other qualities and made her less objectionable. Even if only slightly so.

I saw that, as Griffith Richards had said, she had cut herself adrift: from her sisters among the maids of honor (all except Bridget), from the other courtiers, from all those who loved Queen Catherine and felt sympathy for her. Being the king's mistress isolated Anne from others, especially since the King's Great Matter had split the court into two camps, those whose desire to serve King Henry came before everything and everyone else, and those who were loyal to the queen and her cause.

As to Anne's family, I had not observed any of them closely enough to be able to say whether or not they would be her allies, should she need to call on them. She and her sister Mary were rivals—at least Anne considered them to be so, according to Bridget. The others were all but unknown to me, though I often saw Thomas Boleyn at court, walking swiftly, usually carrying a satchel full of papers, bent on some errand or other and looking as though no force on earth could deter him from his fixed purpose.

Griffith Richards sniffed. Muttering "all the worse for her," he went away, leaving me to watch the sleeping Anne and ponder his words. He was right, King Henry was, most likely, Anne's only ally. A powerful protector indeed—for now. But what of the future? What if Emperor Charles chose to send his armies to invade England, to save Queen Catherine from the threat of the king's nullity suit? Would Henry abandon Anne, just as he had ridden off and abandoned her on their ride together? Just as he had left her to fend for herself as the dreaded sweat descended on England, bringing so much fear and pain and death in its wake?

* * *

A spare supper was served, and the queen sat down to eat it, insisting that I share her table.

"We can hardly keep to our usual ceremony here, Jane," she said. "I will be glad of your company while I sup."

We had not eaten much when we heard a horse gallop into the courtyard below. It was a messenger, sent by Will to say that the chamber gentleman Thomas Tyringham had died but that he, Will, had left Tyringham's estate and was at another nearby estate near Woldringham, with his two young friends.

I knew, of course, who the "two young friends" were: my nephews Henry and John.

"And are they well?" I called down to the rider.

"I believe so, madam," came the response. "Though there's many a poor soul who's well in the morning and in his coffin by evening."

"What of the sweat in Woldringham?" I wanted to know.

"That I cannot say. But I was told to tell you that the nuns of St. Agnes's are in good spirits, and their guest thrives."

So Cat was surviving the disease. This was a great relief, and I chose to assume that Will and Henry and John were all right.

I thanked the messenger and threw down a coin to him, then returned to the table with the queen.

The following morning Anne was slow to rise and ate little. Her spirits brightened a bit when, with a small commotion in the courtyard, Bridget Wingfield arrived at the palace and, since she showed no sign of the sweat, was allowed to join us in the queen's apartments. Queen Catherine was still in her bedchamber but the rest of the household came at once to greet the newcomer.

We were very glad to see that she brought with her some supplies and provisions, casks of wine and oil, flour, salt fish and even a few baskets of vegetables from the Wingfield estate at Darenth. She also brought news.

"Is the king with you?" Anne asked Bridget at once.

"He was, but now he has gone to Tittenhanger, to his tower there. He is all alone in the tower room. He lowers a basket out the window four times a day for his food. He occupies himself in reading and concocting new remedies for the sweat. In truth, he is terrified of it. More terrified than any of us I think.

"Oh, and Jane," she went on, "my husband has had a letter from your brother Edward. Most of those in your family are tolerably well, but your father is ill."

"Is he likely to die?" I asked.

Bridget shook her head. "No one can say. But most of them do, once they start to stink. Once the sores appear."

God help me, I confess, I prayed for my father to die. If, as many said, the sweat was divine punishment, then surely no one deserved it more.

"There is a letter for you, Anne. From His Majesty."

"Read it please, Bridget."

Bridget looked embarrassed.

"Would you not rather read it by yourself, to yourself?"

"I am tired," Anne said, and indeed her voice was listless. She leaned on one arm. "Read it. I care not who hears."

"Sweeting," the letter began, "fear nothing from this passing scourge. If we are cautious, and use good care, we will not be afflicted. Women are not taken as often as men. Take manus Christi and mix it with vinegar and wormwood, rosewater and brown bread crumbs. Smell this often and eat little. Purge your rooms each day with fire. If you can put living spiders into a pouch around your neck the poison will not enter through the heart. I would send you more potions but my apothecary Sartorius is ill and dying. Do not sleep! Else you may not wake.

"Yours from the heart of one who desires you above all things, and will soon send you a shooting glove for us to take hunting. Fear not for want of grain but fasting will drive out sickness."

The letter was signed, "Your Henry, heart and soul."

I noticed that Anne was nodding off as Bridget was reading the king's letter. He cautioned against sleep. I wondered if I ought to wake her. I reached out to touch her shoulder, meaning to shake her gently and rouse her.

Her shoulder was wet.

I gasped, loudly. I couldn't help myself. We all knew what wetness meant. Sweat!

"Anne, wake up! Anne!"

She murmured a few words.

I backed away. "She feels wet. Her skin is hot," I said. With a boldness that surprised me, I grasped her arms and raised them high, as Will had done to me when he came to Greenwich just as fear of the sweat was gripping the palace and the town. I was looking for sores, blisters, evidence of the disease.

Sure enough, in the hollows of Anne's underarms were angry red pustules. She had begun to shiver.

"Oh my Lord," I heard Bridget cry out. "My Lord, preserve her! Preserve us all!"

"The moat!" Griffith Richards shouted. "Throw her into the moat!"

He went to the largest window in the royal apartments and, grasping the metal bars, gave a mighty tug on them. There was a crash of tumbling masonry as the old stones and mortar gave way, to reveal a clear if narrow opening. An opening barely wide enough for a small woman to squeeze through.

But Anne is not a small woman, I thought. Still—

Griffith Richards picked Anne up and hurried to the window. She kicked and squirmed, struggling to free herself from his strong grasp.

"No, wait!" It was Bridget. "Not that!"

"It is the only way," Richards insisted. "Otherwise we will all perish. Would you have that on your conscience?"

"Don't wait!" the servants were chanting. Their faces reflected no dread, only a cruel glee. Griffith Richards had been right. Anne was hated.

Had Will been with us, he would not have hesitated to do the thing that would save us all. Yes, I thought. Do it. Do it and be done with her . . .

Richards was stuffing Anne's struggling body through the opening in the stonework. She was kicking vainly and crying out for Henry.

"Stop!"

At the sound of Queen Catherine's voice, the gentleman usher hesitated, looking back over his shoulder at his royal mistress. But then I heard him say "no" and he resumed pushing and shoving Anne's resistant body through the narrow opening.

"Stop this at once! It is my royal command! My husband would never allow this!"

I saw Griffith Richards's large hands grow slack. He hung his head, though he still kept his hold on Anne's bulky gown.

"We are Christians, not savages!" Catherine was saying. "Release that woman at once!"

Richards loosened his grip and stood aside. I saw him grasp his short sword.

Sobbing, sweating, Anne was managing to pull herself back into the room. No one went to her aid. We were all too much in fear of the disease.

"Come with me, Anne," Queen Catherine said calmly, walking toward the doorway. "I will make up a bed for you in the laundry. I will bring you food myself, if no one else will. Lord willing, you may be restored to health by means of the king's preservatives. And may God have mercy on your soul."

EIGHT

WE had no physician to treat Anne, in her room at the opposite end of the palace. She complained that the room, which was in the laundry, among the washing tubs, was dark and damp, though I thought to myself, how can she know that it is damp when she herself is soaking wet with the dripping of the sweat? I chided myself for even thinking of such a question, and tried to imitate the queen's charitable attitude. For the queen, we all knew, had saved Anne's life. Her command to Griffith Richards had come at the last moment; had she not intervened, Anne would have drowned in the moat.

And though no one said it, we all admired Catherine for her forgiving attitude toward the woman who was her husband's mistress. The woman he intended to marry.

It was not long before Cardinal Wolsey, who, as my brother Ned liked to say, had eyes and ears everywhere, learned that Anne was ill with the sweat and sent Dr. Barchwell to the palace to treat her.

He was a tall, outsize man whose grey hair was thinning, and who smelt of the ointments and potions he carried in his bags of medicines. His boots were crusted with mud, his riding cloak dirty from the road. We led him into the palace and offered him what food we could spare. He said little but ate greedily, frowning when we told him we had very little wine and needed to preserve what we had.

"For the Lady Anne, and any others who may fall ill," I explained.

"If the servants don't get at it first," was the doctor's cynical response. "I need a bed," he added gruffly. "I have not slept in two days."

Griffith Richards took the physician to an antechamber where he could rest.

"Fire," I heard him mutter. "Light fires in the sickroom, where the Lady Anne lies. As many fires as you can." Then he lay down to sleep.

We lit fires in the laundry and brought in as many candles as we could find, until the entire area was ablaze with light. Fire was believed to purge sickness—and also to induce a trancelike state in which healing happened quickly.

When Dr. Barchwell awoke he washed and dressed hurriedly and then, taking his bags of medicines, went down into the laundry to see Anne. I went with him. Anne was shivering beneath her blankets, visibly weaker than the last time I had seen her, clearly succumbing to the fearsome disease. Her eyes were wide and full of fear.

The doctor produced a leather pouch and strode rapidly to one corner of the room, where spiderwebs spread themselves in dark clumps against the walls. Heedless of the spiders' poison, he scooped up several of the webs and poked them down inside the pouch, then pulled the leather thong tight so that the wriggling spiders could not escape.

"Fasten this around her neck," he said to me, handing me the pouch. Anne was wearing a gold chain and I hung the pouch from it, near her throat.

"Have you any bread?" he asked. "Brown loaves, not white."

I assured him that we did. We had not yet eaten all the loaves Bridget brought with her. I went upstairs to get the bread and when I returned I crumbled it as the doctor instructed. He combined the crumbs with the herbs and liquids he was mixing.

Over the next hour, as Anne slipped into a faint and the room filled with the pungent odors of vinegar and rosewater, musk and wormwood and other scents unfamiliar to me, the doctor prepared a powerful remedy.

"It is the king's own formulation," he said. "He swears it will cure the sweat. Only it did not save his own apothecary. The poor man died."

Dr. Barchwell placed the strong-smelling concoction next to the narrow bed where Anne lay.

"Now we wait," he said.

"Shouldn't we try to wake her, to make her drink the draught?"

"No. It is the scent of it that heals."

I did not question this. I merely sat quietly at Anne's bedside, the doctor beside me, intently watching for any change in her appearance. From time to time he reached out and touched her arm.

"It is the manus Christi," he said at one point. "It is having its effect. She is drying up. The manus Christi is healing her, Lord be praised."

And just before midnight, our long vigil at an end, Dr. Barchwell told me he would not be needing my help any longer.

"She will survive," he said, and I saw, for the first time, the smallest of grins on his solemn features. His entire face seemed to relax, the lines of tension in his forehead and around his mouth grew less deep.

"It is well," he added. "The king will be pleased."

The doctor stayed with us for several days, continuing to watch over Anne in her recovery and preparing fresh batches of the healing medicines that had preserved her.

His long weary hours of anxious watching had taken the last of his strength. He looked drained and haggard, his eyes shadowed and ringed with dark circles. He looked as though he had passed through an ordeal of illness himself. Though we urged him to rest before leaving he refused, saying that he was needed, that there were so many others to treat. We saw to it that he had provisions and then sent him off, spent and weakened as he was, on his next errand of mercy.

So many were dying, we knew. I worried constantly that I would hear the dreaded news that Will had succumbed. Instead I had a dream.

It was more than a dream, it was a premonition. I dreamed that my nephew John was sick.

I awoke from my dream and left almost at once for Woldringham, never doubting that the queen, had I consulted her and asked her permission, would have sped me on my way.

I rode as rapidly as my horse could carry me, along dusty narrow roads and across meadows where the last of the wild flowers still bloomed, along with grasses and weeds. I knew that Will had taken the boys to an estate near the town, but which estate? Once I arrived in the vicinity of the town, I began to make inquiries. I soon discovered the answer.

"Ah, you must mean Peregrine Lavington's house," I was told. "All the sick children are being taken there." If John was indeed ill, then I reasoned that he might be at this house. I followed the directions I was given and soon found myself riding down a lane among orchards, the trees sweet-smelling and heavy with fruit. The July sun was hot, a heat haze rose from the earth and I almost wished it would rain, if only to offer some relief. Presently a large house came into view—a mansion, dilapidated but still sturdy, its soft yellow walls crumbling, its thick roof slates beginning to crack and separate from one another. Thatched cottages surrounded the old house, green with moss; the lawns and once luxuriant hedges that spread outward from the structures were neglected.

"Have you brought us another?" asked a woman who came to the door in answer to my knock, her eyes full of concern. She wore no cap, instead her curling grey hair was caught up in an untidy knot and the apron she wore over her bodice and skirt was none too clean. I took her to be a laundrywoman.

"I have not brought anything," I said. "Only myself. I am Mistress Seymour, of the queen's household, looking for Will Dormer and the boys he has with him, Henry and John."

"My good Mistress Seymour," the woman said kindly, "you ought not to be here. There is sickness in this house. I beg of you, find somewhere else to go."

Just then Will appeared in the doorway, a small child in his arms. A girl. He looked harried, but when he saw me, he grinned.

"Jane! My dear! I see you have met Peregrine, selfless soul that she is. She has opened her house to the children. The sick ones, the ones left orphaned by the sweat. All the unwanted ones whose families have died. She is compassion itself."

Peregrine Lavington shrugged. "All the monasteries and convents are full, they cannot take in any more of the afflicted. So this house becomes a hospital. It is a good use for it."

"I had a dream," I told them. "I dreamed that John was sick with the sweat. Is he here, with you?"

Both Peregrine and Will were silent for a brief moment. They exchanged glances. Then Peregine spoke.

"I'm sorry, Mistress Seymour, but your little friend John is very ill indeed. I see now why you are here, despite the sickness. Come, let me take you to him."

Dread rose up in me as I followed Peregrine inside the old house. I had been right. John was ill and in need of my love and care.

The drafty old mansion was falling down. The walls were full of wormwood and smelt of mold, but the rushes on the floor were clean and I caught the scent of fresh herbs amid the moldy odor. A cacophony of children's voices reached us as we went up the stairs, some shrieking, others crying, a few giggling and even singing. Each room we passed through had many beds, and in each bed, I saw, were several children. Some were mere babies, others, I guessed, were as old as thirteen or fourteen—more than old enough to be chasing crows in the fields or helping with the coming harvest.

In one small bed a child lay unmoving, his white body being wrapped in winding sheets by two women. As soon as they finished their sad task, and carried the dead boy out into the corridor, the bed was laid with fresh linen and Will put the little girl he was carrying down on it and covered her with a thin blanket.

"We have so many ill here, Mistress Seymour. Not all who come here die, but so many do! A few recover and they stay on to take care of the others. I am grateful for their help. As I am for Will here." She smiled at Will, then led me into another noisy room.

My nephew John was lying in bed, curled into a ball, like a sick puppy, the runt of the litter.

"He has been with us for several days," Peregrine told me. "He has survived so far. A good sign."

"His grandfather's namesake," was all I said. "Little John Seymour." I sat down on the low bed and put my hand on John's damp forehead. I did not shun contact with him, as I had with Lavinia and with Anne. I did not care, in that moment, whether or not I became ill; my only concern was for the boy. John made a faint sound, a muffled grunt. He did not open his eyes.

"His brother is very worried about him," Will told me. "But I keep Henry away from here, to preserve him from the sweat. I have apprenticed him to an archer in the royal guard. He boards with the archer's family."

My nephew Henry was a sturdy boy, tall for his age, already an athlete at six years old, a good rider and able to handle his small crossbow with some skill.

"You would be proud of him, Jane. He carries the quiver for his master, and is learning to lead his warhorse. He will be a soldier in the king's armies one day. He is strong, and does not flinch."

"And he has not come down with the sweat."

"No."

I was concerned about Henry, to be sure, but from the moment I saw John I was preoccupied with him. I rubbed his body with an ointment Peregrine recommended, a mixture compounded with treacle and wormwood, rosewater and the time-honored remedy called Rasis Pills. I eased his sore head with the juice of daisy leaves. I tried to keep him from falling asleep, remembering the warning in the king's letter to Anne, though he was very drowsy. I tried to feed him turnips, which were said to be very beneficial in strengthening the sick and bringing them back to health, but he spat them out and cried. In the end I gave up.

Hour after hour I sat on his bed, soothing him, singing to him, praying over him and smiling down into his small face, hoping that my presence would give him ease. From time to time Peregrine looked in on us, and I marveled at her tireless attention to the many children under her charge—not to mention her own ability to stave off the pestilence.

"How is it you do not fall ill, Peregrine?" I asked her. "What preserves you, when so many others succumb?"

"I almost wasn't preserved," was her blunt reply. "I was ill. Like the others. But I recovered."

"The Lord has spared her," Will remarked, "to help these little ones."

I was drawn closer to Will than ever before in those sad days, and often went to him for strength and comfort. He enfolded me in his arms, I put my head on his chest and closed my eyes, thinking how grateful I was for his love. We kept watch together by John's bed, and when John slept—as he inevitably did—we helped with other tasks: feeding sick children, washing them when they were first admitted to the house (many of them were filthy, having slept in ditches while roaming the countryside on their own), wrapping them in their small winding sheets when all hope had left them.

I did what I could, and I mourned. Will and I mourned together, and comforted each other.

Will came up to me and tenderly ran one finger along my cheek. "Are you sorry you came here, Jane dearest?"

I shook my head. "No," I said softly. "Despite everything, I am not sorry. I am with you." I kissed his cheek. "And there is so much love in this place. So much caring. It is beautiful to see, to be a part of."

Peregrine's mansion was more than a refuge, it felt like a small community, a village, a vast united family arising amid the ruins of the disease. The children stood by one another, not quarreling or fighting. There were no strangers among them, only family. Family brought together by need—and by grace.

I slept on the hard floorboards beside John's straw mattress and tried to ignore my own symptoms which, I hoped, were not symptoms of the sweat but of a fever. An ordinary fever, one that would not kill me.

I had a headache and my stomach hurt. It was all I could do to drink a cup of soup. My muscles were clenched in pain and my bones ached. I was so anxious!

I watched Will for signs of pain or fatigue but like Peregrine, he seemed to go on doggedly through the days, sleeping little at night, all his concentration on the children and the need to comfort them and give them relief so that they could endure the assault of the illness and overcome it.

By my fourth day in Woldringham I knew, deep down, that my little nephew could not survive much longer. I had the sense that we were waiting—not for John's return to strength but for his valiant struggle to end. Time seemed suspended. There were no minutes or hours, only the immeasurably long wait for his release.

Everything within me cried. All the sorrows of the world seemed to gather in the weakening body of one small defenseless boy, fatherless, motherless, and in the care of strangers.

And yet not strangers. For they gathered, the other children who had survived the ordeal of the sweat unscathed, as if they knew what was approaching, and made a circle around us. Around John, lying quietly on his bed of straw, one small weak arm reaching up to rest against my neck. Around Will, beside me, ever near, and around me, lost in tears, barely able to face my nephew's final moments of life.

They encircled us, silently, benevolently, and we waited together.

I was assailed by wild thoughts. Angels, I thought, as I tried to wipe away my tears. They are angels on earth. Ministering to us, as the dark angel of death passes over us.

My heart broke then, for I felt John's hand slip down off my arm, and he fell back into senseless, lifeless nothingness. No more than a puff of wind. A billow of smoke. A fallen petal. A distant bell. One small life that was no more.

The season of the sweat passed. The dead were buried, and with the advent of crisp fall weather, the number of new deaths dropped, and life began, slowly, to resume its everyday pattern.

Thomas Tyringham's estate at Croydon passed into other hands, Edward Woodshaw's duties at the Maidens' Bower were taken over by Henry Norris, and then by others less intimate with the king. Anne Boleyn's sister Mary mourned her late husband Will Carey, and was said to have found comfort with another man, a soldier in the royal guard. The king engaged a new apothecary and replaced his deceased chamber gentlemen as well. Anne managed to find a new maidservant and promptly forgot the name of the old one who had been carried off by the sweat.

One thing she did not forget: how swiftly and eagerly Griffith Richards had reached for her when it was clear she was infected, and how vigorously he tried to push her out the palace window. It seemed to me that she never again looked at Richards in the same way as before, and I noticed that she stayed as far away from him as possible, and never went near the largest window in the queen's apartments, the window from which the bars had been torn out, the opening just wide enough to accommodate a body.

Within a few weeks all was restored, after a fashion. Will

took me back to Woldringham to visit my nephew Henry, and I embraced him and rejoiced to see how he had grown, and what a strong, brave boy he was becoming. I was very glad that Henry was alive and well, but I still grieved for John. And in my grief—heaven help me!—I cursed God again and again for sparing my villainous father (who had, after all, lived) but allowing my innocent nephew to die.

I cursed God, I cursed the sweat, I cursed life itself, for I saw all too clearly that there was a darkness loosed in our time, and that we all had to fear that we might, in the end, fall under its unsparing hand.

NINE

THE Cardinal of Santa Anastasia, Lorenzo Campeggio, arrived in England with the first frosts of that autumn in the year 1528, sent by the pope to hold a hearing on the vital issue of the king's nullity suit.

At last, a man of great authority, of the highest standing in the church next to the pope himself, was among us and the king's increasingly grave doubts about his marriage to Queen Catherine could be confirmed. Then Queen Catherine would have to take her leave to make way for the woman King Henry preferred—Anne Boleyn.

I was dismayed to think that the queen might be cast aside, but I knew that the decision Cardinal Campeggio made would not be a theological one, rather one arrived at through a trial of strength. The strength of King Henry and whatever allies he could muster pitted against the might of the Emperor Charles and his prisoner Pope Clement.

We maids of honor saw the Cardinal of Santa Anastasia often, for he was the king's guest at banquets and other official gatherings, his red satin robes magnificent, his sad-eyed, jowly, wrinkled old face conspicuous among the faces of the king's advisers and those of the English clerics who deferred to him so pointedly. Cardinal Campeggio was, for a time, the most important man at court, even more important than his colleague Cardinal Wolsey, who in addition to his high clerical office was chancellor of the realm. Hundreds of horsemen made up Cardinal Campeggio's immense retinue, huge gold crosses brought from Rome were carried before him wherever he went. English men and women knelt when he passed by, and crossed themselves, and asked his blessing, and he wearily complied—though it was evident to all that he was not only tired, he was in pain.

Gout tormented the distinguished visitor from Rome (as it did my father), and several times while sitting at a feast or attending an official gathering we saw him suddenly clutch the arm of the man sitting next to him with a grimace of anguish on his face. At such times he had to be helped, limping, from the room.

We knew that he suffered from fierce, excruciating pain in his toe, pain that often spread into his feet and legs and brought with it a burning fever. When his attacks came on he could do nothing but lie quietly in a darkened room—a room was always prepared and waiting for him, should he need it. After a few days he would be well enough to return to his honored place at court, but he never knew when the pain would return.

"All I know is, this gout of his had better not cause any delay in the hearing he has come to preside over," Anne announced, putting on the shooting glove the king had given her and holding it up to be admired. And it was admirable—it fitted her like a supple second skin.

Ned laughed when I repeated Anne's comment to him, scoffing at Anne for thinking only of immediate personal matters, as she so often did.

"The cardinal will indeed proceed as slowly as he can," my astute brother remarked. "And for far more important reasons than his own ill health. He must act with the greatest care lest he offend the Emperor Charles, above all, for the emperor is now master of the Holy City and the pope's safety lies in the emperor's hands. What is more, he must avoid giving offense to the French king—who has now become the emperor's friend and ally. With these constraints, it is hard to see how the cardinal can placate our English king and give him the judgment he seeks."

Ned had explained to me that this signing of a peace agreement between the emperor and the French king was a blow to King Henry's hopes, for it left England without an ally. Vulnerable to an imperial army's attack. But it was a great boon to the cause of Queen Catherine—an answer to her many prayers.

"You see, Jane, how all things work together for good to them that love the Lord," the queen said to me, her plain face shining with hope and confidence. "First a great pestilence was sent to harry England, and punish us for the wickedness of our king and his adulteries." ("And for all the Lutheran books the Boleyns and their kind are reading and circulating," Ned added.) "Now the gout has come to afflict the cardinal, and arrest his work here on the pope's behalf."

And indeed it did seem, just at that time, as though King Henry was less sure of the outcome of his nullity suit. Too many forces were arrayed against him. There was much talk of change—radical change—from highest to lowest in the way people regarded one another. Monks such as Martin Luther defied the pope, and were busy organizing an entirely new church, so it was said. Peasants in the German-speaking lands were overturning the social order and rebelling against their masters. Holy writings, always in Latin and outside the understanding of all but a few learned men and a tiny handful of learned women, were being translated into the common tongue so that all might read and understand them. ("And debate their meaning," was Ned's sardonic comment.)

Where would it lead? No one could say, but all in authority were troubled by the changes we were sensing. And in the light of these changes, King Henry seemed less eager than before to separate himself once and for all from his wife. To be sure, he kissed and fondled Anne in the cardinal's presence, showing her a degree of tenderness and affection in public as if they were already married. But at the same time he allowed Catherine to continue her life at court—having given up on attempting to bully her into entering a convent—and gave her a place of honor at banquets and treated her with respect. I had not heard him shout at her since the outbreak of the sweating sickness, though I could not help remembering that when the king rode off from the courtyard of Greenwich Palace his only concern was for his son Henry Fitzroy's safety, and not his wife's, and throughout the duration of the epidemic he did not send a single letter to Catherine—only to Anne.

Like Cardinal Campeggio, the king was troubled with a painful ailment that fall, and on into the winter. We heard that his new chief apothecary was treating him for a severe inflammation of the bladder, and there were rumors of a worse ailment as well. The gossip among his chamber gentlemen, who were certainly in a position to know the truth, was that the king might be suffering from a tumor in his testicles, for he was known to be mixing herbs and experimenting with new compounds, searching for a remedy and had even sent a messenger to the great university of Bologna to seek the best medical knowledge.

As always, worries arose over the succession. If the king should indeed be suffering from a tumor, a tumor which might make it impossible for him to father more children, then the nullity suit would lose its importance. There would be no need for him to part from Queen Catherine, Anne could simply become his mistress and the throne would pass in time to the prince, Henry Fitzroy. The weak, perpetually unwell Henry Fitzroy, who was noticeably absent from the banquets and other public events to which Cardinal Campeggio was invited.

Months went by, and no progress was made toward the holding of the hearing on the nullity suit.

"You see, Jane, it is just as I have always said," Catherine commented to me one evening after meeting with Cardinal Wolsey and some of her other prominent supporters. "All things work together for good to them that love the Lord."

"And to them who have the imperial armies at their back," brother Ned put in. Ned was always to be found at the cardinal's right hand, it was said he would soon be in line for a prominent position in the royal household. He was not as important a figure as Thomas Cromwell, Cardinal Wolsey's lawyer at Gray's Inn; Cromwell, master of argument and debate, ever cool and unemotional, surveyed the royal court like an eagle waiting to swoop down on his prey. He watched, missing nothing, for his chance to strike—and when he struck, it was said, his victims struggled in vain. I was revulsed by Wolsey, but Cromwell I feared, for his mind was quick and his words clever, and his heart, I felt, was a rock of ice in his thick chest.

When after nearly nine wearisome months the solemn legatine court was at last convened, with the Cardinal of Santa Anastasia presiding and all the bishops and archbishops, the court officials, the legal advisers and attorneys in attendance, all eyes were not on the king and queen, but on Anne Boleyn.

To be more precise, they were on Anne Boleyn's belly. Was she pregnant or wasn't she? The French ambassador started a rumor that she was, the Spanish ambassador denied it, the Bishop of Rochester indicated that his thoughts were above such sordid things, and Anne herself, who enjoyed being the center of attention, smiled to herself and said nothing.

I could not bear to look at her, and I could tell that the other maids of honor—we had some new ones among us just then— were uncomfortable at best to be in her company. Because Anne was believed to be the king's mistress, we were all under suspicion. I had heard mutterings among the courtiers about the "maids of dishonor" and I was offended. I hoped no one could imagine that I might betray the queen.

Dignified and gracious as always, Queen Catherine entered the court on the arm of Griffith Richards and made an eloquent plea to her husband, swearing that no taint of incest blemished their marriage since she and Henry's brother Arthur had never slept together as man and wife.

Her sincerity was overwhelming, her arguments convincing. But the attention of the onlookers in the great hall was elsewhere. Was the next king of England a growing mound under Anne's skirt? Did she look bilious, as pregnant women often were? Was she blushing? Was she wearing a new jewel, one the king might have given her when she told him she was going to have a child?

Day after day the court was reconvened, and the gossip continued to flow, until a month and more had passed and still there was no resolution of the central issue. News arriving from Italy was dire. The emperor's power was growing, he dominated all. And he, through the pope, had given the ultimate command: there must be no decision made in England about the nullity suit. Only the pope could judge the King's Great Matter. And he would do so—at a time of the emperor's choosing.

His voice cracking with strain, a look of defeat in his rheumy eyes, the Cardinal of Santa Anastasia adjourned the legatine court without having made any decision and limped out of the great hall, his red satin robes trailing behind him. Few among the shocked spectators knelt to honor him, or crossed themselves, or called out to him to bless them. Instead there were audible hisses and curses, and among the Boleyns and the king's supporters, cries of dismay.

But I was smiling. I smiled all that day and the next, and when Anne glowered at me I smiled all the more. It seemed to me that right had triumphed, at least for now, and the gossipers and the belly-watchers would have to wait for another time to have their day.

Jane Popyngcort was dead.

She was dead in Flanders, hundreds of miles away.

Word reached us just as the court was leaving to go on progress. It was said that Jane had been riding with others in the household of a Flemish nobleman when they had been set upon by thieves. In the resulting mayhem, few of the women had survived.

"Do you suppose she was ravished?" Bridget asked in hushed tones.

Anne Boleyn turned her head away, as if unwilling to consider something so dreadful. The other maids of honor, most of whom had not known Jane, were wide-eyed with surprise and fear, though Anne Cavecant merely shrugged.

"I'm sorry if she suffered, of course," Anne Cavecant said, "but you must admit she was never really one of us. She was too aloof, always wearing those odd clothes, always keeping to herself—"

"Perhaps she was shy," someone offered. "Her English was so poor."

"No," Anne Cavecant insisted. "She was not shy. She was proud. She looked down on us. She looked down on all the English."

"Was that why she went back to to Mechelen?"

"No," Bridget said smugly. "She went back—"

"Because she had to, that's all," Anne Boleyn interrupted brusquely. "It was her own business, why she left—not ours." Anne gave Bridget a sharp look.

"We must pray that her end came mercifully quickly," was Queen Catherine's pious response to the startling news of Jane's death. "She was my friend for twenty years and more. She joined my household long ago, when I married King Henry. She was always loyal to me, staunchly loyal. I will honor her memory. We must all honor it, by remaining silent about things that are now forever beyond remedy."

I heard nothing more about Jane's death, but I pondered the very strange circumstance and wondered whether there was more to it than a random attack by thieves. The king, I noticed, said nothing at all about Jane's passing, even though at one time—if the stories were to be believed—he and Jane had been lovers. She had once meant a great deal to him. And she had known his secrets, including the secret of his intimacy with Anne Boleyn's mother. The secret, Bridget had said, that had led to Jane's leaving the court, with a heavy chest full of coins.

Clearly the news of Jane's death made the king very uncomfortable, but whether it was because he had once loved her or for another reason I could not discern. He never liked to think or speak of death, or to hear about it. He had not gotten over his fear of the deadly sweating sickness; he shuddered when reminded of it, and dreaded its return. Queen Catherine confided to me that he wore a pouch of live spiders around his neck to ward off the illness.

I remembered that Jane had been vague about her plans when she left England. "I am going home," was all she had said. She had no definite plans. She had spent her last hour in England with Queen Catherine. Just the two of them alone. Were they reminiscing, or were they, possibly, discussing the future?

Somehow I felt certain that what happened to Jane was linked to the king's nullity suit, and the abrupt departure of Cardinal Campeggio.

How nervous and unsettled we all felt that summer! Some said the sweat would return for sure, others that the emperor's soldiers would descend on England, to defend Queen Catherine. Our local militias were drilling, armed with rusty knives and short swords and some with nothing more than pitchforks, as the peasant rebels were said to use. There were all sorts of stories and rumors swirling about, and we could not escape the everpresent feeling that change was in the air, and that the old ways and the time-honored authorities were under assault.

I went to visit my family at Wulf Hall and found there nothing but awkwardness and tension. I sensed that I did not dare to mention Cat or young Henry, or poor John, dead and in the common grave for the children at Woldringham. My very presence seemed unwelcome—in contrast to the noisy, enthusiastic welcome Ned received when he arrived at the manor. My parents could not say enough about Ned, how rich he was becoming (and indeed he was wearing finer and finer clothes, the higher he rose in the cardinal's service and the more the king noticed him and gave him tasks to perform), how hand-some he was getting to be, what an important man at court and so on. I nodded and smiled but said little.

"When are we going to have a wedding, Ned?" my mother asked with a broad smile. "I hear you have been making inquiries about noblemen's daughters."

"He's in no hurry, woman," my father put in. "He has his duties at court to think of. Let him marry when he has fine houses and lands of his own, and a stable of splendid horses, and chests of gold under his bed."

I could hardly believe that they were talking this way, as if Cat and her sons had never existed. I knew that Ned had lost no time in having his marriage to Cat annulled, but that did not cancel out the years of Cat's presence within the family, or the years of loving and nurturing the children. My mother had been especially happy to be grandmother to Henry and John. I knew she had been very fond of them both.

Hearing what I did, I wanted to shout that my relatives were unfeeling, and that Ned was cruel beyond imagining. I felt cut off from my family, cut off by my ongoing ties to Cat at St. Agnes's and to my surviving nephew Henry, by my concern for them, and by my bitter feelings toward my father.

But I held my peace. I sensed that no one in my family would tolerate any outbursts or accusations from me.

I saw how my relatives looked at me, and I knew what they were thinking: she is too old to be still unmarried. (In that summer of 1529 I was twenty-three.) They pitied me. I overheard my father remark, unkindly, that it was no wonder I had no husband, for I had little to offer a man, not a very pretty face or a very fine figure.

"Lavinia Terling," I heard him remark to the owner of a neighboring estate, as they were walking out into the fields. "Now there was a prize. The face of an angel, and the body of Eve in the Garden of Eden." I heard the men laughing, and thought to myself, how would they feel if they heard women talking about them like that?

There was little warmth or comfort to be found with my relatives, and when I returned to court I was once again in the thick of the tense undercurrents of feeling between Queen Catherine and Anne. The sharp jabs, the accidental shoves and prods that made our days unpleasant were unleashed in full force. The queen's supporters in her household sneezed when they saw Anne, and found more and more ways to show her disrespect without actually doing anything overt. The Boleyns and their supporters—and I could not help but notice that their numbers were growing—fought back with cruel remarks and flashes of malice.

We had heard King Henry refer to Anne as "my little puffball," and now we all called her that, mockingly, along with other names: gypsy, vixen, she-wolf, hellhag. We snickered at her moles. We pointed out "the mark of the devil"—her double fingertip—when she put on her shooting glove or drew attention to her hands to show off her costly jeweled rings. We stared at her belly. She lashed out at us and called us worse names, to be sure—but we had the best of the ongoing battles. Or so we thought.

We could not know what lay ahead.

TEN

We could tell that a rainstorm was coming. The air was still and close, heavy and damp, dense with heat and full of the rich, cloying smells of high summer. The storm had already broken downriver, toward Greenwich; we saw, in the distance, white strokes of lightning and heard faint rumbles of thunder.

We had been staying at the riverside house of William Skeffington, a groom of the chamber, and because we had too little to occupy us, we were fretful and ill at ease.

The house was pleasant, large and well kept, bordered by green lawns that stretched down to the river shore and, on all sides but the water's edge, surrounded by woodland. At the king's request, most of the servants had been sent away, and only Bridget and I, Anne Cavecant and one other from among the maids of honor—a pallid, retiring girl called Margaret—had been ordered to accompany Anne to the house as her companions and servants. Yes—servants! We who had always been together in the queen's household were now, for a few days at least, expected to form a sort of household for Anne, who was being raised to a higher status among us.

It felt strange and awkward, it rankled with us, to be expected to do for Anne what Anne herself had always been asked to do for the queen. We attended to her clothes and helped her with her toilette and waited on her—just sat and waited—for her to order us to do some trifling service or other.

Because she was uncomfortable in her new role, Anne was ill-humored and demanding; she adopted a tone of injured dignity, as if nothing we did could satisfy her. Bridget put up with this better than the rest of us did. I think it actually amused her to watch the disgruntled looks on our faces and Anne's hardened demeanor. Anne Cavecant was reproachful, full of hidden malice and muttered threats of revenge. ("Who does she think she is? Double-hearted, double-fingered witch!") Young Margaret, who was too new to the queen's household to understand what was going on beneath the surface of things, was quiet and anxious; she wept when Anne upbraided her and suffered under the lash of Anne's tongue, while I, I was my usual self: observant, quietly rebellious, watchful and full of distaste for all that was going on around me.

During those few days my desire to be away from the court— once and for all—came back again with great force. If only the *Eglantine* had not foundered, I thought. If only it had carried Will and me to the haven we sought in the New World! And Henry and John with us! We would have escaped the fatal sweating sickness, we would be savoring the delights of a virginal world, far from England and its travails.

But I knew that it did no good to ponder things that could not be, or to dream of an impossible future. I had to make the best of my circumstances. So I comforted poor little Margaret, and taught her a thing or two about how to deal with a harsh mistress, shook my head with Bridget over Anne's imperious demands, and waited in the near-empty house, with the louring clouds darkening and the muted drumroll of thunder coming closer, to do Anne's bidding.

We had only been staying in the house a short time when, seemingly out of nowhere, we heard a noise. A sort of buzzing noise at first, like a swarm of angry bees. But soon we discerned voices within the buzzing, and then the sound of tramping feet, and we realized that a crowd of people was approaching the manor. They were coming along the narrow road that led from the nearest village through the woodland to the grounds at the back of the house, where the stables and outbuildings were.

The king was not with us. He had been in the wood hunting since early morning, and had taken most of a troop of guardsmen with him. Only a few of the guards had been left behind to protect us—though I'm sure no one thought any sort of protection would be necessary.

As the tramping feet and shouting voices came closer we became apprehensive. The crowd sounded hostile, and they were shouting Anne's name. A few times before there had been groups of Londoners who gathered in angry knots to shout abuse at Anne and to express their support for Queen Catherine. They had been quickly dispersed by the soldiery long before they came close enough to the palace to present a threat.

But this crowd sounded as though it was far larger, and far more noisy and angry, than any we had seen or heard of before. And we were very isolated, much too far from the capital for comfort.

"We must hide in the cellars," Anne Cavecant said, her voice shaky and anxious. "We can get down inside the flour barrels."

But there was no time for that. I thought, could we get up onto the roof? But we did not know the house, we did not know how to get up onto the leads.

"It's the damned queen! She's sent them!" came Anne's accusing voice. She had a small crossbow that Henry had given her, a beautiful thing adorned with beaten gold. It sat among her things, waiting for her to go hunting with the king later that day. She fitted an arrow to the bow and went to stand at a window.

"Better not do that," Bridget cautioned Anne. "Better stay out of sight. With luck the king will hear the commotion and come back, with the rest of the soldiers."

But minutes passed—many long, leaden minutes that felt more like hours—and the king did not return. Instead the crowd came ever closer, louder and noisier than before, the noise like the rumbling of the storm, rolling in waves of sound like the muffled booming of cannon. A vast throng of skirted marchers swung into view, red-faced and hostile, armed with knives and sticks, pitchforks and broom handles, coming down the road toward the house,

"They're all women!" Anne Cavecant said, amazed. "So many women!"

And indeed they were all in skirts, many with kerchieves covering their heads, shouting "Whore!" "Strumpet!!" "Devil's demon!" They were shaking their fists in the air vigorously.

I looked more closely. Those fists were large, and the arms to which they were attached were large too. The women were exceptionally tall, it seemed. And exceptionally graceless. Stocky. Hefty.

They were men! Clearly, they were men dressed as women!

Puzzled, I looked around at the others.

"It is the emperor's soldiers, dressed like women, come to murder us all!" piped up timid Margaret.

"Nan Bullen! Nan Bullen! Come out, and show yourself! Whore!"

They swarmed among the outbuildings, making the horses whicker and whinny and stamp their feet from fear.

If only the king would come! I thought. And then I realized, he may be frightened just as we are. What could he and his relatively few guardsmen do against a large crowd of angry men, even men in skirts?

"Quick! The boats!" It was Anne, already beginning to run along the corridor toward the wide staircase that led to the front door. She carried her crossbow, and had to hold her skirts up lest she trip over them, even so she ran with a fleetness that surprised me. (I should not have been surprised, she was such a nimble dancer.) We followed, with the guardsmen soon overtaking Anne and preceding her out the wide doorway onto the lawn that led down to the river, to where a dock stretched out into the water. Several wherries were tied up, waiting for custom. The wherrymen, seeing us running toward them, quickly untied the boats and, as we reached them, helped us aboard.

"Take us across the river!" Anne commanded.

"But the king—"

"It is the king's command!" Anne shouted. "Take us at once!"

The boats full, the wherrymen complied, their oars plunging and dipping into the dank river water, fighting the current and making for the opposite bank. And then, as if in response to some higher command, the storm broke, water sluicing from the dark clouds and drenching us as we held on to the sides of the pitching boat, the yelling and roaring of the crowd on the shore blending with the crash and peal of thunder resounding up and down the river, drowning out everything but its own urgent, resonant growl.

"It's time I had a household of my own," Anne told King Henry sharply after we returned to Whitehall. We were in the queen's apartments, as always. Henry had come there in search of Anne, and Anne, still angry after our escape from the threatening crowd, turned her demands on the king. Queen Catherine stayed in her bedchamber, away from the raised voices.

"I want my own guardsmen," Anne said. "Fifty of them, a hundred. Two hundred. I want my own army!"

"Aha!" said Bridget to me, too softly for Anne or the king to hear. "Puffball's revenge!"

"I can hardly give you your own army, sweetheart," the king was saying, half amused, half annoyed, "but I will make sure your guard is strengthened. And I can have that woman silenced—if I must."

"What woman?"

"The one who sent the crowd after you. The one they call the Nun of Kent."

The Nun of Kent! Her name was soon to be on everyone's lips, for she was said to work miracles and to have the gift of prophecy and—most important of all—to see visions of the Virgin Mary, visions in which she received guidance to pass on to all the faithful.

It had been this nun, this Elizabeth Barton, an anchoress at St. Agnes's (where Cat was being held), who had indeed set the mob of irate men against Anne, and told them where they could find her. She had had a vision, she said, a powerful, divine vision of Jesus being led to the cross.

"She has seen Our Lord," Griffith Richards told us solemnly. There were only a few of us near him, but as he spoke on, more gathered.

"She has heard Him speak. She has seen Him with His hands bound, a rope around His neck, dragged by cruel soldiers to the mount where He is to die. In this vision He speaks to her."

"What does He say?" the shy Margaret asked, wide-eyed.

"He says, 'It is King Henry's sin that has led me to this death. He must sin no more. He must flee from the woman who has led him into sin. That woman must be hunted down like a savage beast. She must be slain.'"

Hearing the gentleman usher repeat the nun's words I could not help but recall his eagerness to thrust Anne through the aperture in the queen's apartments at Greenwich. He had wanted her to fall into the moat and drown—not only because she had the sweat, but because of what the Nun of Kent said about her. That it was Christ Himself who condemned her.

"She saw the cross being raised, and the nails being pounded into Our Lord's hands and feet," Richards continued. "She witnessed His agony, His slow, painful death. He suffered greatly—and all because of the king's transgressions."

The gentleman usher's powerful words lingered. Several dozen people had gathered to listen to him.

"Have you heard the nun recount her visions then?" I asked.

He nodded. "Many go to St. Agnes's to hear her—and not only to hear her, but to follow the divine commands she relays. Remarkable things are witnessed in the convent. There are statues there that weep, and unearthly voices that wail. Surely the nun is the true voice of God."

It was both wondrous and alarming, this spreading conviction that the Nun of Kent was hearing the voice of Our Lord.

Anne was terrified.

"You see," she said again and again to King Henry, "I must have a household of my own, and my own guardsmen. This Nun of Kent is my enemy, and she means to kill me. She sent these savage men in skirts, with their knives and their pitchforks, to murder me and all those with me."

The king did not respond, but nodded, twisting one of his rings around his finger, a habit he had, I had often noticed, when he was ill at ease.

"If she is as powerful as they say, an entire army may not be able to conquer her. The force of the divine is far stronger than any earthly army."

He sounded resigned, as if he realized that it would be foolish to resist the divine will. Yet he doubled the palace guard, then tripled it. He gave Anne a dozen guardsmen of her own. And as an added protection, he shrewdly summoned the nun to his presence and sought her prayers.

I had been intending to visit St. Agnes's in order to see Cat, and now that the convent's best-known sister was attracting so many admirers and followers, it occurred to me to go, not as a member of the royal household, but as a pilgrim. I borrowed a simple gown of coarse fabric from one of the kitchen maids, and put on over it a long grey cloak such as pilgrims wear when visiting the shrine of St. Thomas at Canterbury or other holy places. With the plain hood of the cloak covering my head and much of my face, and without any of the jewelry or fine trimmings I usually wore as a woman of the court, I did not stand out from the others who were riding or walking along the dusty road that led southeastward toward the coast. I rode a horse of little value, and the groom that rode by my side had a mount that was equally humble.

As we rode along we heard snatches of talk.

"She's a miracle worker. She prays for sick folk, and they are healthy again."

"She raised a man from the dead."

"No! Only the Lord Himself can do that!"

"The Lord and the nun."

"They say she was a poor girl. A serving girl. She nearly died of the pox, or the plague. But the Virgin Mary came to her and healed her. She's had visions ever since."

"The king is afraid of her. He wants a new wife, but the nun says he mustn't have one. If he marries a new wife he will die. He must stay with our good Queen Catherine."

"The nun can pray for a miracle. That Queen Catherine will have a strong son to be our next king."

"That would be a miracle indeed. Just like Sarah in the Bible. She was an old woman, long past the age of bearing children. But the Lord sent her strong sons."

The stream of talk was endless, some of those on the road were singing, others praying aloud. I looked around at the pilgrims nearest to me and thought, were some of these the men who dressed as women and pursued Anne and the rest of us? Did the Nun of Kent really have the power to turn pilgrims into cutthroats?

It was with such unsettling thoughts that I entered the convent grounds and joined the large throng gathered there. A nun offered me a cup of water from the well. I drank deeply and wiped my dusty face. The nun smiled, watching me. Her smile was kind and genuine and I thanked her.

After handing the reins of my horse to the groom I joined others and was led inside the wide double doors to an entrance hall and then to a special room that contained nothing but a rather shabby woman's garment, deep green in color but quite faded, shapeless, and spread out on a low bed. All those around me were kneeling in reverence before this garment and I imitated them. I heard a woman say, "That's what she wore when she first saw the Virgin." Other rooms held similar objects: the holy nun's prayer book, her handkerchief, a rather dirty glove. No one was permitted to touch these things, only to kneel in adoration of them.

"But she's not a saint," I heard someone say in an undertone.

"She will be," came the response. "All these things will be holy relics one day."

In the large candlelit room devoted to the newly completed shrine—the shrine that, so it was said, was attracting pilgrims from as far away as Exeter and Thetford—people fought for space, carrying in the sick and dying and laying them before the gleaming altar. Babies cried, moans came from the lips of the sufferers as statues of the saints and of the Virgin Mary looked down, expressions of kindly compassion on their carved wooden faces.

As I stood in the doorway I saw a small figure moving among the sick. A woman, a very ordinary-looking woman, short and rather stout, touching each one gently as she passed. Her lips were moving but the noise in the room was so very loud that I could not hear what she was saying. I saw people reaching out to touch her clothing as she passed, and then I realized that the garment she was wearing was very like the one displayed in the first room I had entered. I knew then that it was the nun herself who was ministering to the sick.

Presently the crowd seemed to part, to make room for the nun to pass out of the room.

"She goes to her prayers now. She comes again to see the visitors at eventide."

I rested then, lying down amid the others on the stone floor, thinking, this is the hardest bed I have ever known. Yet it was appropriate, for apart from the great gilded altar of the shrine, everything in the convent was spare and austere. Some convents were luxurious, St. Agnes's was not.

I was awakened by the clamor of bells. All around me, people were rousing themselves. We went into the chapel, where, in contrast to the noisy scene in the shrine room, there was a reverent quiet. Presently a small door opened at one side of the room and the nun entered, dressed as before, and accompanied by a group of attendants in long white robes such as oblates wear. I scanned their faces. One seemed very familiar. I looked more closely.

It was Cat.

I stared. Could I be wrong? But I was not wrong. It was Cat, my sister-in-law, wearing a long white robe and looking far healthier and better fed than when I had seen her last.

Cat! I wanted to cry out, but did not dare. Instead I continued to watch, with the others, as the nun stepped forward and began to speak, her voice sweet and her smile radiant. A hush fell over the eager crowd as her words reached us, and I felt—or thought I felt—a faint stirring in the air, a breath, a subtle wind of the divine.

ELEVEN

“T HE devil is among us!”

Such a powerful voice, to emerge from the narrow chest of such a small woman.

“He is using the king’s lust to lead all England astray!”

Murmurs of assent greeted the nun’s rousing words. Heads were nodding. At the mention of the devil people were crossing themselves.

“One woman bears the devil’s mark!” The nun held up her small hand, and turned it for all to see. “I have five fingers. So have all of you. But this woman, this one evil woman, has six! The devil has put that demon finger on her hand, to show that she belongs to him.”

The woman sitting next to me shuddered, and I could feel an almost palpable sense of horror passing through those around me. I thought, this is Anne the nun is talking about. Not a demon, just a woman. A woman with an odd cleft finger.

“A struggle is under way,” the nun was saying. “A great

struggle, between the forces of light and the forces of darkness. The fate of England's soul rests with the outcome of this battle. It is all foretold in the Bible. We live in the time told of by Saint John in the Book of the Revelation. He saw it, all those years ago. He knew what the outcome would be."

"Tell us, tell us," I heard people saying. I looked around me, and saw anxious faces, frightened eyes. They were clamoring for answers to the alarm they felt, for an end to the terrible uncertainty that was preying on them. I shared that fear, though I did not share the desperation that I saw in those frightened eyes, those tremulous voices.

"It depends on you. On us. We are God's warriors. If we fight well, we will win. The Lord will win, and the devil will be sent back to hell."

"The Virgin has shown me a great battle to come," she began again, after a pause. "The greatest of battles, in which the earth shall be cast into the sea and the armies of darkness shall be utterly destroyed. The Virgin has shown me the future," she added, her face radiant. "I rejoice in it, as shall you all. But before it arrives, there shall be a time of dire testing. We shall all be brought low. None shall escape, no, not one."

She broke off, shaking her head, as if in an effort to emerge from her visionary state. And then she said an odd thing.

"I have seen a ship," she said. "Carrying a man, a man sent by God to help Queen Catherine. He has come among us. He will tame the vipers in the court. For the court is nothing but a nest of vipers."

These words seemed to me to clash with the earlier part of her message. Instead of being part of a general message, these words were very specific, about a very specific man, a man who had come to the royal court recently. I had no doubt the nun was speaking of Eustace Chapuys, the imperial ambassador, sent by the emperor to represent his interests and to aid Queen Catherine. I not only knew who Ambassador Chapuys was, I had often seen him, for he came to visit the queen frequently, and she sometimes urged me to stay and be present during their colloquies.

She welcomed his visits and his assistance in her difficulties resulting from the king's nullity suit, but I knew that he disquieted her. He had no piety, and Catherine preferred people around her who were of strong faith. Beyond that, Chapuys was an ill-favored, hard-featured Savoyard, clever like my brother and Cardinal Wolsey, and while the queen found his cleverness reassuring—for he had a quick and incisive grasp of her situation and was full of suggestions for how she should deal with it—she disliked Italians and distrusted them. I admit that I shared her prejudice. It seemed to me that the ambassador was eloquent, yet untrustworthy; words slipped off his tongue with ease but they were not words one ought to believe.

And now the nun was telling her followers that Ambassador Chapuys was a man sent by God.

I tried to remember when it was that I had first heard of the Nun of Kent, and realized that it had been just at the time Cardinal Campeggio left England to return to Rome. Just when the legatine court was disbanded, having failed to render the judgment the king had been so eager to receive: the judgment that the royal marriage was no marriage at all. Ambassador Chapuys had arrived in England near that time.

Had the nun's visions begun at precisely the time when the queen's need for support was growing? When she needed her rival Anne Boleyn to be vilified?

I put my questions to Cat, later on that afternoon, after the nun had finished delivering her message and the pilgrims were leaving the chapel. The nine women in white who formed the nun's escort—with Cat among them—were filing into an adjacent room, and I followed. No one stopped me or challenged me.

I went up to Cat at once and kissed her and told her how very glad I was to see her. She kissed and hugged me and then, reaching for my hand, quickly took me aside.

"Everything has changed, Jane," Cat said, keeping her voice low and looking over to where a small group of priests was standing, watching all that went on. "As you see, I am no longer kept locked away. The nun protects me. I am useful to her, and to the queen's cause. I know things about the family—your family, that used to be mine as well—that Ambassador Chapuys wants to know. As long as he wants me to help him—and help the queen—I will stay out of that horrible locked cell." She had been bright-eyed, but as she spoke of the locked cell, just for a moment, she looked bleak. How unthinkable her suffering must have been, I thought, shut away there, kept from seeing anyone, and believing that she would spend the rest of her days in that same lonely, grim stone-walled room. Yet now I knew I had to add to it.

"Cat," I said, wishing I did not have to convey what I needed to tell her, "I have some very painful news."

At once her features grew clouded, and she nodded sadly. "About my dear John. Yes, I know he has gone to be with the angels. The nun told me."

"But hardly anyone knew. How did she find out?"

"She is a true prophet, Jane. She knew when he died, and was very kind to me when she told me."

"I tried to do my best for him and for Henry. Will took the boys away when the sweat began to spread in Croydon."

"I know. I'm grateful, Jane, for what you have done for my

boys—you and Will both. You didn't abandon them. Without you, they both might have died."

"At least Henry is doing well," I said. "He seems to grow bigger and stronger each time I visit him. He can draw a bow as well as a boy twice his age. Will thinks he will be a warrior one day."

I went on to tell Cat about Henry and the family he was living with, about how impressive he was, intelligent and resolute. She smiled.

"I will write him. Can you make sure my letter reaches him?"

I nodded.

As we talked on, about all that I had seen that day and my conjectures about the nun's revelations and the arrival of Ambassador Chapuys, I saw that Cat continued to keep her eye on the black-robed priests who hovered near the nun and her handmaidens. There were some half dozen of them, youngish men, not venerable bearded fathers, energetic men who talked in excited voices. I could not help overhearing their conversation—and realized that they were speaking in Spanish. Eventually one among them, a handsome, dark-haired man, approached us.

"Jane, this is Father Bartolome. He came with Ambassador Chapuys. He is staying here at the convent."

"For now," the priest said, turning his dark, curious eyes on me. "And you are Catherine's sister who serves the queen."

I nodded. "I am, although my brother Edward would tell you otherwise."

"I know what has happened in the family," the priest said. "I have heard about the estrangement. Your brother, if I may say so, is going against the laws of God and the church."

I did not quite know what to say to that, so I said nothing. The priest continued to regard me as if expecting a reply.

"I hope you are not one of those who reads blasphemous Lutheran books and ponders challenging the authority of the Holy Father. In Spain, we reserve our harshest penalties for such persons."

I looked at Cat. Why was this priest asking me such a question? I remembered the stories I had heard, from Queen Catherine's Spanish ladies in waiting, about the torturing of heretics in Spain, who were burnt alive or had their limbs pulled apart by cruel devices until they screamed in pain. I had heard of the Holy Office, the church court that condemned people to horrible deaths. But surely such investigations into religious error had nothing to do with me—or did they? For had I been questioned, I would have had to admit that Lutheran books had indeed found their way into our royal court, and out of curiosity, I had glanced at them.

I was curious to read for myself what it was that the former monk Martin Luther was telling his followers, how his teachings differed from the teachings of the pope and of the church of St. Peter. The church of Rome.

I had heard often enough that many learned scholars respected Luther's teachings as founded on deep and solid learning as well as on high moral standards. Yet his writings were denounced, the books themselves burned as dangerous, insidious works of devilry. As far as I could tell, these books brought to light corrupt practices in the church, exposed the making of profits from the forgiveness of sins (which act of exposure seemed to me noble and moral), and were in favor of a pure and spiritual trust in divine mercy.

If this was Lutheran teaching, I privately thought, then it was a kind of Christianity I could embrace. But I was no theologian, perhaps there were dangerous teachings hidden within the appealing new doctrines. Perhaps it took a far subtler and more learned mind than mine to determine where the truth lay.

I knew that I was not alone in finding the teachings of the former friar Luther to be of interest. Among others, Anne and her brother George both read Luther's writings, and King Henry too had acquainted himself with the books of the renegade monk. He condemned them, to be sure, but at least he read them first. Perhaps, I thought, it was the mere fact that I was a member of the royal household that brought me under suspicion from the black-browed priest.

"I assure you I am no follower of Luther," I told Father Bartolome. "Queen Catherine can vouch for my faithful devotion to the church of Rome."

"Ah! But even to use such a phrase as 'church of Rome' brings you under suspicion, Mistress Jane. There is not a church of Rome and a church of Luther. There is only one true and apostolic holy church, presided over by His Holiness."

"I shall guard my words more carefully," I said with a slight bow.

"Jane," Cat said, "we must talk again. I have much to tell you. If you will stay until tomorrow, I will see you then, and give you a letter for Henry." She kissed me on the cheek and moved away, and to my relief, the priest moved off after her.

The warm spring sun was shining down on Chevering Manor, the Dormers' estate, on the day Will's sister Margery married my father's cousin Godfrey Seymour and the Dormers and the Seymours were officially united.

Margery had asked me to be one of her bridesmaids and Will stood up for the groom, who was all nerves and whose gold-trimmed doublet quivered in the sunlight.

There had been a sudden thaw in the frosty relations between our two families, a warming brought about by Ned's rapid rise in royal favor and the Dormers' eagerness to profit from his success. Today's festivities were a sign of this newfound warmth and congeniality, and my presence as a member of the wedding party was significant, as I was well aware.

Our families had been neighbors and friends for as long as I could remember, it had only been the discovery of my father and Margery together that had caused the abrupt and seemingly irreparable breach between them. But when Ned had approached Will's father Arthur Dormer, offering him the office of Under-Groom of the Confectionery at an entire thirty pounds per annum, and had added to that the promise that in the very near future he might be made Door-Keeper to the Court of Wards and Liveries, Arthur had immediately accepted and offered to make amends.

"After all, it isn't as though your father can hide in the storage room with any more of my girls, eh?" Ned told me he had said. "His gout keeps him in bed all the time now—alone. Am I right about that?"

Ned had acknowledged that our father was indeed very seriously afflicted with gout, and could barely walk any more. His days of seduction, of adultery, were over.

"And my Margery requires a husband. What about your cousin Godfrey, that lost his wife? He's no Adonis, but he's a fair huntsman and keeps an adequate table. Do you think he would have her?"

Ned's imitation of Arthur Dormer made me laugh. He could be wickedly amusing when he chose. His imitations of the great men of the court were devastating. He even dared—in safe company, of course—to imitate the king. But he seldom allowed himself to be lighthearted, work engulfed him more than ever after Cardinal Wolsey died and he was appointed to the much sought-after post of gentleman of the chamber to the king. Beyond that, he was often to be found in the company of the new power at court, Thomas Cromwell. I knew Ned saw himself as Cromwell's successor. As the king's future right-hand man. Perhaps, even, as chancellor of the realm.

Will and I danced with abandon at the wedding, and drank deeply of the abundant country ale. As dusk was falling Will helped me up onto a cart and drove me out into the fields, fresh with new growth and fragrant with early flowers. He spread a blanket and cushions across the wooden floor of the cart and lay down, reaching for me to join him. I nestled into his warm arms.

It was not easy, in the hours that followed, to keep our joint resolve and resist making love. Deep, sweet kisses, caresses that left me breathless and Will choked with desire: these we allowed ourselves, as the twilight faded to midnight blue and the sky became studded with brilliant stars, but we held back from going further. We saved that for our wedding night.

"Soon, Jane, soon," Will said. "The life we have hoped to make together is within our grasp now. Before long it will be our wedding day—and then, ah then, our wedding night."

Will had lost no time in speaking to his father about our continuing wish to marry, and had been assured that the Dormers would not stand in our way. Indeed, so changed was the entire situation between our families that Arthur Dormer hoped our marriage would come swiftly. Once we were married, he expected to be offered an even more impressive array of court offices. And with these offices, he said, would surely come his chance to buy a larger and finer estate than Chevering Manor.

"This house will belong to you, Will," Arthur Dormer had said. "Just as soon as I can afford to purchase a larger property nearer the capital. One more fitting for an under-groom of the confectionery—or, of course, any other offices that may chance to come my way."

"So you are to become a gentleman farmer, Will," I said, half teasing. "And I can learn to shear sheep and plant flowers, and help the cottagers when they are in need, while you improve the breed of our cows and make sure the steward is doing his job properly."

"And most important, we can have a family of our own. We can leave the court behind."

He took my hand and raised it to his lips.

"Are we agreed then, Jane?" he asked tenderly. "Shall we do this?"

I looked at him, at the loving, boyish face, the tousled blond hair, the warm blue eyes. I was so very, very fond of him in that moment. I nodded.

"Yes, dear Will. Yes."

Mr. Skut was very glad to be called back to the queen's apartments at my request. He rubbed his hands together in happy anticipation.

"Ah, Mistress Seymour," he said, his smile broad, "am I to hope that the time has come to complete the beautiful gown? Is a betrothal to be announced?"

"Indeed it is—at last. I trust the gown can be altered to fit a slightly older, slightly more world-weary bride."

He motioned to his assistants who brought forward their baskets of cloth and began unpacking their contents.

"Of course we shall have to alter the bodice and sleeves, to bring them up to date. And perhaps we ought to add different trim at the neck and adjust the petticoats. Since the Lady Anne has come to prominence, and her wardrobe draws all eyes, all the ladies at court must follow French fashion. Which is to say, they must follow Lady Anne's fashion."

I was only too aware that Mr. Skut's comments were true. Anne's influence on dress was paramount, and—I had long felt—quite intrusive. She changed her gown three or four times a day, and demanded that we all follow her example. And it seemed as though she not only changed her gowns often, she changed their design, their ornaments, their colors. It was impossible to keep up with her quicksilver taste. One day she had Mr. Skut's seamstresses, their needles flying, sewing gold acorns on her skirts, the next they were ripping out the acorns and replacing them with sparkling aglets. True-loves were embroidered into puffed sleeves only to give way, shortly afterwards, to strips of black sarcenet or Bruges satin.

It was all quite dizzying—and, in my view, quite excessive. Anne needed the distraction of her obsession with dress because without it she was overcome by her fears. She needed to give orders to others so that she could forget that she herself was in thrall to the king, to her relatives, to the king's hostile subjects. I felt I was beginning to understand her quite well. Not that understanding bred sympathy, quite the reverse, I'm sorry to admit.

Mr. Skut was going on about the need to alter the bodice and sleeves of my beautiful wedding gown, as the sleeves were laid out and the cream satin petticoats spread between two carved benches. He reached into a basket and held up a length of delicate lace. He placed it against the satin, then shook his head.

"Too yellow."

He rummaged in the basket again, and brought out several more samples of lace, rejecting each in turn.

"Perhaps this is what you seek." It was the resonant, musical voice of the king—a voice I had heard so often raised in quarrelsome anger that I was startled to hear it in a pleasant tone.

He had come into the room holding up a length of Venetian silverwork, intricately woven in delicate metallic threads. Mr. Skut and his assistants bowed deeply.

I curtseyed—and at the same time gave a little gasp.

"How beautiful!" I said. "But surely this ought to be saved for one of Your Majesty's velvet doublets, or to trim a pair of silver stockings—"

"There are plenty more," King Henry responded. "I believe the ship that brought this trim brought twenty or thirty boxes more like it. And enough silver to buy and sell most of my palaces," he added in an undertone.

"Is it from Venice?" I had heard that some of the finest silverwork was made in Venice.

"Yes—but the silver itself is from the mines of Alta Peru, in the Americas, mines that belong to my wife's nephew Charles. It is about these mines that I have come to see her."

With these words his voice darkened, and he dropped the length of gleaming silver as he made his way toward the door of the queen's bedchamber. I quickly picked up the shimmering, snakelike bands.

"Instead of lace, could you not trim the neck of the bodice in this?" I asked Mr. Skut, holding out the woven strand.

"It is not customary to trim a wedding gown in such an adornment—" the dressmaker began, then quickly added, "But of course if the king advises it—"

I handed the silverwork to one of the assistants, who began to measure it.

"I shall need more," Mr. Skut said.

"And more you shall have," was the king's last utterance as he strode from the room, in search of his wife.

TWELVE

H ERE, little Pourquoi. Here, little one."

Anne went from room to room in her suite of apartments, calling and whistling. Her favorite lapdog was nowhere to be found.

"Someone stole him, I know it!" she cried, growing more and more exasperated and fretful as she searched and called frantically. "Someone who hates me!"

It was no use reminding her that Pourquoi had run away at least a dozen times, being a nervous creature, ever in search of escape, and that he had always been found.

"Jane! Anne! Bridget! Help me!"

Obedient to her demand, we fanned out into adjacent rooms, calling for the little dog and clapping our hands and whistling. I saw Bridget raise her eyebrows and smile, as if to say, what can we do but humor her?

We were no longer in Queen Catherine's much diminished household; Anne Cavecant, Bridget and I and a dozen others who had served the queen now served Mistress Anne Boleyn, who had won out in her clamorous urgings that she be given a household and staff of her own. The king had granted her wish—partly, I felt sure, in order to humiliate Queen Catherine, who persisted in maintaining her marital rights and relied on her nephew to defend them.

I felt at times like a shuttlecock being tossed between opponents in an endless game. My services, and those of the other women, were hostage to the shifting tides of power; sometimes the queen appeared to be in the ascendant, sometimes Anne. But at the moment we served Anne, and so it fell to us to help her try to find the missing Pourquoi.

Calling and whistling, I went into a small room with windows looking out on the privy garden. A workman stood at one of the windows, carefully removing a section of decorative glass. He bent to his task, long fingers stretched delicately across the fragile surface. A pane bearing Queen Catherine's badge and emblem were being replaced by another with Anne's white falcon.

He turned to look at me as I entered the room. His gaze was calm, open—and admiring. The look in his brown eyes was warm. He smiled.

"Mademoiselle," he said, his voice as warm and pleasant as his glance. He was tall and lean, well-built and with a workman's strong muscles whose outlines were plain beneath his laborer's smock.

As soon as he spoke I felt drawn to him, charmed and mesmerized by the sound. Though he was a common laborer, a glazier though evidently a skilled one—and I a gentleman's daughter I felt no barrier between us. I took a step toward him, then another, and returned his smile.

"Have you seen a little dog?" I heard an unaccustomed softness in my own voice.

"No, mademoiselle. But if I see him I will come and tell you."

There were dozens of workmen repairing and improving Anne's suite of rooms just then. Stonemasons, carpenters, joiners and painters. The sounds of hammering, scraping and shouting surrounded us. Yet it was as if the noise suddenly ceased. I no longer heard it. I was content to stand where I was, looking into the man's welcoming brown eyes.

"May I trouble you for a drink of water, mademoiselle?"

He spoke with an accent. His voice was soft, musical. Bemused, I turned and went into Anne's bedchamber. A pitcher of watered wine was kept beside her bed. I poured out a cupful and took it back to the glazier. He drank it thirstily, at one draught, then wiped his mouth with the back of his hand. I watched him drink, admiring his throat, the perspiration along his jaw and on his arms and hands, the dark hair that fell in waves to his shoulders.

He held out the empty cup and as I took it, our hands touched. Once again I noticed his long slender fingers. Neither of us withdrew from the slight, soft touch. His hand was rough. I felt heat rising from my fingers where they pressed against his. Heat, and an excitement I had never felt before.

Reluctantly, after what seemed a very long time but was probably only a moment, I pulled my hand back, only to hear the glazier say, "I sometimes forget my tools and have to return for them quite late at night. If I were to do that, should I find you in the courtyard?"

I did not hesitate. "Yes," I said, and with a smile left him.

Dazed by what had just happened, I went to rejoin the search for Anne's little dog, who was at length discovered cowering under Queen Catherine's prie-dieu, taking refuge from the priest I had seen at St. Agnes's, Father Bartolome.

"Get away from my dog!" Anne shrieked when we entered the queen's apartments. The entire search party had gone there together at Anne's command, after Griffith Richards had sent word that Pourquoi had found his way to Queen Catherine's suite.

The black-robed priest was kicking with his fierce-looking boots underneath the low kneeling bench, where the whimpering Pourquoi had tried to hide himself. When the priest heard Anne's command he looked up at her—a most un-priestly look—and resumed his kicking, harder than ever so it seemed.

I hate to see any animal being attacked or mistreated, and at once I rushed to the prie-dieu and, narrowly avoiding the menacing boots, reached under it and brought out the trembling little dog. I handed him to Anne, who snatched him out of my arms and ran out of the room.

Father Bartolome was staring at me. I scrambled to my feet, my gown and petticoats a hindrance. No one helped me.

"I see it is the little reader of Lutheran books!" the priest exclaimed, his black eyes stony. "The one who comes as a pilgrim to see the wonder-working nun at St. Agnes's, so she can repeat to the king's accursed mistress what she has seen! You are nothing but a spy!"

"And you are nothing but Ambassador Chapuys's creature!" I burst out.

"I am the queen's new confessor," Father Bartolome announced gravely, suddenly altering his tone of voice, his expression, his posture. He became the reverent, beneficent man of God.

"It is only too evident to me what you are," I retorted, "and I shall make it known!"

* * *

He was there, waiting in the moonlit courtyard of the palace, when I made my way along the quiet hallways and by the least used, least guarded stairways to the outside. Sleepy guardsmen reclined on benches, there was no night watchman to be seen.

"Mademoiselle!" I heard his urgent whisper. "Over here, mademoiselle!"

He was under the eave of the brewhouse, so deep in shadow that all I could make out was the tall, lean length of him, a thin cloak covering his shoulders, his hair brushing the sides of his narrow, handsome face, his eyes bright even in the dimness.

He held out his hand and beckoned me into the shadows. I went to him gladly. In an instant I was enfolded in his strong arms, pressed against him, his chest against mine, his lips kissing my ear, my neck, my throat.

"You are here!" he murmured. "I wasn't sure you would come."

I could not resist, I wanted to say, but I could not speak, his mouth was on mine and I felt a force rise up within me that overpowered me completely.

"Ma chère mademoiselle, mon ange, ma fleur, ma petite—"

He lifted me up and carried me into the brewhouse, lit only by a single candle, burning beside a mound of straw covered by a blanket. When he laid me down I reached for him, wanting him beside me, wanting his mouth on mine again, and soon I was lost in his embrace.

So easily, so naturally, did I leave girlhood behind that night and not with dear Will, but with a stranger. By the time the candle guttered and went out, I had blossomed into womanhood, my body's bloom as inevitable as the unfolding of a flower. He told me his name: Galyon. He called me his love. He promised we would meet again.

I found King Henry in the tiltyard, mounted on Coeurdelion, his favorite warhorse, with Henry Fitzroy on his pony trotting beside him. He was trying to teach the prince to jump, assuring him that the pony already knew how, that all the boy had to do was touch his spurs to the beast's flanks and hold on.

But Fitzroy could not bring himself to attempt the jump. Time and again the king encouraged him—even dared him— and time and again the prince turned the pony's head sharply at the last minute and avoided the hazard.

"By all the saints, boy, how will you fight the French if you can't jump a hedge no higher than a snake's garter?"

There was no answer. Fitzroy hung his head.

"I hurt, father," he managed to say at last, his voice weak. "My stomach hurts." And he cupped his hands over his velvet doublet where the pain was.

The king wheeled Coeurdelion and spurred him to gallop. The great horse thundered down the length of the tiltyard, his hooves raising dust and his thick blond mane flying. Then the horse wheeled again and returned the way he had come, stopping suddenly and with a great whinnying just short of the prince on his frightened pony.

"You hurt?" Henry shouted. "You have a bellyache? Pah! My head is about to split open, my leg feels like some damned villain stuck a lance in it and as for my balls—" He swore graphically, then grunted. "As for my balls, well, you'll know about that pain soon enough, when you're older. Fight the pain, boy! Learn to fight the pain, or you'll never fight the French!"

"My tutor says we must fear the soldiers of the emperor, not the French," the prince managed to say.

"I'd like to see your tutor put on armor and take the field," was the king's sarcastic response. "His bones would turn to water before he took a step, right enough, weakling that he is." He paused, then added, "Though he isn't hired to be a soldier, he's hired to teach you Greek, and that he does very well." King Henry, who had a good deal of learning himself and admired scholars, was quick to modify his comments.

While I watched, the king tried again to convince his son to be bold and jump the low hedge, but the effort failed, and in the end Henry got down off his horse and slapped the pony on the rump, sending the boy away toward the stables.

It was then that he caught sight of me, and beckoned me over to where he was standing.

"Oh, that boy, that boy," he was saying to himself, shaking his head. "Between the boy and the lawyers and the women, like two cats squabbling—"

I assumed that by "two cats squabbling" he meant Anne and Queen Catherine, but I had nothing to say to that, and so was silent.

"What is it, Jane?"

"If Your Majesty pleases, it is about the silver mesh trim for my gown."

"Yes, of course. You need more of it, I take it."

"Mr. Skut requires more, Your Majesty."

"I shall have it sent to him tomorrow."

"Thank you, Your Majesty." I hesitated. "There is one other thing."

"Yes?"

"The queen's new confessor, Father Bartolome. He isn't what he seems."

"Oh?" There was amusement in his king's eyes.

"He is Ambassador Chapuys' man. A spy."

"Of course he is. But then, better the devil you know, eh? Is it not so? All Spaniards ought to be sent to the bottom of the sea, as Anne loves to say!"

"Not all Spaniards," I said stubbornly. "Not my former mistress, the queen."

The king frowned. "Watch your words, girl. Learn from your brother and bend with the wind. Right now the wind is not in the queen's favor. Indeed, a tempest is brewing. A tempest that, if I'm not mistaken, will blow the queen clean away. Or send her to the bottom of the ocean!"

THIRTEEN

By the time Mr. Skut brought my finished wedding gown to the palace and I tried it on, I was feeling ill at ease about marrying Will, and all because of Galyon.

Not that the gown was any less lovely than the last time I had seen it—in fact it was lovelier than ever, with the glittering silver trim all in place and the sleeves tied on properly and the elegant, whispering petticoats and undergarments spread out to their full extent, their length barely sweeping the rushes on the floor.

"We'll have to shorten that skirt," Mr. Skut was saying, indicating to his assistants how much of the shimmering pale blue satin would have to be hemmed. "You're not a very tall girl, are you," he added, more to himself than to me.

"And when is the wedding?" the dressmaker asked me presently, in a brighter tone.

"I don't yet know. We are waiting until our home is ready." Will had been repeatedly assured by his father that Chevering

Manor would be ours, but first Arthur Dormer had to find a house and land near London, and move out of his former residence, and that was proving to be difficult. So we waited.

I could not help thinking that the delay was providential. Maybe I wasn't supposed to marry Will. Maybe I was supposed to wait for Galyon. After all, this was not our first delay; in the beginning there had been Will's parents' refusal to permit the marriage, because of my father's seduction (I preferred to think it a seduction) of Will's sister. Then had come my decision not to run away to the Spice Islands with Will aboard the *Eglantine,* and the ship's foundering. And now there was the matter of the house, our house, that was not yet ours, and might not be for some time.

Providence, I had always believed, worked to bring about good results we cannot foresee. It governed our lives and determined our destinies. So when Will's father ran into problems time and again in acquiring a new residence, I had to believe it was more than coincidence. I had to believe that the hand of the divine was at work.

How else to explain the number of times Arthur Dormer had tried, and failed, to become the owner of a property worthy of his new standing at court?

If only I had never seen Galyon, there at the window, and felt the irresistible force of his presence! If only I had not gone to meet him in the darkness, and felt the roughness of his hands, the softness of his lips, the press of his muscular body, the long, lean strength of him. Had I never known what deep and joyous pleasures he could arouse in me, I would surely have been content to go on as I was. But now that I did know, could I ever be content again?

"I do believe you are more slender than when this gown was first fitted," Mr. Skut was saying. "We shall have to take it in."

I was not surprised to hear the comment, for I had been eating little, the excitement of my meetings with Galyon had taken away my appetite. We had only been together a few times since our first midnight meeting, but each time the attraction had been stronger than the time before. Each meeting had left me eager and impatient for the next—and at the same time unsettled, out of balance with myself. I felt at times as though I was basking in the delicious warmth at the end of a long summer season, waiting for the weather to break and the storms and cold to come rushing in.

For of course my dalliance with the alluring glazier could not be anything but a fleeting, rapturous dream. A passing wonderment. Here I was, after all, preparing for my marriage to my long time love and best friend. Preparing to leave the court with its poisonous quarrels, harms, traps set for the unwary, its ever unfolding intrigues. I would marry Will the gentleman farmer, mild-mannered and sweet. We would begin our new life together. The fleeting season of joy with Galyon would pass, and the storms and perils of real life would begin.

But with Will I would never know rapture. Of this I felt certain. How could I marry a man who could not share with me all that I had discovered with Galyon?

And what disturbed me at least as much, how could I keep to myself the secret of my betrayal? I had always confided in Will, I had never lied to him. But this secret I had to keep. I would never, ever, tell him about Galyon. This troubled me, and as so often happened, Bridget Wingfield read my mind.

"You are not yourself, Jane," she said when she came upon me one afternoon when I had been brooding over my dilemma. "Are you worried about becoming a wife?"

I sighed—and she took my sigh as acquiescence. She sat down beside me.

"Are you worried about the pain of becoming a mother?"

I nodded—though the pain of childbirth was not, in fact, in my thoughts.

Bridget moved closer to me.

"I have heard the most alarming story, just a few days ago. From a midwife who has delivered hundreds of babies. She told me about a healthy woman whose monthly courses ceased—but her belly did not swell."

"But if her belly did not swell, then where was the child?"

"In her side," Bridget whispered.

I had never heard of this. I wanted to hear more.

"Her side swelled, a little," Bridget went on, "and then she got very sick and died."

"And she did not have the sweat, or the plague?"

Bridget shook her head slowly.

"How horrible."

"The midwife says it can happen. A sign of an unnatural child."

"A child not meant to be born," I said, thinking, a child whose death was decreed by providence.

We were both silent for a time. These were solemn matters.

"To be sure," Bridget went on eventually, "there is no reason for you to fear such a terrible outcome. I believe it to be quite rare.

"I was nervous and unsure before my marriage too," she said. "All was arranged by others. Richard was much older. I barely knew him. I never had the chance to choose him, because the choice was never mine to make.

"I liked him," she went on, "I did not love him, of course—how often do married people love one another? And if they do, how long does it last? But I thought that Richard and I could be content together. I was sure he would never be cruel to me."

She looked at me sympathetically. I longed to confide in her, but I was wary. At length I began, uncertain how much to say.

"I am not nervous, exactly. I dread thinking about this. I haven't talked about it to anyone, especially not Will. But the truth is, I'm no longer certain Will is the man I want to marry."

"Oh dear."

I looked up at Bridget, hoping to find sympathy in her eyes, her expression. I saw only a patient attentiveness.

"I've tried not to think about this, but I can't help it. No matter what I do, I can't prevent these doubts from flooding into my mind."

"Is there someone else?"

Bridget's words opened a wound. My eyes filled with tears—tears of guilt and shame and remorse. I did not answer her right away. But then I wiped impatiently at my eyes and said, my voice low, "Yes."

To my surprise Bridget laughed.

"Oh, is that all!" she trilled. "I fell madly in love with an archer in the king's guard during my engagement. But I came to my senses. I knew I was only acting out of fear. It wasn't a real attachment at all. I was trying to find a way to avoid doing the thing that frightened me. Thank goodness I realized it and sent the archer away. He married someone else—a woman of his own sort, a butcher's daughter from Plymouth.

"Tell me honestly, Jane, is this someone of yours a man far below you, someone your parents would never approve of?"

I nodded.

"And someone you could never bring to court, who would never be welcome as an equal among us?"

Ruefully, and with a sigh, I nodded once again.

Bridget shrugged and spread her hands.

"Then don't you see? All you are doing is defying your family—especially your father, judging from what you have told me about him, and what I have heard from others—and defying the social rules we follow here at the royal court. Am I right?"

"I don't know. All I know is that since I met him, I feel different. I am different. I can never go back to being the old Jane again."

She patted my hand.

"Think about what I've said. I never regretted marrying Richard, and the archer never crosses my mind, or the butcher's daughter either."

The Christmas season approached, and the dozens of grooms and valets in Anne's growing household all had new liveries. Embroidered on the servants' new coats, in large letters, was the message "Grumble who will, this is how it's going to be!"

It was a stark challenge to Queen Catherine and her supporters, and no one could mistake the meaning of the words.

Nor would anyone mistake the fact that Anne was wearing looser gowns, and complaining often of illness, and demanding quails' eggs and pomegranates and marchpane and other delicacies as pregnant women often did. As ever, the eyes of the court were fixed on Anne's belly, and whether her loose gowns were meant to accommodate a telltale swelling or disguise the fact that her symptoms were all a ruse, no one could say. Not even those of us who served her.

The challenge of the servants' liveries was not lost on Queen Catherine, who immediately ordered new coats for her own grooms and valets, embroidered with the words "Queen Forever."

Fighting broke out between the men of the two rival households, their brawling an incessant annoyance to the king, who at last, in exasperation, sent Queen Catherine away to Oatlands for the Christmas season and ordered her not to return.

Anne had won—but King Henry was put out with her.

"Why must you go out of your way to stir up conflict?" he snapped. "Why can you not be content with all I have given you, all I have done for you? Is it not enough that you demand your own household, your own army of guardsmen? Must you use them to provoke quarrels?"

"The guardsmen protect me against that damnable Nun of Kent!" was Anne's retort. "And against the Spaniards, the supporters of that woman who calls herself your queen!"

Back and forth the accusations flew, until the king limped out of the room—only to return, not long afterward, his mood contrite.

"Pardon me, sweeting, puffball," he began, taking Anne's hand and kissing it. (I could not help but notice that he never took the hand with the extra nail, always the normal hand. I never spoke of this to anyone, but I often wondered, had anyone else noticed?) He spoke and acted as if unaware of those of us in the room, he did not care who heard him.

"It was only my leg," he went on, his tone pleading. "My painful leg. You know how it rouses me to fury."

Anne nodded her forgiveness, but there was a smile of triumph on her lips.

The king had reached the age of forty, and it was evident he was feeling the weight of his years. He had grown heavy and fleshy, his handsome face rounder, his chins multiplying. (I counted three.) He walked with a golden walking stick and when in his worst pain, leaned on Charles Brandon's strong arm. Ever fearful of a return of the sweating sickness, he continued to wear a pouch of live spiders at his throat, which made Anne laugh and tease him.

The nullity suit languished, its outcome uncertain and with no final resolution in sight. The king's impatience deepened, and gave him headaches—or so we heard him tell Anne. We did not look forward to Christmas, and as the wintry days grew shorter and darker, the pageantry and foolery of the Christmas season, the gift-giving and solemn worship, held none of their usual joyful appeal.

Besides, with the rains and frosts of December, work on Anne's apartments ceased, and my opportunities to spend precious hours with Galyon grew fewer.

"Grumble who will, this is how it's going to be!" I told myself, echoing Anne's new motto. It was no good lamenting how things were, or complaining. For now, things were as they were: with Galyon, with Will, with the conflicts and the unhappy Christmas to come.

The days passed, and I did not see Galyon, or receive a message from him. Always before, when something had happened to keep us apart, one of Anne's grooms would send me a message.

I grew worried. Had something happened to Galyon? Was it possible that Will had found out about us, and attacked him? Will was generally a peaceable man, but I had never given him any reason to be jealous. I could not be sure of what he might do if he discovered that another man had become my lover.

I waited, anxiously, then just before Christmas I went to the groom who relayed Galyon's messages to me in the past.

"He has gone back to France, mistress," was the groom's response when I asked after Galyon. "He has gone to spend the Noel with his wife."

Our traveling party strung itself out in a long dusty line of carts, wagons, mounted guardsmen and footsoldiers, winding slowly along the sun-swept Dover road. It was September of the year 1532, I was twenty-six years old and still unmarried (a disgrace, for a gentleman's daughter), and was preparing to embark with the rest of the royal party for France.

The months had gone by quickly since our last troubled, quarrel-blighted Christmas season, a season I was eager to forget, and events were moving rapidly toward a long-awaited conclusion. King Henry and Anne were living as though they were already married, as though the failed nullity suit was no more than a minor inconvenience and the king's decision to cast aside the pope's authority over his marital life was the inevitable outcome of a long and unjust struggle.

For the king had, at last, freed himself from the burden (or blessing, however one might see it) of submission to the church of Rome. He had taken the radical—many said heretical—step of declaring himself to be the head of the church in England. He had joined the rebels who, like Martin Luther, renounced the primacy of the Holy See and severed the time-honored unity of Christendom.

And for this he was condemned, bitterly and unceasingly, by those loyal to the pope.

Anne, however, was overjoyed. She had triumphed over Catherine at last. She was on her way to the French court, as King Henry's chosen companion, and her forty-eight trunks were filled with silken nightgowns embroidered with miniver, kirtles of purple and blue and green damask, gowns of russet and crimson velvet trimmed in cloth of gold. The king had indulged her every whim in preparing for the journey to the French court, for he would not have it said that his bride-to-be was anything but magnificent in her dress, a worthy future consort and the future mother of a line of kings.

Anne had begun to boast about her own mother's descent

from King Edward I (ignoring her father, who, as everyone knew, was a mere commoner). She held herself with a newfound authority, looked at others with a condescending stare, and affected an air of superiority and command that I found hard to endure.

"Jane!" she would call out to me, "take little Pourquoi for his walk! Bring me my satin sleeves! The ones with the diamonds! Jane! Where is my cloak of Bruges satin? Find it!"

We were kept busy fetching and carrying, bringing pillows for her back and footstools for her feet, ever mindful that she might possibly be carrying the king's child and so we might in fact be serving not only Thomas Boleyn's haughty daughter but the next king of England.

Certainly Henry was lavishing more costly gifts on Anne than ever, from fur-trimmed gowns to gold-trimmed headdresses to delicate damask slippers to velvet and satin cloaks in numbers too high to count. A dozen dressmakers and countless assistant seamstresses were kept busy cutting and fitting and sewing Anne's beautiful garments; precious stuffs were brought to the palace in quantity to be turned into much admired gowns and petticoats. And beyond the clothing were the jewels the king showered on Anne. He ordered his jewelers to remove the largest rubies and diamonds from his own bracelets and rings and make them into sparkling necklaces for Anne. Catherine was ordered to turn over her gems to the royal treasury as well, and they found their way (much to Catherine's anger) into Anne's treasure hoard of valued stones.

And to complete Anne's honors, she was elevated, amid grand ceremony, to the rank of Marquess of Pembroke.

Clad in a mantle and gown of crimson velvet trimmed with ermine, while all the prominent nobles and officers of the court looked on, she knelt before the king as her patent of nobility was read out and the gleaming golden coronet was placed atop her dark flowing curls. Trumpets sounded and the choir sang a Te Deum of thanksgiving before the court celebrated the event with feasting and pageantry.

Once she was made a marquess, Anne's hauteur rose to new heights. Her demands grew, the punishments she imposed became more harsh. She dismissed a royal valet for allowing little Pourquoi to relieve himself on a pair of her satin slippers lying on her bed. And not only was the unfortunate valet dismissed, but all the valets were deprived of their usual special privileges (their right to keep candle ends, the heels of manchet loaves, discarded points and laces) for an entire month—and a winter month at that.

She was very particular about the embroidered counterpane on her bed, with its elaborate border of cloth of gold and its heraldic white falcons. At the least sign of a wrinkle in this bedcovering she would give a shout of dismay, call for one of the grooms and insist that the counterpane be pressed and straightened—on pain of immediate dismissal.

Worst of all, Anne became not only imperious but vengeful. When a tearful mother came to her to beg her to intervene to prevent her son from being hanged, Anne's response was cold.

"He has gone wrong," she said. "He has been found guilty. Let him be hanged!"

"But all he did was to steal a small coin—and not for himself, but for our neighbors, who do not have enough to eat! He is only sixteen years old, he is a kind boy—"

"Laws are made to be obeyed—and enforced," was all Anne said, turning aside from the sorrowing woman. "He must pay the price for his misdeed."

I thought of Anne's pitiless words as we rode along on our way to Dover, Anne in her litter, the king mounted on Coeurdelion (though riding pained him), the rest of the members of the royal household in carts or on horseback, the soldiers on foot. We had to stop often when carts lost wheels or horses went lame or wagons overturned, spilling their contents into a ditch. The slow speed was wearing, I wondered whether we would reach our destination before nightfall. I saw Ned ride past, trying to clear the road of obstacles, shouting to the outriders up ahead and calling out when he spied hazards.

Ned had become indispensable to the king as the most capable of the esquires of the body. He was efficient and always managed to get things done, often things others found impossible. Any time he saw a task, no matter how menial, being badly performed, he asked for permission to take charge of it, and usually succeeded. He seemed tireless, his determination and strength of will carried him through.

So it was on this ripe fall afternoon, with the slow progress of the long royal traveling party. Ned had taken over, and was making headway when, as we rounded a turning in the narrow rutted road, we found ourselves facing a startling, unexpected sight.

Atop a hill, looming above the roadway, stood a high wooden cross, at least three times higher, I judged, than the tallest man in the procession—the king. Beneath this stark wooden symbol stood a small woman in nun's garb and nine attendants in long white tunics.

It was the Nun of Kent and her acolytes, including my sister-in-law Cat. Arrayed before the cross, they could not fail to capture the attention of everyone in the royal procession, and I heard gasps of alarm and awe and cries of "The holy nun!" "The Nun of Kent!" before the long line of horses and vehicles came to an abrupt halt, the horses pawing the ground and whinnying nervously.

For the nun, her voice strong and far-reaching, was addressing us all, and the sound of her words was chilling.

"For your sins, I shall send down plagues upon you, saith the Lord," she was saying. "Adulterers! Fornicators! O thou guilty of wickedness in high places!"

"May the demon of lust be cast out, and the angels of mercy restore godliness to the throne of England! May she who bears the devil's sign know the wrath of the Lord!"

I saw that the king was sending guardsmen to climb the hill. All around me I heard murmuring among the royal attendants.

"They say she casts out demons—she heals—she can even raise the dead—"

"The woman is mad!" the king was shouting. "She speaks blasphemy! She babbles!"

But the nun had more to say.

"For your sins, O king, and the sins of your Jezebel mistress, the Lord will send plagues upon England. First will come a plague of frogs!" I heard gasps from those around me. "Then will come a plague of lice, and of flies. Then the Lord will send a great sickness, and many cattle will die, and horses too, and the sickness will endure without ceasing, until boils cover all human flesh, and the entire earth is afflicted past endurance." Moans arose from many throats at these words.

"Silence that woman!" the king was shouting to the guardsmen, who were scrambling up the hill toward the nun. As they approached the immense cross I saw the nine women who attended the nun scatter, and I wondered whether Ned had recognized Cat among them. I didn't dare look at him, not wanting to quicken his suspicions. He believed Cat to be locked in a cell at the convent of St. Agnes's. He would have no reason to think Cat might have been liberated in order to serve the Nun of Kent. Unless—

But I did not give this more thought, for the nun had reached her final prediction.

"Finally the Lord will raise his hand and smite the evildoers with one last plague," she thundered. "The firstborn son of the adulterer and his Jezebel mistress shall die!"

Hearing this Anne shrieked, Henry swore, many of those around me crossed themselves—as I did—our lips moving in prayer. And the guardsmen, reaching the nun at last, silenced her with savage blows and tied her limp body with ropes and took her away. In less time than it had taken her to announce the coming plagues the hill was bare and there was no more sign of the stunning sight we had witnessed. Only the stark high wooden cross, rising above the road, lonely and silent.

FOURTEEN

S HE'S not at all what I expected."

"The clothes are good, but her body—well—hardly any bosom, and that nose! The mouth too big, she looks as though she could devour a horse—"

"And those hands! Well, I know what they say in England, the hands of the devil, or the fingers of the devil—"

"Good, thick hair. Straight, but good."

My French, however flawed, was quite fluent enough to understand the comments I overheard the French courtiers make about Anne. They speculated endlessly on her looks, her clothes, her dancing (this, they agreed, was above reproach), her height (not tall enough), her belly (was she or wasn't she?).

They snickered, they called her every foul name, every name applied to the women of the streets. They made fun of her walk, the way she gestured with her hands, her favorite posture when irritated (one hand on her hip, a scowl on her face). They drew six-fingered hands on the palace walls, alongside stout phalluses.

We had not been at the palace of Chambord more than a few days before I began hearing these unflattering remarks and observing the mockery. The French had never liked the English, that much I knew; King Francis and King Henry were meeting to carry out a pretense of friendliness and bonhomie that neither of them truly felt. We were instructed to be gracious to the ladies of the French court but we felt no real friendship or courtesy toward them, and we heard their smothered laughter and their whispers whenever we left the rooms in which we met.

There was much sniggering about Anne's illicit relations with the king, her haughty manner, her lack of graciousness. I heard King Francis's valets betting with each other how quickly King Henry would discard Anne, and who his new love would be.

But at the lavish banquet held in honor of Henry and Anne in the immense grand salon with its tapestries in glowing tones of blue and deep red, green and gold and ochre, its brilliant painted ceiling, its long tables covered in gold and silver plate, Anne was treated as though she was already queen.

Her device, the white falcon, was embroidered on cushions and borne by the king's guardsmen on their helms and even molded into spun sugar and served with sweet wine. She was accorded every honor, and addressed as a noblewoman (for she was, after all, Marquess of Pembroke). No one mentioned the name Catherine of Aragon; it was as if Catherine had never existed.

Between the many courses of the banquet, poets read verses composed for Anne, and musicians played dances and songs dedicated to her. We heard her merits praised and admired again and again; her beautiful black eyes, deep and dark as onyx, her swanlike neck, her long slender tapering fingers, her smooth skin, the perfect oval of her face.

I had to smile at the contrast between this courteous formal praise and the jokes and jibes I continually overheard. But then, everything about our reception by King Francis was artificial, part of a calculated show of cordiality between the English and French designed to thwart the designs of Emperor Charles.

"Nobody takes any of this to be sincere," Ned remarked to me during the banquet. "It is all for show. But the alliance is very serious indeed—and King Francis's acceptance of what our king has done in putting aside his wife is vital."

"Anne is a pawn on a very large chessboard," I said.

Ned looked at me appraisingly. "Very astute, for a girl," he said. "I could not have put it better. Mind you never say anything like that when the king can hear you."

During the banquet I noticed that Anne was looking at me—really looking, and not just glancing past me as she usually did, taking in my appearance as she did the furnishings of the room, the number of attendants nearby, the wrinkles or lack of wrinkles in her counterpane. She was looking at my gown.

I was wearing the beautiful pale blue and cream satin gown Mr. Skut had made for my wedding, the sleeves and bodice somewhat altered to match the cut and style currently favored at the French court. The glittering silver mesh trim that had been the king's gift to me drew attention to the gown, I saw the French queen's ladies admiring it and commenting to one another.

Anne's own gown was very grand, and quite becoming—a sweep of russet velvet with black lambs' fur at the neck and on the full sleeves. Yet as the evening went on she seemed more and more preoccupied with my gown, staring at it and frowning. Eventually she beckoned to me. I went to stand before her as she sat, surrounded by golden plates and goblets, the king sitting beside her, engaged in conversation with one of the French noblemen.

"Jane," Anne said evenly, in a tone of voice I knew well. It was a tone she used when she was about to make an accusation.

"Yes, Milady Marquess?"

"The trimming on your gown. Where did it come from?"

"From Peru, if I'm not mistaken."

"And have you been in Peru recently?"

"No, milady."

"Then how did you come by it? Did you steal it?"

"Of course not."

"I'm waiting for an answer."

I glanced at the king, but he did not appear to be listening to what we were saying. The musicians were playing, there was a buzz of talk and laughter in the vast room, the chink of cutlery and the clatter of serving plates and goblets made it difficult to overhear what others were saying.

"It was a gift, milady."

"A very costly gift."

"The giver is wealthy." I did not want to reveal that the trimming came from the king. Anne was very jealous. I hoped that King Henry would come to my rescue with some gallant comment that would satisfy Anne. But he took no notice.

"And just who was this mysterious gift-giver? A suitor perhaps? At last, someone who hopes to marry you?"

The jibe stung, especially since Anne was not yet married herself and was older than I was. And besides, Will and I had been promised for more years than I could remember.

"No, milady. Not a suitor."

"Then who?" Her voice rose in exasperation, and conversation near us died down. The musicians stopped playing. King Henry turned to look at Anne.

"What is it, puffball?"

Anne took a drink of her wine.

"This girl will not tell me where she got the trimming for her gown. I think she stole it."

"Aha! A thief in our midst!" He winked at me, stood and strode slowly toward where I was standing. He towered over me.

"We shall have to bring her to justice," he boomed out. "Councilor Cromwell!" he shouted, "come into court!" Every eye in the room turned to Thomas Cromwell, who, playing along with the charade, got up from the banquet table and joined us.

"Lord Councilor, what is the punishment for theft?"

"To be stripped naked and whipped without mercy, Your Majesty."

"Well then—"

"But my crime is unproven, sire," I interrupted, taking the risk that my participation would be welcomed. "There must be witnesses against me."

"Who will bear witness that this girl is a thief?" The king looked around the room. Silence, broken only by a ripple of laughter.

Out of the corner of my eye I saw Anne, looking annoyed, fidgeting in her chair.

"There, you see?" said Henry, turning to Anne. "She is innocent. Pure as the driven snow."

More laughter greeted this pronouncement.

"What's that? You scoff at the idea that a pretty young unsullied girl, a girl who has been at court—how many years has it been, Jane?" I held up seven fingers. "A girl who has been at court for seven years, might not be innocent?" He looked shocked.

"I will not be mocked in this way!" Anne said, standing up and preparing to leave the room.

"Stay where you are, wench!" Henry said sternly, then quickly resumed his pantomime, so quickly that his flash of anger passed without breaking the ribald mood. "Besides," he said to the banqueters in a light tone, "I know how the girl got the trimming! I myself am the gift-giver, and no one else." He reached over and hugged me lightly, reassuringly, and then gave the disgruntled Anne a kiss on the cheek. He waved his hand at the musicians and they resumed playing. Anne sat down heavily, scowling, and I took the opportunity to scurry across the room, out of the way, and take my place among Anne's other attendants. It was a long time before I caught my breath.

Dozens of servants brought in steaming platters and laid them before the banqueters. Hardly had I glanced down at the food on the platter before me when I heard a loud shriek.

It was Anne. Another terrified shriek followed, then she cried out, "Frogs! It is the plague of frogs!"

Sure enough, on the silver dish in front of me were arrayed hundreds of frogs, steaming hot and covered in sauce.

Anne sprang up and ran from the room, wrenching her body past the king's clutching hands.

FIFTEEN

I saved her," Catherine whispered from where she lay, a small, frail-looking figure in the wide, intricately carved canopied bed. "I saved her life. How could she turn against me so brutally? Has she no feeling?"

I had come to the remote rural palace of Buckden in Huntingdonshire where Catherine of Aragon was living, a large if somewhat dilapidated fortresslike mansion set in a modest hunting park, far from London, far from all that was going on in the court and country. King Henry had sent me to Buckden with the distasteful task of giving Catherine the latest and most important news from the court: the news that he had married Anne.

I made the journey to Buckden filled with chagrin and sorrow. It was my duty to deliver the news of the king's marriage, but I had rarely been given a more distasteful task. Queen Catherine, my mistress for so many years, who had favored me and had always been a model of courtesy and charity, was now shunted carelessly aside, an insult to her Spanish royal blood and an even greater insult to her years of pain and sacrifice as King Henry's consort.

She had done her part, played her thankless role with uncommon grace. Now I had to tell her that after all her struggles and years of dishonor, the king was going to marry the very woman who had caused all her misery.

"I ask you, Jane," Catherine was saying, "how could the Great Enemy do to me what she has done, when she owes her very life to me?"

Catherine began to cough, and tried to raise herself up on one elbow. The effort to speak tired her and left her hoarse. Ever since she had been sent away from court and banished to Oatlands the previous year, with King Henry refusing to see or communicate with her, she had been plagued by fevers and rheums. Her Spanish doctors bled her and purged her again and again, but she did not recover. Rather she seemed to worsen, or so I heard from her long time gentleman usher Griffith Richards on his visits to the capital. Each time she received word of the king and Anne, Richards told me, she seemed to grow more frail, though she fought to retain her dignity and in particular, refused to give up her claim to the title of queen, though the king had ordered her to be addressed as "Princess Dowager."

I sat down on a bench beside Catherine's bed. She lay back against her pillows and reached out to me. I took her hand.

"I wish I had found Your Majesty in better health," I said. "I will pray for your swift recovery."

I looked over at Catherine's familiar prie-dieu which stood near the bed, and it was then that I noticed, in the shadows of an alcove, the dark figure of Father Bartolome, sometime companion of the Nun of Kent and now Catherine's confessor.

He nodded slowly, sending a chill up my spine. I did not nod back.

I returned my gaze to Catherine.

"I'm sorry to say that I have come on an unhappy errand for the king. He wishes me to tell you that he and the Lady Anne were married recently. She is to be crowned before long."

"And has she quickened?" was Catherine's question.

Somewhat startled, I answered that there had been no official announcement of a pregnancy, and certainly no announcement that the child had quickened, or leapt into life, within the womb. Midwives, ever cautious, waited for this vital sign before assuring women that they would be giving birth.

The princess dowager merely shrugged. "He would never have married her unless she was bearing his child. Though from what I hear of her, the child could be anyone's. That handsome young musician Mark Smeaton, for instance. They say he is in love with her. Or the rascal Weston. Or her old love Wyatt. Bridget Wingfield used to be full of stories of Anne's seductions."

"Yes, I have heard some of those stories."

Catherine coughed again, and Father Bartolome came out of the shadows to offer her a goblet of wine. She let go of my hand and took a sip, then another. It was hard for me to believe I was hearing such words from the former queen. She seemed coarsened, embittered by her banishment from court, her rural exile. Where, I wondered, was her usual attitude of Christian forgiveness and fortitude? Why hadn't I found her on her knees, kneeling at her prie-dieu?

"Do you know what day this is?" Catherine asked when she had soothed her throat and was able to take my hand again and resume talking. "You don't remember, do you? It's the anniversary of the birth of my little New Year's Boy, the only one of my sons who lived long enough to be christened."

"I was only a child myself when he was born, milady," I reminded her. "That was a long time ago, before I entered your household."

Catherine waved one thin, long-fingered hand. "No matter," she said wearily. "The priests say God governs all. He took every one of my sons to Himself before they were out of the cradle. And my daughters too, all but my dearest jewel Mary. Perhaps He will take Anne's sons in the same way. The Nun of Kent says He will."

I smiled. "The nun has called down all the plagues of Egypt on Anne's head. And Anne is terrified."

I told Catherine about the royal banquet at King Francis's court, how Anne had caught sight of the platters of frogs and shrieked in terror, thinking the plague of frogs called down by the nun had arrived.

"Has she quickened yet?" Catherine asked again.

"No, milady," I assured her.

"Then there is nothing to be concerned about. And meanwhile, there are the reports from the Flemish court. But then, I'm sure you have heard those already."

"What reports?" I asked, suddenly intrigued.

"Father Bartolome knows more than I do."

I looked at the priest, who approached Catherine's bed once again.

"The Great Enemy's sins are being brought to light," he told me solemnly. "It is said that she caused the death of Jane Popyngcort, and that she has tried to poison others who stand in her way."

I remembered well how the Flemish Jane, always an outsider to our circle as maids of honor because of her foreign ways, had suddenly left the English court years earlier and gone home to Flanders. According to Bridget, Jane had been paid to keep secret what she knew of King Henry's relations with Elizabeth Boleyn, Anne's mother—relations which belonged to the distant past, when the king was a youth. Bridget had said that, had the truth about the king and Anne's mother come to light, he could never have married Anne. The Holy Father would not have allowed their union.

I remembered well the chest full of gold Jane took with her when she left our court, the valuable new jewelry she had proudly worn, the hurried meetings and secret conversations that had gone on just at the time she left. Clearly she had been bribed to leave the court. And then, not long after she left, we received the news that she had died suddenly, the victim of robbers as she was traveling.

"The Great Enemy is much hated," Father Bartolome was saying. "Those who know the truth about her are revealing it."

"Is it being said that Anne is a murderess?"

The priest nodded.

"But such reports could be nothing more than slanders. Courts are cesspits of lies."

"Those who were in Anne's pay have come forward. There can be no doubt of her guilt."

"And I saved her life," Catherine murmured, letting go of my hand. "Perhaps I should have let her die. Poor girl! She has become a spider, entangled in her own treacherous web. May the Lord have pity on her." Once again Catherine sank back into her pillows, closing her eyes and sighing deeply. Taken aback by what I had just heard, and not wanting to spend any more time with the disturbing Father Bartolome, I got up to leave, looking down, before I did so, at Catherine's pale face and bending down to kiss her soft cheek.

Anne rode in splendor through the freshly swept London streets on the day of her coronation procession, her litter draped in shimmering cloth of gold, her mantle of royal purple furred with thick ermine, her long fall of black hair flowing down her back under a circlet of flashing rubies.

Her hands with the extra nail—the mark of the devil—were hidden under a large bouquet of lilies and gillyflowers. Her prominent belly was shrouded under her wide crimson gown and the long rope of large pearls that hung from her graceful neck drew attention to her handsome face and dark eyes—the eyes, so it was said, that had won the king's love years earlier.

I had to admire her on that day, she was at her best. We maids of honor had spent hours dressing her, brushing out her thick rope of hair, brightening her skin with unguents and applying tinted powders to her lips and cheeks. She was excited. Her hands shook as she took her place in the litter and we smoothed out the long skirts of her gown.

This is her moment of triumph, I thought. Her ultimate victory.

But as soon as the procession set out along Fenchurch Street the jeering catcalls began, the crowds parting to allow her litter to pass but voices calling out curses and bawdy insults and laughing in mockery as the royal procession went by.

"Harlot!" we heard people cry. "Whore!" "She-devil!"

The royal marshals were quick to strike out with their batons but the cries and insults continued.

"Great Harry! Take back your wife!" "Burn the witch!" "Put her in the stocks!"

Londoners had been taxed heavily to pay for Anne's coronation and the celebrations surrounding it, and they resented having to pay for the exalting of a woman they detested. They shouted out their slanders as Anne passed in her litter. They saluted Queen Catherine and blessed her name. They predicted disaster for the realm and for the king.

And in truth we had to wonder, as we heard the protesting voices and all the slanders, whether indeed the forces of darkness had triumphed. Anne's exaltation frightened the Londoners as much as it angered them. If good queen Catherine could be displaced and her disreputable rival Anne crowned, then surely the power of the divine was tottering. Where was the Lord, where were His angels, when the witch was borne past in all her finery?

Our progress was interrupted again and again by musicians playing lively tunes, actors reciting long speeches and spectacles staged along the route. The noise was quite overwhelming at times, and I felt my panic rising, hemmed in as I was by the press of people and the constant clamor of their jibes and outcries. By the time we reached the Strand I was quite overcome, the stench of unwashed bodies and street odors making me nauseous and the feeling of being trapped by the drunken spectators, dancing and singing and flinging themselves about with abandon, making me desperate to escape.

Bridget, sitting next to me in our litter, sensed my mounting desperation and held me back.

"Only a little farther, Jane," she said. "Remember, this is Anne's day. We are here to serve her. Think how hard all this must be for her, with the baby kicking and her stomach upset as it nearly always is."

Anne's baby had quickened, the midwives had assured the king that she was past the dangerous early months when she might miscarry. It was the last day of May in that year of 1533. The prince was expected to be born at harvest time.

Though the coronation went forward the following day without incident, with Anne crowned by the new Archbishop of Canterbury Thomas Cranmer, there was an abiding sense among the Londoners that the very order of nature had been shattered. Now that the royal harlot had been made queen, there were rumors of strange lights in the sky and ominous rumblings under the earth. Great fishes a hundred feet in length beached themselves in the Thames, so it was said, and in every parish, the number of people who drowned or hanged themselves in despair rose alarmingly.

Saddest of all, on coronation day, as the new queen feasted on a banquet of twenty-seven dishes and we all dined with her, we heard cries of alarm and anguish in the streets outside. For hundreds of hungry Londoners, eager to enjoy the royal bounty in food and wine spread out on tables in the open air for them to share, pressed in too closely and many of them were crushed to death.

It was a sign that the Lord was punishing England for the transgressions of its ruler. One more sign among many that a change had come, a darkness had fallen over the kingdom, and nothing in our lives would ever be the same again.

I had been avoiding Will for months, but I could not avoid him forever. Our paths crossed often at court, for, as Ned had once predicted, Will was destined for preferment and had all the qualities needed to rise high in royal service. The all-powerful Thomas Cromwell had singled Will out and recommended to the king that he be made principal chamber gentleman to the prince, Henry Fitzroy. His promotion to that post soon followed. And as Fitzroy, who at the time of Anne's coronation was fourteen years old, was being put forward by the king at every opportunity, given a prominent role in every ceremony and occupying a place of honor at banquets and other great occasions, Will too was on constant view, and we were often thrown together.

At the time I thought it ironic that Will, who had always insisted that what he wanted most was a quiet life in the country, far from any undue attention, as far away as possible from the bustle and intrigue of the royal household, should now be rising ever higher at the center of power around the king.

Each time I saw him he looked older, more weighty in both mind and body (his waist had definitely thickened), less the eager, sweet, affectionate boy I had known and cherished since our childhood and more the man of affairs—not with Ned's ruthless edge but with the purposeful walk and serious demeanor of a high official, preoccupied with important matters. As Henry Fitzroy's principal chamber gentleman Will received not only a very substantial income but valuable extra funds; like his father, he was appointed to many offices—Collector of the Fifteenth, Armorer of the Tower for Powder, Constable of the King's Castle of Etall—and was paid a handsome sum for each, though the actual labor was carried out by subordinates. His newfound prosperity was evident in his costly doublets and fine linen shirts trimmed in Belgian lace, his jeweled caps and doeskin gloves, the flashing rings on his stubby fingers and the heavy gold buckles on his shoes.

There was a definite change in his manner as well. Whenever I saw him, it seemed, he was barking out orders to his underlings, criticizing them impatiently for being slow to carry out his commands or for making errors. I overheard him one day reprimanding a young clerk who had erred in tallying a tax. His voice was shrill, his words harsh and unsparing.

"Can't you do anything right?" he was saying. "From the first day you were appointed to work under me you have had to be watched, and corrected, and prevented from doing harm making wrong entries in the records."

He went on, continuing to raise his voice in criticism while the young clerk looked down at his feet, his face flushed in shame.

"I—I'm doing my best, master," he said. "I have no talent for this work. I am a cordwainer by trade—"

"Then what are you doing here?" Will barked, more impatient than ever. "Did you lose your way, and stumble into the tally room?"

"No, master. I was sent by Master Cromwell."

"Then I must inform Master Cromwell that he himself has made an error. He has chosen badly. Very badly indeed!"

Will's choler brought tears to the young clerk's eyes. I felt very sorry for him. I wanted to intervene, but held back. Something told me all was not well with my betrothed. I needed to wait until we were alone to talk to him about it. In the meantime it was clear to me that my Will, who had once wanted to be a gentleman farmer, had become a gilded courtier with a tense, nervous edge to his voice and a merciless attitude toward those who disappointed him.

One morning he sent me a message to say that he needed to speak with me urgently. I changed my gown and put on my costliest gold-trimmed headdress—a recent castoff from Anne—in an effort to match his splendor. But when we met, I found that Will had little attention to spare for my appearance. He cared only for the warning he had come to give me.

"Jane," he said when he came up to me in an antechamber of Anne's apartments, "you must guard the queen's kitchens. See that the entire staff is sent away if you feel you must." The urgency in his tone alarmed me.

"But why?"

"Someone is poisoning the food," was Will's curt reply, his

expression grim. "The prince has had a narrow escape. Last evening after supper he had only taken a few bites of his food when he began to feel queasy. The plate was removed at once and all the dishes given to the beggars who wait at the outer door for scraps." He frowned, shook his head, and then went on. "Two of them died. Another is dying. There can be no doubt. It was poison."

"Do you know who has done this?"

"We suspect the Spaniards, naturally. Or Ambassador Chapuys imperial spies. They want to disrupt the succession. Henry Fitzroy is the king's designated heir. They may try to poison Anne—and kill the infant in her womb."

"I will tell the queen at once," I began to say, turning to go, but Will stopped me, taking hold of my arm. His grip was gentle, but firm enough to make me pause.

"You must be cautious about whom you tell about this, Jane." He lowered his voice, and looked around the room. "It is possible, you see, that Queen Anne, or those around her, may be responsible."

I looked at Will. "You mean—"

"Yes. There is no need to say the words."

Was it possible? Had Anne sent a poisoner to put some deadly substance in the dishes prepared in Henry Fitzroy's kitchens? I remembered what Father Bartolome had said about the story being told in Flanders, about Anne's having arranged the death of Jane Popyngcort.

"Remember," Will was saying, "anyone who hinders her plans in any way could be vulnerable."

I let the full weight of Will's words sink in. If the dark accusations were true, then any one of us, including me, might be at risk. I did not want Anne for an enemy!

"But surely, by showing concern about the safety of her food, the loyalty of the kitchen staff, I am proving my own loyalty to her," I protested.

"Unless the result is different from what you expect. It could be that in your rigor to cleanse the Augean stables of her kitchens, you flush out a poisoner who is in her pay!"

While pondering this worrisome outcome, I could not help but notice that along with his fine clothes and serious demeanor, Will was acquiring the elevated speech of the cultivated royal servant. Augean stables indeed! Will was a gentleman's son, he had been tutored in Latin and knew the Greek myths—as did I, to an extent, having been allowed to sit quietly by from time to time and listen while Ned was being tutored. But this was a change indeed from the Will I used to know.

"I will try to use discretion," I told Will. "Meanwhile, I will avoid dining altogether." This made him laugh, and for a moment I thought I glimpsed the old familiar Will under the carapace of his newfound gravity. His expression softened, I glimpsed the old fondness in his blue eyes.

"Jane, about our plans—our hopes—" He sighed. The subject was uncomfortable for him. "My father continues to promise that Chevering Manor will be mine one day, but that day seems farther and farther away." I noticed he did not say, "Chevering Manor will be ours one day."

"There is a cottage on the estate that my father would let me have, to live in, but as my duties keep me here in London—"

"As do mine," I interjected. "And I quite agree, a cottage would not be suitable. Not suitable at all." Though even as I said this I thought, there was a time, not too long ago, when Will and I would have rejoiced in a cottage of our own, our own garden, our own family. But that had been before Galyon.

In truth I was relieved at what Will was saying, though what he said next came as something of a shock.

He was looking down at his feet, always a sign, with Will, that he was embarrassed or guilty.

"I ought to tell you, Jane, just to be completely honest, that it might be best if we no longer considered ourselves to be promised to one another. Given our circumstances."

I heard regret in his voice. Regret—and remorse.

Yet I heard myself agree with alacrity. I felt only relief.

"You will always be—like a dearest sister to me, Jane. I will always love you like family."

I had to smile. In the past Will's family—and my own father's misdeeds—had prevented my marriage to Will. Surely the mention of family brought as much anguish and sorrow as it did comfort and reassurance. Or was I thinking only of myself?

That evening, still pondering all that Will had told me, my stomach rumbling from hunger (for I could not bring myself to eat what was brought to us from the royal kitchens), I joined Bridget Wingfield and several of the other maids of honor in preparing for bed.

It was a time for confidences. One of the young maids, Arden Rose, Lord Edgewater's daughter, was about to marry a diplomat who was leaving soon for France and confessed to us that she was unsure about how she would be treated by the French women—and by her husband-to-be, who was a commanding man and a very critical one. Anne Cavecant told us of a lump in her side that seemed to be growing larger and that the king's own physician could not account for. She was fearful and asked us to pray for her.

"At least the queen's midwives are full of good news," Bridget Wingfield told us. "The baby kicks lustily. They say he will be big and strong like his father. A warrior. A jouster. A man of many abilities—above all a kingly man."

"Do you think he will be named for his father?" Arden Rose asked. "Will he be the ninth Henry?"

None of us knew what to say to that. Anne did not like us gossiping about her baby, or speculating about his name or when he would be born. The astrologers had made their calculations as to the day of his birth, but they were keeping their calculations secret.

"There already is a ninth Henry," put in the sour Anne Cavecant. "Henry Fitzroy."

"Don't let the queen hear you say that!" Bridget snapped. "She doesn't want the royal bastard anywhere near the court. She and the king quarrel about him all the time—especially now that he is to be married to the duke's daughter."

Henry Fitzroy was about to marry his long time betrothed Mary Howard, daughter of the Duke of Norfolk, in a lavish ceremony that was almost on par with a royal wedding. Tongues wagged endlessly about why the king was continuing to keep his natural son so much at the center of things. Was it because he feared Anne's son might not be a suitable king? Did he want to promote a rivalry between the two boys, one a weakling on the threshold of young manhood, the other as yet unborn?

"September fifth, that's the wedding day," Bridget told us. "And from what I hear, there will be at least three other weddings at the same time—at least three of the prince's gentlemen marrying three of Mary Howard's women."

Bridget looked pointedly at me. "I believe, Jane, that your old admirer Will Dormer is to be one of the bridegrooms. Am I right?"

I opened my mouth, then shut it again. So that was why Will wanted to make it plain that our engagement, however long it had lain dormant, was at an end. Because he planned to marry someone else.

"Yes," I managed to say. "Yes, I believe he told me he plans to marry."

"He was quite good-looking once," Bridget mused. "No wonder you were in love with him. But he's gotten quite fat—and much too impressed with himself. You're better off without him."

And I was, I thought. Bridget was right. Yet at the same time I felt a pang. For I still wanted a husband, a home, a family, children, a future. Now I had lost that dream. A dream I had once shared with Will, and could never have with Galyon, no matter how I treasured our moments together.

Life was moving on, passing me by. That summer, the summer of Anne's coronation, I was twenty-six years old, nearly twenty-seven. I was already long past the age of ripeness for a marriageable young woman.

I lay down on my narrow bed and tried in vain to settle myself for sleep. Dark thoughts crowded out my drowsiness. I could not rid my mind of a disturbing image, an image of Will with a much younger, vivacious, pretty girl, dancing with her, pledging himself to her in church, his face brightening into a wide smile with her beside him.

I had let Will go. What would happen to me now?

My feet felt cold, the thin blanket that covered me left me shivering. Galyon's feet were always warm, but Galyon was elsewhere, and we would never share a marital bed, with all its warmth and comforts.

Unable to prevent myself, I sank lower and lower into despair. I felt as if I was standing at the edge of a black pit, looking down into a well of loneliness. Aloneness. Into a future in which I would never have a family of my own.

My time had come and gone, I told myself. I would be a spinster. The fate every girl dreaded most.

I gave way to tears—but then, before long, another image came into my mind. A lovely fantasy in which Galyon and I moved into the cottage on the Chevering estate. In which we planted our garden, raised our children, and lived in a dream of happiness for the rest of our lives.

If only, I whispered to myself. If only! And then my fantasy slipped into reverie, and I was dreaming.

SIXTEEN

MAY I speak to you, sire?"

I had found King Henry in his private retreat, the tower room where he mixed his medicinal formulas and read his treatises on alchemy. Though it had been five years since the terrible outbreak of the sweating sickness, he continued to wear around his neck the small pouch of live spiders that was said to keep the dreaded illness away, and Anne often joked about how the king would hang an elephant around his neck if he thought it would keep him free of disease.

He sat at a table, hunched over pots and jars of powders and liquids. He looked tired, I thought. His shoulders were rounded, his brow furrowed. Though still a magnificent figure when he stood before the court in his doublets of purple velvet trimmed in gold, the tallest man in the room, his head held high, his growing baldness hidden under a rakish cap studded with gleaming jewels, it was apparent to those of us who had lived alongside him for years that he was aging. He limped heavily on his sore leg. Headaches plagued him, and the other affliction no one wanted to mention except in whispers—the pain in his swollen testicles—was by all accounts getting so much worse that it often forced him to take to his bed and call for his physicians.

"What is it, Jane? I am just preparing some sorrel for a posset. The farrier tells me that it soothes aches in horses—why not in kings, eh? By all the saints, my leg aches . . ."

"I'm very sorry, sire. I wish I had a posset of my own to offer you," I said with a smile.

He looked up at me and smiled back. "Your presence is always soothing."

"I feel I must tell you something disturbing. Will Dormer confided to me that poison was put in the prince's food—poison that could have killed the boy, and that killed several men after they ate of it. Will fears an imperial plot to remove the prince and possibly also to threaten the queen and her child."

The king made a dismissive gesture.

"That was no poison, that was spoiled fish. Or rancid wine. It happens, even in the best kitchens, with the best precautions."

I was silent.

"But sire, what if Will is right? What if a poison was indeed added to the food? Would it not be wise to make certain nothing like that happens in the queen's kitchens? To make certain she remains safe, and her child too?"

He studied my face.

"Jane, is there something I need to know? Is there someone I ought to suspect?"

"If I knew for certain, I would not hesitate to say. Only—"

"Yes. Go on."

"There is a man, sire, who makes my blood run cold whenever

I see him. I first saw him at the convent of St. Agnes's. He was with the Nun of Kent. Now he has become the princess dowager's confessor. He is called Father Bartolome."

Henry frowned, then with a sudden, lithe movement got up from his chair and went to the door of the small room and flung it open. All at once he seemed to throw off his weariness. He moved like a much younger man.

"Get me Crum, at once," he said to the guard who stood outside, then turned back to me.

"Now then Jane, I want to know everything about this man. What he looks like, what he has said or done to make you suspicious of him." I told King Henry what little I knew. While I was talking the squat, hefty Thomas Cromwell hurried into the room, out of breath, squinting at me and making his obeisance to the king.

"Crum, ride to Buckden with a dozen of the guard and seize the princess dowager's confessor. He calls himself Father Bartolome. Find out what he knows of the poisoning of the prince's food. And turn out every servant in the queen's kitchens, from the cooks to the turnspits."

Cromwell looked startled. "Even her favorite cook, the one she brought from Paris?"

"Especially him. Now go!"

The secretary hurried from the room.

"You are quite right to raise the alarm, Jane. And you are brave to tell me of this Father Bartolome. Crum will show him no mercy."

I hesitated, then, as the king sat down again at his table, I felt emboldened to go on.

"There is something more, Your Majesty. I am reluctant to mention it, fearing that it may anger you."

"What is it?"

I took a deep breath. "It concerns the death of Jane Popyngcort. Rumors at the Flemish court—that is, it is being said—"

"Out with it!"

"It is being said that Jane Popyngcort was not killed by robbers, but by men in the pay of Queen Anne. The men have confessed—"

Henry slammed his fist on the table, making the pots and jars on the table bounce.

"Confessed under torture, no doubt! Of course Anne is being slandered! They hate her! But she is no more guilty of murdering that woman than you or I are." He glared at me, and for the first time I felt afraid. "Don't you see that it is all a conspiracy? Even my saintly wife—I mean the princess dowager—is not above such tricks and stratagems."

He sighed, then gave me a baleful look.

"Ah, Jane! We live in such dangerous times! Thank heaven the imperialists have not come after us with an army—not yet—but they still may. And I—I who once led an army of my own into France, when I was a young man—" He shook his head. "I could not do it now, not if my life and the realm depended on it. I could not even enter the lists and compete in the jousting on Anne's coronation day. My damnable leg was too sore." And reaching under the table he began to rub his leg, his expression rueful.

"Sit down, Jane, and keep me company. I am feeling old today." He smiled as he spoke.

I sat on a dust-covered bench, doing my best to wipe it first with my petticoat.

"Sire, there is one more thing I would like to ask, though it is certainly yours alone to divulge or keep secret. I have always been curious about Jane Popyngcort—about what she knew from the past that could have been an obstacle to your marriage to Anne."

Henry spat.

"That whole business was before I became head of the church. When England was still obeying His Obstructionist the Pope."

"Yes, of course. It is of no consequence now. Yet—"

"Very well, Jane. Ask your question," he said indulgently. "What we say here shall not go beyond these walls."

"Sire, did you really do what Jane said? Was Anne's mother really your mistress?"

To my amazement the king burst into laughter. "Who remembers? I was only a boy, I was drunk, I had just had my first great victory against the French. What drunken young warrior can remember all the women he has been with?"

For a moment a happy youthful smile lit his face.

"It doesn't signify, either way."

"But Jane was given a chest of gold coins and sent away, because she swore that Lady Boleyn was your mistress."

"Yes, and she should have been shut in the Tower as a traitor, for spreading such slander. Anyone will say anything, Jane, if they are paid well enough to say it." He sighed once again. "Now, you must leave me to finish making my posset, or I shall have to lie awake all night with the pain in this leg of mine." He raised his hand in a gesture of dismissal.

"Please forgive me for disturbing you, sire."

"That's all right, Jane. Come again—when you have happier news to bring me."

I lay in Galyon's arms, the warm scented air of the soft summer night filling my senses, the quiet around us broken only by the gurgling of the stream and the sleepy murmur of birds.

To my great surprise and delight, Galyon had been brought to England to work on the enlarging of Anne's apartments, one of a crew of three hundred French craftsmen lodged in a village near the capital. The labor would take many months, he said happily; we would be able to see each other often and without fear that each meeting might be our last. It was as close as we had ever come to enjoying a daily life together, as close as we would ever come.

Galyon had become a master glazier, and as such was entitled to a spacious, well furnished lodging while he worked in England. Often in the evenng, as dusk fell, I met him and we rode together through the darkening orchards and meadows to his house, where we supped together and then went to bed, sometimes in the cool of the upstairs bedroom, sometimes, as on this night, out of doors, at the bottom of the garden, near the stream.

He kissed my forehead softly, then looked over at me. I saw such love in his clear blue eyes, a great depth of love. I thought, what more could I ever ask of life than this?

I drank in everything about him, his familiar scent, his strength, the tautness of his muscles, the curve of his lips, the fullness of his mouth. The gold stubble on his cheeks and chin, the way his hair fell over his forehead.

We stayed as we were, without speaking, for a time, as the moon rose and its light touched the leaves of the trees with silver.

"Jeanne," he said at length, "I have had a letter from my wife, Solange. She is still living with the parish priest of our village, and they are having another child. But something has changed. Père Beignet is no longer a priest. He has renounced the Roman faith. He has been excommunicated."

"Like King Henry."

"He is plain Georges Beignet now, and he wants to make Solange his wife. They have begun attending services conducted by a follower of Jean Calvin. In this new church of Jean Calvin it is possible to obtain a divorce and remarry. Solange means to divorce me."

"Just as King Henry, by becoming head of his own church, divorced Queen Catherine." I thought for a moment, then said, "That would make you a free man."

"Not in the eyes of the church, the true church."

"Surely what matters is the belief that resides in the heart, not in the definitions of theologians."

He shook his head. "I don't know, Jeanne. I truly don't know. Surely it is wrong to overturn in a few years what has taken centuries to build. What is sanctioned by the Holy Book, by the mass, by all the saints—"

I pondered his words, looking out at the stream, watching the moonlit rippling of the water.

"How many lovers, do you imagine, have lain together in this place, over the long centuries since the world began? Watching the moon rise and set, taking their pleasure together, sharing what is in their hearts? While gods and goddesses have come and gone and the world has changed from pagan to Christian and now—some say—back again?"

Galyon laughed. "And how many priests like Père Beignet have seduced the wives of their parishioners?"

"Luther and Calvin and King Henry all say the Roman church is corrupt and unworthy. That it needs amending."

"And yet—the king did not set aside his old queen and take a new one because of his belief—rather he has adjusted his belief to serve his lust. And if I recall my catechism, lusting after what is not rightfully yours is against the Ten Commandments."

"All I know, dearest Galyon, is that my heart is at ease, and overflowing with love, when I am with you. If that is wrong, then I will take my punishment. I will burn in hell."

He bent and kissed me. "We will burn in hell together, my love." And after that, we were lost in each other, until at last the moon began to set, and there was a chill wind off the river, and we made our way across the dark garden to the house.

The summer wore on, the time came for Anne to take her chamber to await the birth of her son.

The entire court was in a constant state of expectancy. When would the child be born? Would he be delivered safely? Would the queen survive?

Nothing else could go forward until the delivery was accomplished, or so it seemed. We paced, we went for long walks through the yellowing grasses. We hunted and gathered fallen apples. Most of all we watched the queen for signs that her delivery was approaching.

She withdrew formally and with great ceremony into the interior of her apartments, where six midwives were in constant attendance and no men were allowed. She would remain there, as custom decreed, until she had given birth. Meanwhile those of us in her household—a much larger household than before her marriage—waited to serve her, to do her least bidding.

The summer days dragged by, the air was hot and full of dust. We maids of honor and bedchamber women did our best to keep ourselves amused in the outer rooms of Anne's apartments, playing card games, doing embroidery, reading and, as always, gossiping. There were so many more of us than in the past, Anne insisted on a larger household than Queen Catherine had had. Besides Bridget and Anne Cavecant, there was the young, pretty heiress Elizabeth Wood, Catherine Gainsford and Honor Grenville, Mary Scrope whose teeth were yellow but who was of acceptable appearance in all other ways, Margery Horsman who I found amusing and half a dozen others. It annoyed Anne that her uncle Norfolk's mistress Elizabeth Holland had to be given a place within her inner circle, but when she complained she felt the keen smart of the king's displeasure, and so ceased to complain.

We waited through the long hot days and sweltering nights of late summer—and then, one night, I was awakened by a terrifying scream.

It was Anne.

"Her pains have begun!" someone cried. We hurried into Anne's bedchamber and found her out of bed and standing, disheveled and slapping at her night clothes, her long black hair in disarray, cursing and shrieking.

"The lice! The damnable lice in the bed!"

The midwives, in a frenzy of distress, were pulling at the linens and elaborate counterpane of Anne's magnificent bed, the pillows and bedcurtains, in an effort to remove the vermin.

"A tincture of chamomile and dock will take down the swelling," I heard Mary Scrope say. "Our apothecary always advised that, for lice."

But Anne only screamed again, and flung a fat pillow at Mary.

"You stupid fool! It's that hateful woman! That nun! First she brought the frogs, and now it is the lice! She's cursed me!"

I remembered the chilling prophecy of the Nun of Kent, delivered as we traveled along the Dover road. First would come a plague of frogs, then lice, then fleas . . .

"Lice leave the body of the dying," Bridget whispered.

Anne's hearing was keen. "And am I dying then?" she shouted as she tore off the last of her garments. "Is that what you are telling me, Bridget? That I am going to die? That my baby is going to die?" She rushed out of the room, leaving us to cope with the lice and the fouled linen and the wrath of the king, whose loud voice I could hear in the corridor outside.

Anne would have to be calmed, a fresh bed would have to be made up for her. I felt something crawling up my arm and looked down, pulling up my sleeve. It was a louse, its body black and swollen. I slapped it, leaving a spot of red. My blood.

I could hear, through the wall, that Anne's screams had turned to sobs. I wondered if this fear and excitement would bring on her labor. She was due, the midwives said. Her son could be born any day or any night.

As I thought this I could not help remembering the most alarming part of the Nun of Kent's curse. "The firstborn son of the adulterer and his Jezebel mistress shall die," she had said. Could it be true? Were the lice fleeing the dying? And if they were, what would it mean for us all?

SEVENTEEN

THE birth chamber was darkened, the heat from the braziers stifling. Thick curtains over the windows shut out the afternoon sun. A cloying odor of musk and lavender, sickly-sweet, overlaid the smell of opium. It was hard to breathe.

We had been called into Anne's bedchamber to witness the birth of her child, so that no one could say afterwards that the baby was not drawn from her womb. A long table with plates of comfits and goblets of wine had been laid out for our refreshment, but we could hardly bring ourselves to nibble at the food. In the wide bed, Anne writhed and screamed and sobbed, cursing the stern-faced midwives who pressed mercilessly on her belly.

"Let me die!" she cried, her face wet with tears. "Let me die!" In her delirium she reached out for her absent mother, pleading with her to ease her pain, then drew her hand back in terror. "Send the heralds!" she called out weakly. "The queen is dead!"

I prayed that she would not die, that her agony would soon end. But hour by hour her suffering only seemed to grow worse, and still the child would not be born.

At length the chief midwife lost hope.

"I can do no more," she announced, wiping her hands on her dirty apron. "She is in a condition beyond my skill. It is the Lord's will that she shall come to Him. She and her child."

We tensed. Was this to be the outcome of our long vigil, and Anne's long anguish? Would Anne die? And if she did, how would the king fare?

I had eaten nothing for many hours, yet I could not bring myself to eat of the comfits or drink of the watered wine. I could not, I felt that I must not.

I remembered how Anne had looked when she lay at Greenwich, so very ill with the sweat. We thought she would die—yet she had been spared. Why? So that she could bring shame on the realm, and die giving birth to the king's child?

"Let the priest come," the midwife was saying, her face resigned. "It is time. We have done all we can. The last rites must be given."

Bridget went to Anne's bedside and sat down on the bed, disregarding the strict rules forbidding anyone to approach the queen without being summoned or spoken to. She took Anne's hand and murmured, quite tenderly, "Shall we give up then, Nan, shall we let you go?"

I held my breath. Moments passed. Then I heard a small noise. It was Anne, stirring, moaning. As I watched, her body stiffened, the sign of yet another contraction. Her face grew red. While Bridget continued to encourage her, Anne took a deep breath and made a mighty effort to expel the child.

And with such a groan as I had never heard come from a woman's lips, she began to succeed.

"The little head! It is the little head!" All at once the midwives were stirred to urgent action once again.

Into Bridget's waiting hands, the midwives clustering around to aid her, the tiny infant emerged into the world, slippery with blood, still bound to Anne by the thick cord sprouting from its small stomach.

Whispering an incantation, the chief midwife cut the cord, then gasped.

The room was so dark that we could not at first see what had shocked her. Then came the fateful words.

"No! It can't be!"

"Oh, Lord God in heaven, it is. It is—a princess."

"Cancel the tournaments. Take out that cradle of estate. Bring in the other one, the wooden one. Draw back those curtains. Let us have some light!"

The king's orders were swiftly obeyed. Anne was asleep, her tiny daughter, washed and put to the breast of a wetnurse, had been wrapped warmly in a swaddling cloth and laid in the lovely old cradle of carved wood. The splendid golden cradle of estate, lined in purple velvet, its small counterpane trimmed in royal ermine, was removed; it had been meant for a son.

The king, as soon as he was told that Anne had given him a daughter, had sent all the midwives away and shouted for the astrologers.

"Kill the whoreson villains, every last one of them!" he shouted. "I'll have them racked! I'll have them thrown in the Tower and whipped!"

But the astrologers, who had also heard the news from the birth chamber, had swiftly departed, as had all those who were waiting in the corridors and outside.

"Shut down the kitchens," I heard the king snap. "Tell the cooks to give all the food to the beggars at the gates. There will be no banqueting tonight!"

It was the opium, Anne insisted as soon as she had recovered enough to find her tongue and struggle to her feet. She had been given too much opium during her terrible labor. No doubt the princess dowager, the former Queen Catherine, was to blame. Or her wicked accomplice, the Nun of Kent. The nun cast spells and worked demonic magic. Her dark magic had turned the boy in Anne's womb into a wretched girl.

Hadn't the Nun of Kent prophesied that Anne would not bear a living son? Had she not sent the plagues of frogs and lice to torment Anne as she waited for her child to be born? There was magic in those damnable creatures! They had been the familiars that worked the nun's dark spells!

It was no good reminding Anne, as Bridget and I and many others did, in an effort to soothe her fears, that the Nun of Kent was locked away in a royal prison. She could still do harm, Anne said sharply, and I saw a flash of fear in her eyes as she spoke. She could still act through her familiars.

And one of those familiars, I knew, was not only free but had been seen at court. Father Bartolome, the black-robed priest who had become the princess dowager's confessor, had eluded Thomas Cromwell when the latter went in search of him at Buckden. He had disappeared—only to be glimpsed among the crowds at court, always fleetingly, his shadowy presence just out of reach. I had seen him myself, or thought I had, on more than one occasion, slipping in or out of a dimly lit room, hurrying along a dark passageway, even at the christening of the royal child. Anne's small, pale, weak little daughter who was given the name Elizabeth and who everyone said would not live long.

Imprisoned or not, Anne was clearly terrified of the Nun of Kent, who continued to have visions, and managed to report what the heavenly voices and visions told her to others in the prison who spread the word throughout the capital. She claimed that Christ Himself appeared to her while in her captivity, moaning in agony from the wounds He bore, and told her that He could never be free from his pain until King Henry ended his adulterous, accursed marriage to Anne.

Because of the furor she caused, the nun was moved to the Tower. But immense crowds gathered on Tower Bridge and in boats out in the river, watching and praying and hoping to hear more of her revelations. Sick and dying people were laid at the fortress gates, and on the shore, and some, it was said, were made whole. Truly the nun was one of the Lord's own, touched by His holy hand, while the wicked Queen Anne who bore the sign of the devil was cursed. And the realm still waited for, and longed for, a prince.

"That woman cannot be allowed to live," Anne announced to the king once she had recovered from her ordeal in childbed. She was in the throne room, her arms folded, her head held imperiously high.

"She has cursed me. She is evil. She is the pope's familiar."

Her voice could be heard across the vast room, where dozens of officials, messengers, servants and hangers-on gathered in order to be near the king and, if possible, to approach him for favors. There was a brief lull in the din of talk, then it gathered volume once again.

King Henry, who was engaged in a game of chess, the checkered board and carved ivory pieces spread out on a low table in front of him, did not look at his wife but let out a chuckle.

"The pope's familiar, is she? What do you think of that, Madge?"

His chess partner was Madge Shelton, Anne's blond, dimpled cousin. She sat across from him, wearing a gown of a delicious strawberry pink color, a color most becoming to her rosy cheeks and full red lips.

"I can't imagine." Madge toyed with her queen, rubbing it and nudging it slightly, uncertain where she meant to move it.

"She must be executed! At once!" came Anne's demand.

"I have never liked a woman with a shrill voice," King Henry remarked, to no one in particular. "It upsets me. It makes my leg hurt."

Madge held out her goblet.

"Here, Your Majesty. Have some more of this posset. It will do your sore leg good."

The king took the goblet and drained it, then handed it back to his chess partner, allowing his hand to rest lingeringly against hers.

"Where is the prince?" Henry asked my brother Ned, who was among those standing closest to him, watching the progress of the game.

"Playing at quoits with his companions, sire. Shall I bring him to you?"

The king nodded, then looked across at Madge. "Your posset is giving me ease," he said in honeyed tones.

"I'm glad, sire." Her bright smile was tinged with invitation.

Anne stamped her foot, but only those of us in attendance on her paid any attention.

Before long Henry Fitzroy came in, escorted by three other boys. The scrawny, weakling boy prince had grown into a delicate, leggy, undersized young man, though he appeared to be no more than a boy. He was dressed, as always, in imitation of his royal father, in a rich robe of ermine-trimmed velvet and a jeweled hat with a feather. The fullness of the robe could not entirely disguise the fact that his arms and legs were as thin as twigs, but his long face had lost its sickly pallor and in imitating his father he had taken on something of King Henry's domineering, arrogant manner. It was evident to us all that he thought himself to be very important indeed.

Among the three boys accompanying the prince was my nephew Henry.

Ever since the tragic year when the sweating sickness had carried off Henry's younger brother John, Will had taken it upon himself to oversee Henry's upbringing, and had recently brought him into the prince's household, where he soon became Henry Fitzroy's favorite companion.

Raised by one of the king's former guardsmen, Henry had taken his foster parents' name, and was called Henry Glyndell. He remembered little of his early childhood; he had rarely seen his busy father and his mother had thought it best to let him believe that she had died.

Ned showed not the slightest sign of recognizing Henry as he entered the throne room. Having disowned both his small sons years earlier, when he disowned his wife Cat and had her locked away in the convent of St. Agnes's, he had never spoken of the boys since—at least not to me. It was as if he had forgotten about them entirely. And he had no idea that only one of them was still living.

"Ah, my prince," the king cried when he saw Fitzroy, smiling broadly and beckoning him to come closer.

"He looks well, does he not?" the king said to Madge. "Fit to govern this realm, when the time comes."

"My child is heir to the throne of England!" Anne fairly shouted, but at a wave of Henry's hand, she was escorted

hurriedly from the throne room, her protests drowned out by a
chorus of rude boys chanting "Nan, Nan, the devil's dam" amid
a ripple of laughter.

The fickle court had lost no time in shifting its fragile
loyalties from the never popular Queen Anne to Henry's newest
favorite. I knew the whims of the courtiers, I had seen them
in operation often enough. Whoever was in the king's favor
gained widespread approval, whoever was out of royal favor was
shunned, lest their disfavor rub off on others.

"And how is your newest daughter," Madge ventured to ask.

The king dismissed the question with a gesture.

"A scrawny little thing," he said. "Barely hanging on to life.
The mother was not strong enough to produce a son."

"Ah." Madge's beautifully shaped eyebrows were raised. "And
does that mean, Your Majesty, that she may not have an
opportunity to produce another child?"

The talk in the room subsided. The question hung in the air.

"Why speak of such things," Henry said at length, "when
there are pleasures to be had here and now?" And as he spoke
he moved his rook.

"Checkmate," he said, smiling and glancing at Fitzroy, who
applauded his father's finesse, the entire room joining with him
in a thunderous chorus of praise.

My father's health was failing.

He had fallen down the new staircase at Wulf Hall and was
so injured he could not get out of bed. No amount of opium
could ease his pain, nor help him to breathe. Ned and I traveled
together into Wiltshire to see him, having been cautioned by
his physicians that we would need to be respectful and subdued.

The least upset, they said, could be so alarming to him that he might stop breathing altogether.

Despite this warning I could not help but cry out when I glimpsed him, his shrunken form heaped with woolen blankets, a stubble of white beard on his sunken cheeks, his eyes red and his mouth drooling. He had become an old man, a helpless old man.

"Father," I managed to say, suddenly feeling like a child once again and kneeling at his bedside. "Father, I most humbly ask your blessing." They were the words we had been taught to say when we were children.

I felt him put his hand on my head, then sensed that Ned had knelt beside me to receive his blessing in his turn. I heard a muffled sound and, looking up, saw that the wrinkled face on the pillow was laughing.

"Where are your haughty court manners now, eh?" he muttered. "Where are your grand ways and all your pride?"

Tears washed down my cheeks. All the anger and resentment I had nursed for so many years fell away. The tall, loud, arrogant father who had seduced Will's sister and ruined my hopes for a happy life was more than worthy of my harsh condemnation. But this man, this aging, frail man with the sardonic grin, brought forth only my pity. Though in truth he was far from pitiful; he was full of mockery, making light of my pain.

"Sad little Jane," he was saying, "don't you wish you had been nicer to me? And you, Ned, aren't you sorry you didn't come to see me before this? Have you no sympathy for me, now that I am in my dotage?"

We squirmed under his merciless dark teasing, and he enjoyed watching us squirm—until a spasm of pain struck him, making him grimace.

He began to wave one arm frantically.

"Out! Out!" he cried. "Get out, before I throw a fit!" His voice cracked. He managed to go on. "Don't worry, I've left you money! You'll find out soon enough how much!" And as he burst into choked laughter, Ned took my arm and we left the room together, to the sound of our father's coughing and sputtering and—I could swear—his cackling laughter.

"Jeanne, ma douce Jeanne!" Galyon embraced me with an eagerness that surprised me, an eagerness that had an edge of urgency. I had not been away in Wiltshire long. What could have happened to give his affection such added passion? A terrible thought came to me. Could it be that for some reason he had been summoned back to France? Had the work on the queen's apartments come to an unexpected end?

He had sent me a note to meet him in a dim loft, and there, in the darkness with only the horses in their stalls for company, he told me a story so bizarre that even now, recalling it, I shake my head in disbelief.

"Jeanne, my sweetest, my most precious Jeanne. I do not know what to do. You must help me. You must save me."

I put my arms around him. He was trembling.

"My dearest Galyon, I will do anything for you. You know that."

We sat together beside a steaming brazier, one blanket warming us both, and he went on.

"Jeanne, she came to me, alone, the queen with six fingers, and she showed me a purse of gold coins. More gold coins than I have ever seen in my life. I don't know how many.

"'I must have another child,' she said. 'The king—he is of no worth. He cannot do what a man must in order to have a child.

A strong child. A boy. You must help me or the king will lock me up, cast me out.'

"I knew what she meant. I was frightened, Jeanne. So very frightened. I said, 'Madame, I cannot do this. I cannot.' I was trembling, I was so frightened. I would not take the purse of coins. But I could not call out, there was no one I could turn to. I dared not try to tell the king. He would have sent his men to seize me as a liar and a traitor. So I ran from her, and hid here in this loft until I knew you had returned. Until I could turn to you."

He was panting, it was difficult for him to speak. But I had no doubt that every word he said was true. His eyes were the clear, sincere eyes of a boy. Besides, what he was saying made sense. Anne faced a dilemma—King Henry had all but told me that he was not puissant in bed, as the common phrase went—that he was no longer confident that he had the potency to impregnate Anne. Anne faced dishonor, ruin, exile—or worse—if she remained queen but could not give the king a son. In the past, she had solved her dilemmas through bribery, or murder. (The more I heard Galyon say, the more I believed Anne guilty of causing the death of Jane Popyngcort, and of attempting to poison Henry Fitzroy.) Why should she not bribe Galyon to do what the king could not? Galyon and King Henry were not unalike in coloring; if he and Anne had a son together, the boy would very likely resemble the king.

"Jeanne! Can you help me get away, back to France, before she takes out her anger on me?"

"I will do all I can for you. You know that. I would give my life for you. But we need to think clearly, and not act rashly."

I took a deep breath, then told Galyon of the strong suspicions about Anne, and how after Jane Popyngcort had been sent across the sea to Flanders, she had been killed—most likely by men in Anne's pay.

"There may be nowhere safer for you than right here, my dearest Galyon." Except perhaps the Spice Islands. I suddenly remembered the doomed *Eglantine*, and how Will and I had once hoped to sail far away from the court and its entanglements aboard her. Such a vain youthful dream! It seemed so very distant now, so very naive.

"Stay here, my love. I will see that you have food and whatever else you need."

"But what if I am discovered?"

I had no answer for that. Who was there that I could trust, someone who would be able to protect Galyon and conceal him? There was no one in Anne's household who could not be bribed. I had trusted friends in the princess dowager's household but they were far away at Buckden, and in any case I was not eager to make my own ties to Galyon known. Ned would not help us, Ned helped only Ned. Will had never failed me—but would he protect my lover? Could I be certain that no lingering spark of jealousy or rivalry would arise to divide his loyalties?

I had no answer for Galyon. What were we to do? I looked into his dear eyes.

"Trust me, my love. I will do my best to find an answer. For now, I don't know what to say—except trust no one else!" And with a kiss I left him there, in the hayloft, and made my way back to the queen's apartments, looking deep into the shadows at every turn.

EIGHTEEN

IN the middle of the night Ned roused me from my bed in
the dormitory room I shared with the other maids of honor.

"Quickly! You must dress and ride with me to Wulf Hall! Our
father is dying!"

Groggily I got up and, with the aid of the servants, put on my
riding clothes, while Ned paced impatiently in the next room.

As we rode together toward Wulf Hall on that chilly night,
all my thoughts were of Galyon. How could I arrange for him to
stay hidden and supplied with what he needed if I was in
Wiltshire? Would Anne or her minions discover him? Ought I
to have brought him with us? But no, she would be certain to
look for him—through her spies—at Wulf Hall. Galyon and I
had been discreet, but Will knew of our closeness, and I had
confided in Bridget also, and Galyon's fellow workers too had
seen us together.

I worried, continuing to think of Galyon's plight as we made
our way along the rough roads in the dark, our wagon jouncing

and pitching with every hole and rock and tree branch in our path.

I thought of confiding in Ned, but held back. Ned could easily protect Galyon—but would he? I could not be certain. If I told him the story Galyon had told me, he might not believe it—or, if he did believe it, he might well have Galyon hidden away in a dungeon and then brought out to bear witness against Anne. Ned disliked Anne, she had spoken scornfully to him and had tried to persuade King Henry to remove him from the court. She sensed his opposition and his cunning. If Ned imagined that he could find a way to turn the king against Anne, he would be eager to use it.

I did not want Galyon to become a pawn in the dangerous game of court intrigue. So I held my tongue, and did not confide in my brother.

Once Ned and I reached Wulf Hall we were swept up in the larger family drama surrounding our father's final hours. He did not long outlast our arrival. He lay in his wide bed, his eyes closed, unaware of any of us in the room. At our mother's insistence, he was given the last rites, although that sacrament belonged to the old Roman church and it was unclear whether the new church, headed by King Henry, still acknowledged and practiced it. At any rate the family chaplain gave the blessing and said the prayers, touching the holy oil to our father's wasted body. Soon afterward father's breath ceased and he was still.

We had the consolation of knowing that our father had been shriven, his sins forgiven and his place in heaven assured. How it would have vexed me, only a few years earlier, to imagine him among the saints! Now, however, I could no longer judge his behavior so harshly, for had I not proven my own sinful weakness by sleeping with the married Galyon? Had I not betrayed Will's trust? I was no saint, and I realized I had a great deal to learn about Christian forgiveness.

I could tell that Ned was not troubled by any such scruples of conscience. If he mourned our father, he hid his feelings well; what concerned him above all, in the first hours and days after our father died, was his own inheritance, and his new role as master of Wulf Hall and the entire Seymour estate.

Watching Ned in the days immediately after our father's death I sensed a new mastery about him. It was not that he was greedy for money or for the inevitable rise in status that his inheritance would soon bring him. Rather, I thought, it was a sort of inner growth. He was changing from within, so that he could take charge of the responsibilities that would soon be his.

I could not help admiring my brother just then, for no one had taught him what to do or how to act in his new role. Our father had not provided a good example. He had not managed Wulf Hall at all well, his tenants gave him grudging obedience but cursed him behind his back. From what I knew of father's estates, he had neglected the crops and paid no heed to the villagers who worked the land. His stewards were greedy and uncaring. Yet I could see that Ned was giving much thought to what needed to be done, what changes needed to be made. Perhaps, I thought, he had been preparing mentally for the time when he would take over our father's responsibilities. And I had been unaware of this.

I began to see Ned in a new light. But I still did not tell him of Galyon's situation or his revelations about Anne.

Father was barely laid in the ground before his will was read and its provisions fulfilled. Ned became master of nearly all father's lands and possessions, but there were other legacies, including one for me. Father was generous; he thought me likely to remain unmarried, and so he left me the money I would otherwise have had as my dowry—enough to keep me in comfort, with quite a bit to spare. I was very grateful—indeed I was quite overcome with emotion, I who have always been seen as exceptionally self-possessed and able to cope calmly with emotional situations.

I wept. I said my prayers. And I worried over Galyon, in his loft.

Will was present at the funeral. The Dormers and the Seymours were connected, after all, through Will's sister's marriage to Godfrey Seymour. Will came to represent his family and to offer condolences. Seeing him reminded me of the other Seymour relation who was not present: young Henry, the son Ned refused to acknowledge as his own, and whom Will had watched over and sponsored when he entered Henry Fitzroy's household.

Young Henry! My realization was sudden and swift. My nephew Henry was in London—and I knew I could trust him to deliver food and water and other supplies to Galyon.

I took Will aside and confided in him all that had happened, how the queen had tried to bribe Galyon and how, having evaded her entreaties, he had had good reason to fear her revenge. I explained where Galyon was hiding and asked Will to send a message to Henry, in all secrecy, requesting his help.

I had no doubt Will would want to defend my dear Galyon against Anne. After all, it had been Will who cautioned me that Anne might have plotted the poisoning of Henry Fitzroy. His words had stayed with me. "Anyone who hinders her plans in any way," he had said, "could be vulnerable." Galyon was hindering her plans—and was a threat to her, for if he revealed her attempt to bribe him (always assuming he was believed) then their roles would be reversed. Galyon would be the one who was loyal to the throne and the true succession, and Anne would be the traitor.

Will sent a trusted messenger to London at once to find young Henry, and I felt relieved. I spent several weeks at Wulf Hall, confident that until I returned to my duties at the palace, all would be well.

How very wrong I was! And what a terrible price I paid for my mistaken confidence!

I must now write of the worst time of my life. I dread to choose the words. I dread to write them. But without this unbearable piece of my story, all that came afterward would not have made sense. So write it I must.

May the mercies of heaven follow me as I write these bitter, bitter words.

When I returned to London I waited until nightfall, then slipped into the stables, to the loft where I had left Galyon. I called his name softly. There was no answer. I waited, then called again. But no sound came back to me.

Awkwardly, in my long skirt and petticoats, and without Galyon's strong arms to support me, I climbed up into the hayloft and found there nothing but a pile of clothing and the remains of many plates of food, with rats swarming over the bones and scraps.

I shuddered, recoiling at the sight and fearing what it might mean. Where was my Galyon? And where was Henry?

Late as the hour was, I went in search of Will. He would know. Perhaps he had moved Galyon to a safer place while I was away.

But Will, I was told, had taken Henry Fitzroy into the country on a hunting trip, and would not be back for several days. I assumed that Henry, as the prince's constant companion and defender, had gone with them.

Sick with fear, I returned to the queen's apartments and prepared for bed. I was tired. I knew I could do nothing more that night. I tried to sleep.

In the morning we maids of honor were summoned into Anne's bedchamber. One of the windows, I noticed, was covered with a thick curtain of black velvet, which blotted out the light and drained the color from our faces.

Anne was in bed, wearing a soft woolen bedgown and over it, a warm fur mantle. The room was cold despite the flames that leapt in the fireplace. I shivered, as much from fear as from the chill in the spacious room.

Anne gave us our instructions. We were to prepare ourselves for a visit by the French ambassador and other notables from the court of Francis I. They were expected within a day or two and there was much to be done before they arrived, for the king hoped to strengthen England's bonds with the French against the renewed menace of Emperor Charles.

"I am unwell," Anne said wearily.

"Are we to hope that Your Majesty may once again be with child?" Bridget asked.

"It is possible. Meanwhile another bedchamber must be prepared. I cannot stay here in this ice house." Servants were sent to make another bedchamber ready.

"Why is that window covered?" asked the ever inquisitive Anne Cavecant.

Anne shook her head in annoyance. "One of the workmen fell out of it yesterday. A foolish fellow, a Frenchman."

My heart stopped.

"But those workmen are always so careful," Anne Cavecant insisted. "I have never known one to fall. They strap themselves to the scaffolding."

"This one didn't!" Anne snapped. "He was trying to run

away, or to escape his superiors. He had been hiding in the stables, when he was needed here! Not that it mattered, but it seems he was the only one of the entire work crew with the skill to repair this window and install my falcon badge. I had him found and brought back. But he fell."

"Is he—did he survive the fall?" I heard myself ask, my voice tremulous.

Anne shrugged. "As it happens, he didn't. The king is annoyed. It will take weeks to find a replacement for him, and meanwhile we will not be able to show off this room to the French."

I thought I would die where I stood. I couldn't breathe. The hammering in my chest was so loud I imagined everyone in the room could hear it. My cheeks were wet.

I felt an arm around my shoulders, and heard Bridget saying, "Jane, you look pale. Come, take some wine." The maids of honor were dispersing, and I let Bridget lead me into an adjoining room.

"It was my Galyon, it was my Galyon," I kept whispering. "My Galyon is dead. And Anne killed him!"

For I had no doubt about what had happened, as surely as if I had been there to witness it. Anne had sent her spies to find Galyon, and to bring him to her. She had renewed her offer of a bribe—or perhaps it had been not an offer but a demand. Galyon had refused to do what she asked. And then—I still feel the horror of it now—in desperation he had jumped to his death. Or she had cornered him beside the window opening, and in her fury, pushed him out.

I cried out, and made a dash for the doorway. What did I mean to do? I had no clear plan, only the overwhelming need to destroy Anne. Had I been a man, and armed, I believe I could have run her through with my sword.

Poor Bridget, not knowing what else to do, called for the guards, who restrained me and then held me down, keeping me from any further rash acts, until a physician had come and given me a drink that addled my wits and made me senseless, and I fell into a whirling, dizzying sleep filled with dreams of loss and hopelessness.

Tears! Tears of rage, tears of sorrow, such deep sorrow, all the deeper for being kept to myself. I wanted to kill Anne, I planned to do it in a thousand ways. But I did not. Ever since that terrible time, I have asked myself why I did not. Was it because from childhood I had been told "Thou shalt not kill" and "Vengeance is mine saith the Lord"? Was it because I feared to suffer the king's vengeance, and the pain he would be sure to inflict on me and those I cared about if I harmed Anne?

Or was it because, since I am not after all a creature of impulse—at least not entirely so—I had, in the horrible days following Galyon's death, begun to form the first faint outlines of a more devious plan. A way to take vengeance on Anne that would leave me free of suspicion, but would ensure that in time, my beloved Galyon would be avenged.

Hardly had the first frosts set in before Anne's baby daughter, given the name Elizabeth, was put in the care of her nurse and rockers and sent off to Hatfield. Her birth had mortified Anne and angered King Henry, and her presence was an unwanted reminder of how chance governed the affairs of men—even of kings.

"Why couldn't young Fitzroy have been a girl—and this one a boy!" I overheard the king say as he passed, limping on his sore leg, through Anne's new bedchamber, shaking his head and sighing. "What have I done, that the Almighty should cross me so!"

He was wrapped up in his own thoughts, but not so preoccupied that he did not nod to me and smile as he passed me. I made a small half-curtsey.

"Ah, Jane," he muttered, almost to himself. "Jane, the only one I can trust."

It was not the first time I had heard him greet me with those words. I wondered that he should single me out as uniquely trustworthy. To be sure, the court was rife with deception, but I was hardly free of that taint. I was no innocent. And if the king had known what elaborate deceits and harms I spun out in my fantasies, he would surely have taken back his trust. Still, I valued his confidence, and did not abuse it. And I liked the warm comradeship I saw in his smile.

His smile! Something we saw all too rarely in that troubled time following the birth of the little princess, when the king complained loudly of feeling besieged on all sides—by ill fortune, by the Emperor Charles and his armies, by the new pope, Paul III (the king's old nemesis Pope Clement having died and an equally uncompromising successor having been elected), and above all, by his lordly, nagging wife.

For Anne had triumphed over her disappointment, to become more irksome than ever.

"I am carrying within me the next king," she announced to her household, her face aglow with triumph, her hands over her stomach. "He should arrive, God willing, with the harvest. Prepare the birth chamber."

Greatly surprised, we scurried to do her bidding. We sewed yards and yards of purple velvet to make new hangings for the bed. We had the carved, gilded royal cradle brought in—the cradle fit for a prince. At Anne's command I sent for a statue of St. Margaret, patron saint of safe childbirth, and had it placed prominently in the room, even though some of the other maids of honor objected, saying the worship of saints was popish and therefore wicked.

"The Nun of Kent would rejoice in that statue," Anne Cavecant said when she saw the smiling blue-gowned figure. "The saint would probably talk to her."

"Don't be absurd," said another of the maids. "Statues can't talk."

"And lice can't suddenly appear in their thousands, I suppose. But it happened. I saw them. Lice everywhere. I say the nun has powers, great powers. She could destroy us all."

"And idle talk could make the king angry at us," I said, hoping to divert the flow of gossip, "which would be even worse."

"Bridget," I went on, "where have you put the queen's counterpane? She will be asking for it."

"Demanding it, you mean. I will have one of the grooms fetch it."

In preparing Anne's birth chamber we kept in mind that an exceptionally cold winter was expected. The royal gardeners cautioned us that the onions they were pulling that fall had very thin skins and the thinner the onionskin, the harsher the winter to come. We piled warm bedcoverings over the pallet beds for the six midwives that would attend Anne. We had braziers brought in and ordered a larger supply of coals than usual.

We were careful in making all these arrangements knowing how superstitious Anne was about the coming birth of her child. She had her old bedchamber—the one in which Galyon had died—shut up tightly and sealed. It was bad luck, she said, to sleep in a room where a life had ended through accident. Only it was no accident, I felt sure, and Anne's reluctance to enter that room was the result of a guilty conscience and fear of retribution.

Not only was Anne "pregnant with the king," as she often said, she was about to repeat her triumph at the French court. The emperor had renewed his threat to invade England, and had the firm support of the new pope; because of this, and to ensure that his fragile ties with King Francis remained firmly in place, King Henry had decided to take his courtiers to the continent once again, for another meeting with the French.

Nothing delighted Anne more than the prospect of a new wardrobe, and she insisted on having one made for the journey to France. Mr. Skut and his assistants were kept busy all day and long into the night preparing new gowns, in Anne's preferred shades of deep rose and rich murrey, soft cinnamon and russet brown. There were petticoats and kirtles in the newest style, longer and wider than those in fashion when Catherine was queen, and lace-trimmed, angel-wing sleeves to go with them, soft bedgowns, velvet slippers and a curious kind of new headdress voluted at the sides. Every garment was made with Anne's rounding shape in mind, even the shell-like headdresses. ("To draw attention to the ears, and away from the belly," said Mr. Skut, and Anne had to agree.)

With Anne's quickening, in the depth of winter, came a renewed frenzy of activity—and a squabble. For Henry, ever changeable and unpredictable, had ordered that Princess Mary, Queen Catherine's eighteen-year-old daughter, join Queen Anne's household.

"I will not have this!" Anne cried in exasperation. "I will not have that stubborn, mulish girl near me, with her airs and her popish ways!"

Mary, ever loyal to her mother, refused to accept the outcome of her father's nullity suit and the official change in her mother's status to that of "princess dowager." Mary continued to regard her mother as a queen, and herself as a princess, and was not reticent in calling Anne's tiny daughter Elizabeth a bastard. I thought Mary very brave, and quietly admired her for standing up for what she believed—yet I could not help thinking her a fool. As I was learning in the months following my loss of Galyon, confronting a powerful enemy only led to self-destruction; far better to find a way to win by attacking the enemy secretly, behind the scenes, by indirection.

As I predicted, Mary's obstinate insistence on being called princess and refusing to accept any subordinate role to baby Elizabeth (who was not even present at court in those days) made Anne furious.

"That girl needs a beating!" Anne shouted. "She will be taught to obey, or she will be shut up in a dungeon!" There were quarrels between Anne and the king, long silences, estrangements. Mary gloated—she was enjoying her brief triumph as a source of anxiety to her mother's hated rival Anne—but in the end, Anne won out. She was, after all, pregnant with England's next king, as she never ceased to say. And King Henry, though capable of loud and frightening anger, was a beleaguered man with a sore leg who very much wanted his wife to give him a son.

Mary was sent away. And Anne, in her moment of triumph, made yet another demand. The Nun of Kent, she said, must be executed at once, before she could do any harm to the boy who would soon be born.

Too weary of arguing to resist, Henry agreed. The nun was put to the rack, her frail flesh tormented, until she shrieked with pain and begged to be allowed to die. In her agony, so King Henry said, she confessed that she was no visionary and that the Lord did not speak to her or through her. She was in the pay of Ambassador Chapuys. She was paid to prophesy doom for the house of Tudor, to stir up the English against their ruler and to punish him for putting aside his Spanish wife.

The execution of Elizabeth Barton, known as the Nun of Kent, was set to take place toward the end of April, and Anne announced that she, and all her maids of honor, would attend.

NINETEEN

THOUGH the sun was high and bright in the spring sky, the air was cool. A faint wind blew toward us across the river as we took our places in the innermost courtyard of the Tower, beside the gallows. Thin clouds raced past. Beside me, Anne shivered. She was determined to watch the Nun of Kent die. But she disliked discomfort, and she did not like to be kept waiting. She wrapped her fur-lined cloak tightly around her and tapped her foot on the dusty cobbles, a frown of discontent on her harried features.

After what seemed an endless wait, soldiers began to file out from the inner ward, sharp halbards gleaming in the sun, and formed a half-circle around the prisoner they guarded. She was a small woman, her dirty grey-green garment in rags, her feet bare. She stumbled as she walked, looking down as she went, her long dark hair veiling her face. She was much thinner than she had been when I saw her first in the convent of St. Agnes's, thin as a broomstick, one emaciated arm stretched out in front of her as if beseeching aid or trying to keep from falling.

To the loud beat of drums, she left the ring of soldiers and made her way slowly and shakily up the steps to the platform where the gallows waited: two upright planks supporting a crossbar—the stark, fearsomely simple structure that would soon end her life. A priest mounted the steps after her and stood behind her as she faced the murmuring crowd.

Then something remarkable happened. With a dramatic gesture, the nun threw back her head, revealing her face—a face covered in purple bruises, yet seemingly lit from within by an odd radiance. At the same moment there came a brilliant burst of lightning and, just afterward, a sharp clap of thunder. The first fat, heavy drops of rain splattered on the gallows, the cobbles, the soldiers and the nun herself. The dust beneath our feet turned to mud as more rain fell, until the spattering became a shower and then a torrent. Thunder rumbled ever louder. We were soon drenched, but Anne stayed where she was, next to me, the hem of her gown growing black with mud, her slippers ruined, and the rest of our party—ten maids of honor in all— remained with her.

"Rain from a clear sky!" I heard people exclaim. "The nun is working a miracle!" "It is a sign!"

A herald appeared on the platform, sheltered from the rain by a thick cloth held over his head by two servants as he read from a document.

"Elizabeth Barton, known as the Nun of Kent, you have been found guilty of treason. Though you have recanted your false visions, and admitted to having been paid by enemies of this realm to harm and subvert the authority of His Majesty King Henry, you are sentenced to be hanged for your wicked misdeeds.

Have you anything to say before the sentence of execution is carried out?"

"I have," the nun shouted in response, her voice strong and resonant, "and may the power of the Lord sustain me as I speak His message!"

I felt those around me draw back in awe as the nun went on speaking, the rain letting up just enough to ensure that her words could be heard. It seemed to me, though I'm sure it was merely an illusion, that she stared right at Anne as she spoke.

"Plagues shall harm you! Disaster shall follow you, dishonor smite you, and in the end, death shall find you!" she chanted. "I say to you, Jezebel, that your firstborn son shall not live!"

I felt Anne trembling, and I knew that it was not only from the cold, but from terror.

"Look!" The nun was pointing upwards, into the dark sky. "I see—I see an angel."

Everyone around me followed her pointing finger, including Anne. I could see nothing but low overhanging clouds, sluicing rain. I was aware of feeling very wet and uncomfortable, and wishing that the nun would end her peroration, and that the execution would proceed.

But instead, the nun seemed to be gathering the onlookers more and more into her vision—the vision she described as an angel, wings outspread, descending upon London. I heard gasps, sobs, cries of wonderment, as if others near me were sharing the nun's vision, though it was plain to me that the sky was just sky, the clouds mere clouds. There were no heavenly visitors to be seen.

"I forgive you all," the nun was saying, relaying, so she said, the words of the angel. "Though you take part in wickedness, in the silencing of a holy woman who is a divine messenger. I forgive you all!"

I heard the herald's voice barking an order. Two of the soldiers seized the nun and placed the noose around her neck. Yet she spoke on, undeterred.

"She is coming for me, to take me up to the Lord." She smiled. "I see a green field—" she began, but then her voice was choked off, for the planks beneath her feet had given way and her body dropped, suddenly, rudely. Her neck was snapped.

Many in the crowd dropped to their knees in the mud, crossing themselves and murmuring prayers. Others pointed to the sky. Still others rushed forward to touch the nun's body and tear off pieces of her garment, precious relics to be preserved.

But amid the confusion, the air was suddenly thick with swarms of flies, rising in black clouds to infest and bite and crawl over every inch of our exposed skin. People cried out and struck at the sudden infestation. I slapped at the nasty creatures as I felt them nip and sting my face, my ears and neck, felt them crawling up beneath my garments.

Maddened by the flies, Anne was trying to run, shuddering, tugging at her cloak, her gown, barely able to move because of the sudden turmoil in the crowd. A madness had descended, people were rushing in all directions, trying to escape the flies and each other, running into one another in confusion, crying out, lashing out.

I thought, we will die here. We will be trampled.

Then I felt someone gripping my arm firmly. I turned to see who it was—and looked into Will's resolute, flinty face, his mouth set in a hard line.

"Come," he shouted above the hubbub, pulling me along through the unruly mob, through the swarming flies and the noise, the flailing arms and thrashing bodies. Instinctively I grabbed for Anne with my free arm, and managed to pull her after us.

The next few moments were a blur of confusion and panic. I was aware that I was stepping on squirming bodies, and that I could not stop to help them. I heard Will's voice, and felt his strong grip on my arm, I heard Anne sobbing and panting, I thought I heard the tramping of boots. I felt faint, but gulped as much of the rain-scented air as I could hold and lowered my head and went forward as Will was telling me to do. And finally, as the noise and confusion seemed to grow less, I felt myself pulled into a dim corridor, where burning torches were set into the stone walls and the sounds of mayhem were dimmed.

"Stay here," Will ordered, sitting me ungently down on a hard bench. "I must go back for the others." I sat where he put me, dizzy and out of breath, too weak and bewildered to do anything but wait, glad to be delivered from the scene of chaos, for Will's return.

The arrival at court of a new special envoy from Emperor Charles was a welcome relief. The nobleman was a hefty, strong-looking man, with something of the seasoned courtier's subtlety of manner. His shock of white-blond hair and blue eyes were a pleasant surprise to us; they made him seem forthright, even knightly, while Ambassador Chapuys was small and dark and slippery.

King Henry embraced the German with unaccustomed bonhomie. I knew at once that there was deviousness afoot. I glanced around the room. Ambassador Chapuys was present, and Thomas Cromwell, and a priest I did not recognize, along with several of the king's chamber gentlemen and an array of clerks and grooms.

Henry had asked me to be there, saying I was the favorite friend of the princess dowager Catherine who was, of course, the emperor's aunt. When I learned that my presence would be required I was reminded of what the king often told me, that he trusted me, that I was the only person he could trust. I had never been more conscious of that trust than on this afternoon.

"And was your crossing smooth?" King Henry was asking the envoy.

"As smooth as my master's grand trireme could make it," came the German's reply. He smiled, showing blackened teeth. "It is his newest vessel, with twenty-seven banks of oarsmen. I have never ridden in a swifter ship. It flies over the water."

"I myself have ordered a quadrireme, with one hundred banks of oarsmen," Henry boasted. "The shipwrights are building her now. No ship is larger, or faster." He beamed. "But then," he went on, "I need no array of ships. My great fortresses at Calais and Dover are so strong no foreign army could ever cross the water to conquer England."

"If it pleases Your Majesty to think so," was the German's complacent reply. "As to the quadrireme, I believe it has often been noted that Your Majesty has a natural inclination to all things new and strange."

"Such as yourself," was King Henry's immediate rejoinder. "You are new, and strange, are you not?" He guffawed and clapped the foreigner on the back. Ambassador Chapuys and the chancellor laughed and a tight smile appeared on the German's face.

"New perhaps," he said, stepping deftly out of the king's reach. "But hardly strange. I do not, for example, possess a magic ring, or a cloak of invisibility, as Your Majesty is said to do."

King Henry, taken aback, looked around at the other men in the room, none of whom met his gaze. It was well known that he boasted of possessing a ring that had belonged to Cardinal Wolsey, a ring with a wonder-working stone that was a talisman of protection and a source of occult power. The Duke of Norfolk complained that the king, by turning this ring on his finger and muttering a charm, had cast a spell on him and caused a demon to haunt him.

As to the cloak of invisibility, I myself had seen the king working on it in his Tower room. It was a sweep of buckskin which, he explained to me, would hide the wearer from view once it was treated with a special tincture of wine, horse bones and powdered glass.

"I see I can have no secrets at this court," Henry said gruffly. "As usual, Jane here is the only one I can really trust."

A collation was brought in and the men sat at a table to refresh themselves.

"If Your Majesty pleases," the envoy broke in, "I should like to convey His Imperial Highness's wish that our two realms might join in a crusade against the enemies of Christendom, the heathen Turks."

"Ah, the emperor's old dream, to defeat the unbelievers. It would take a great many triremes to accomplish that, I imagine. Ah well, I have quite enough difficulty trying to defeat the rebels in Ireland. I cannot join in a grand enterprise against the Turk."

"His Imperial Majesty will be disappointed to hear that," the German said. "Especially since you once promised him you would send your armies to the East to fight alongside his own."

"I did promise that, didn't I?" Henry mused. "It was when Charles was here in England, visiting his aunt Catherine. Years ago. He was just a boy then. An idealistic boy."

"A boy who had inherited half the world," Ambassador Chapuys put in. "A very rich boy."

"But a boy nonetheless," Henry snapped. "He used to kneel to me, to ask my blessing. He used to call me Bon Père, his good father.

"'Can we not make a joint crusade against the Turks, good

father?' he asked me. He was a clumsy boy, with a long face. He said too many prayers, as I recall, and rode awkwardly. A bad jouster.

"Well, at any rate, he asked me if we could not ride together against the Turks, and I remember saying to him, 'The King of France, he is the greatest Turk.' And he was. He still is. But that was long ago, before Martin Luther arose among us. Some say he is the greatest Turk now."

The men ate and drank, Henry kept them amused with stories and jokes and at length called in his astrologer John Robyns.

"My Robin here," he said, getting to his feet, "keeps me intrigued by reading the night sky. He has studied the stars and especially the comets. We speak of them often, do we not?"

Robyns, lanky and balding, with a broad brow and wide, bright eyes, told the others about a long-tailed comet that he had been watching.

"It may portend the birth of a son to the queen," he said, making King Henry smile and nod. "Or it may predict disaster. No one can say for certain."

The king frowned.

"Don't be grim, Robin. Be hopeful."

"The skies do not respond to our hopes, as I have often told you, sire," Robyns said, his voice even. "The most we can do is observe, and note the changes in the heavenly bodies, and write down what we see."

"Robin is writing a treatise on comets," Henry informed us. "On how long it takes them to reappear. It is of the greatest interest to me."

"His Imperial Majesty the Emperor also has astrologers who read the heavens," the envoy remarked. "Perhaps they could meet."

Robyns bowed. "If His Majesty wishes it, I am ready to confer with others who study the skies."

"As above, so below," was King Henry's enigmatic response. He looked around at the others. "If we can divine what is occurring in the heavens, then we will know what to expect on earth."

This awkward comment met with silence. It was a time-honored truism, beloved of fortune tellers and purveyors of magic. It was out of place.

I found my voice.

"Speaking of what to expect on earth, does anyone here read fortunes?" I held out my palm.

The priest who was a stranger to me, a benign smile on his elderly face, now came toward me.

"I have that gift, Mistress Seymour," he said.

"Ah! Good!" the king exclaimed. "Now we shall have some fun. Tell us, what is Jane's future to bring?"

The man looked down into my hand, then drew back. I could tell right away that something he saw in my palm alarmed him.

"You must forgive me," he said, his voice faltering. "My gift fails me on this occasion. Perhaps if we wait until nightfall, and consult the stars—"

"Foolish old man!" The king reddened. "Spare us your feeble gifts!" And waving the priest away, he called for more wine and a plate of lampreys, which he proceeded to devour noisily and greedily, biting off the heads of each as if he bore a grudge against it.

That summer, the summer of the year 1534, cattle in the fields and horses in their stables began to die.

At first it was only the weakest, leanest cattle and the oldest horses, broken down, spavined nags who would not have lived to see another winter through. But then, as the first of the crops began to come in, the healthy cows began to die, along with their young calves, and the strong bulls, and the drays that pulled the heavy wagons and even the magnificent warhorses and jousting horses that could carry a man in full armor.

The murrain struck suddenly, and killed surely—but only after the animals had suffered for days, their piteous lowing and bleating and whinnying an agony to those that tried to care for them. King Henry loved his horses, and when word of the sickness began to spread he tried to save the most precious of those in his stables by sending them upriver in his royal barges. But no place, it seemed, was safe; the royal horses reached Reading, only to die there within days; he mourned them, withdrawing into an inner chamber and refusing to see or speak to anyone. When at length he came out, he was filled with blame.

"I should never have let that woman die," Ned overheard King Henry say, then passed his words on to me. "I should never have listened to my wife's demands. What more plagues are there to descend on us? Am I to suffer and die like my warhorses?"

"Take the greatest care, little sister," Ned cautioned me. "You have escaped calamity so far, but everyone near Queen Anne is under threat. I wish you would leave her service."

"If only I could. But she favors me—heaven knows why. She keeps me near her, and the king too wants me at court. He likes talking to me. He says he trusts me."

"You know, of course, that the people blame Queen Anne for the threat of harm to their idol, the Nun of Kent. And for these harms that have befallen us they will have their revenge."

Ned's words stayed in my mind as week after week the plague continued. For with the dreaded murrain came stories, widespread among the Londoners and country people alike, that the Nun of

Kent had not died, that her spirit lived on—and that the curses she had placed on the king and Anne, and on all the English, were still to be fulfilled. There were reports that her ghostly form was seen floating over the capital, hovering over the royal palaces, even haunting the nursery we had prepared for the coming birth of Anne's child.

Anne could not sleep for worrying. She huddled in one corner of her wide bed, alone save for little Pourquoi who lay curled against her under the mound of coverlets, whimpering and snuffling in his sleep. He refused to eat, even though Anne tempted him with plates of shrimp and sweet cream and bowls of pudding—which had always been his favorites. But the food lay untouched. Day after day he languished, while Anne fretted over him and wept and cursed the fewterers who could do nothing for him.

In the end she went to the king, escorted by all her ladies, and told him that she needed to take Pourquoi to the country, away from the poisons of the capital.

Henry regarded us all calmly, and heard Anne's demand.

"Do you imagine that you can save your dog, when I could not save my horses? Don't you know that there is no cure for this plague?"

"I will take him somewhere safe," Anne insisted. "I will protect him. I will not let any other animals come near him. Or sorcerers, or seers or false visionaries in the pay of Ambassador Chapuys."

"It is too near your time," the king said. "You must not go anywhere until our son is born."

"I cannot bear to lose little Pourquoi," Anne said stubbornly. "Would you have me bear our child in a season of mourning, if my beloved dog were to die?"

"He will die soon enough, even if he is not struck down with the murrain. He is an old dog. Now, I will hear no more about this."

But Anne, as always, was persistent. In the end the king threw up his hands and told her she could go to his hunting lodge at Lornford near Cheam, taking only a small group of servants and four of her maids of honor. She chose Bridget and me, along with Anne Cavecant and—at the king's insistence—Bess Holland, mistress of Anne's uncle Norfolk.

"Foolish errand!" I heard the king mutter. "The dog will be dead within a day, and this whim will be past."

All the way to Lornford Anne held her little dog in her arms, beneath her cloak, talking to him soothingly. It was a mournful journey, past fields of dead and dying cattle, the stench of death thick in the air. In the towns we passed through, the markets were all but empty; a few scrawny fowls and quacking ducks were all that were to be seen.

"Where are all the dogs?" Anne asked a town gatekeeper.

"All dead, Your Highness," came the reply. "You'd best guard your own beast before he falls in a faint like the rest."

It was raining when we arrived at Lornford, and there was a chill in the air. No fires had been laid for us in the old hunting lodge, and it was several hours before rooms could be warmed and prepared for Anne and a bed made up. What food was brought to her she tried to feed to the weak Pourquoi, who lay under silken sheets we had brought with us, shivering and whining.

For two days, while the roof leaked ceaselessly and Pourquoi grew weaker and weaker, we awaited the end. Anne sat sleepless beside him, and insisted that prayers be said over him just as if he had been a Christian soul in the last stages of illness and not a small black dog with a fringe of grey at his muzzle. At last, on the third night, Pourquoi gave a final faint cry and fell onto the floor.

Almost at the same instant Anne wailed and clutched her stomach.

"The midwives!" she cried. "I need the midwives!"

But we had brought no midwives to Lornford. The king had ordered them to stay at Whitehall, thinking our stay in the country would be brief.

Bridget and I put Anne to bed and did what we could to soothe her. One of the grooms was sent to Whitehall to fetch the midwives, but we knew it would be many hours before we could expect them, and in the meantime it was clear to us that Anne was in increasing pain. I had attended enough births to feel certain that the seizures that gripped her were something other than the slow, progressively building pains of labor. These spasms were sudden and sharp, knifelike stabs that made her scream in terror.

I could not help but think that her suffering was one more sign of the nun's revenge.

"Is she going to die?" Bess Holland asked Bridget, her eyes wide. "Are we all going to be blamed if she does?"

But Bridget only snorted in derision and waved Bess away so that we could give Anne wine—and not the watered wine we were accustomed to drinking but wine mixed with some of the opium Anne Cavecant always carried with her to soothe her own constant pain from the tumor in her side.

The mixture appeared to make Anne drowsy, yet the fearsome spasms did not subside, but rather seemed to worsen, jarring her cruelly out of her lethargy and making her tear at her blankets and shout and swear at us until we were beside ourselves with frustration.

"It's no good," Bridget said to me at length. "We'll have to try to find a midwife in Cheam."

A hasty search through the town, with two of the royal servants loudly announcing in the king's name that a midwife was urgently needed, produced a frightened, disheveled dam in a dirty apron who could barely bring herself to look at us, much less attend to Anne. She was clumsy, her hands were shaking as she approached the bed, her grimy cap awry and her mouth open in disbelief.

She looked down at Anne, and saw, not only her face, contorted in pain, but her left hand, with its long thin fingers and telltale extra nail.

"It is the whore!" she cried out. "The king's whore! She bears the marks of the devil!"

And before we could try to stop her she had run out of the room, past the servants, shrieking as if a demon was after her.

What happened then makes me cringe, even now, in the telling. For with the aid of Bridget and Anne Cavecant and one other, the cook's assistant, a strong young girl who did not flinch though what she saw and heard were fearsome indeed, we delivered Anne of the burden that was making her suffer.

We delivered her, though what came forth from her distended belly after she had fainted from her agony was less a babe than an unnatural thing, a gruesome prodigy like those glimpsed by the followers of the Nun of Kent and welcomed as signs of divine wrath and punishment.

I will not dwell on its size, or its odd shape, or the way its great round bald head lolled uncontrollably and its stunted arms and legs waggled grotesquely. I will only say that we all gasped in horror when we saw it, and that it did not live. Bridget and I looked at one another, shook our heads, and wrapped the thing in a sheet. It was hurriedly placed in a wooden box and taken to one of the outbuildings. Not knowing what else to do, we left it there.

When Anne revived on the following day we told her only that the baby had not lived. Thankfully she did not ask us anything more. It was as if she sensed that there was something terribly wrong, something best left unsaid. We four who had been present at the birth—Bridget, Anne Cavecant, the cook's assistant and myself—were the only ones who knew the truth. We agreed among ourselves to say only that the baby had not lived.

That night, with Anne sleeping and the others at rest, I walked out alone into the dimness of the forest and thought about all that I had witnessed earlier. Twigs and fallen branches snapped under my feet as I went along, night birds called and I heard other sounds that vaguely frightened me. I knew that there was danger to be found in the forest, especially at night. Beasts walked abroad, wolves and bears and the human forest-dwellers who shunned the daylight and waylaid travelers and the unprotected.

But as I walked on, what kept my attention was not the sounds of the night or its menaces but the faint starlight that shone through the branches of the tall trees, starlight that glimmered on the fallen leaves and broken branches. I came to a clearing and stopped walking. Looking up, I was dazzled by the brightness of the stars. So many, many glowing stars, the familiar patterns I had known since childhood when Ned had taken me by the hand on summer nights and pointed them out to me.

As above, so below King Henry had said. Our fates are written in the skies. His astrologer was watching a long-tailed comet as it crossed the heavens. A comet he believed could predict disaster. And disaster had surely come to Lornford that day, and I had seen it. Yet the skies above me on that night seemed benign, not threatening. I saw no comet, no fiery portent of death. Only a boundless field of sparkling lights, shining down on us all, unreadable and indifferent to our fates.

Anne rested for two more days in the hunting lodge, then we all went back to Richmond, where the king was, and took up our familiar duties.

Anne was pale and quiet. There was none of her customary bluster, no arguments with the king—who, on seeing that she no longer had the belly of a pregnant woman, let loose a storm of anger and then stayed away.

In the quiet of the room where we maids of honor slept, those of us who knew the secret kept our bond of silence. When asked by the others in Anne's household what had happened at Lornford, we said only what was obvious to all—that Anne was no longer carrying the king's child. But we confided to one another, when we were certain no one else could overhear, that in our hearts we pondered the meaning of what we had seen— what Anne herself did not know. Which was that the monstrous thing she had birthed was an ominous sign, a sign sent from God—or from the devil—to warn us all of worse to come.

TWENTY

NOTHING was ever the same after that. The royal marriage soured, the persecutions and executions increased. England lay under a pall. We dreaded the future. I attended Will's wedding and Ned's wedding and wished them and their wives well—but could not in good faith imagine that theirs would be long or happy lives. My own life seemed to lie in abeyance: I no longer had Galyon to love, and I mourned him; I was getting older—soon I would attain the advanced age of thirty—and the pleasures of youth no longer seemed within my grasp. Younger maids of honor joined Anne's household, stayed for a few months, and then married. I watched this happen again and again, and still there was no one for me—nor could I imagine ever loving anyone as I had loved Galyon. Babies were born, some lived and some died. But would I ever be a mother? I thought not. There were times when I wept over my lost children, my drowned hopes. And at those times I blamed Anne.

I blamed her, I savored her suffering. And I bided my time, waiting for my moment of revenge.

Meanwhile more and more victims of the king's justice—many said the king's injustice—lost their lives, their severed heads grinned down from London Bridge. More and more of the king's spies were said to be watching us all, and listening to our every word, and sending in their reports to Cromwell and his minions. Arrests were made, people were taken from their homes and locked in the royal prisons, never to come out again. No one knew who would be next, for as Anne often said, there were eyes and ears everywhere.

Treason was the dreaded word. Traitors. Who could say what lies might be told, leading to false accusations of treachery, and to death? Who would be the next victim? No one was spared, not saintly clerics such as Bishop Fisher or sage men of law such as Thomas More or even pious monks, pure and chaste, who fell under the scrutiny of the royal spies.

Amid it all, the king neglected his wife and spent his time with his favorite Madge Shelton, dancing with her as he had once danced with Anne, wooing her, and taking counsel with his advisers about how he might rid himself of Anne and marry a woman such as Madge who could give him a strong living son. For baby Elizabeth, who continued to surprise everyone by surviving, was only a tiny girl and a girl whose birth many considered to be tainted by the king's adultery. And Mary, fragile, blond Mary who was Catherine's daughter though she was no longer called princess, was also only a girl and chronically ill. And Henry Fitzroy, small and weak and lacking in royal courage, was not likely to live long—or if he did, he was not likely to become a strong king.

Conspiracies were taking shape, and we all knew it, even

Anne. There was treachery in the air. I trembled whenever King Henry summoned me into his presence and asked me to tell him what rumors I was hearing, who was spreading disloyal tales about him or Anne.

"Jane, there is something I must know for certain," he asked me one morning when he was sure we were alone. "I know I can trust you to tell me the truth."

"Yes, sire."

"What really happened at the hunting lodge at Lornford?"

The question took me by surprise, and unnerved me. I took my time in replying. I had never confided to the king or anyone else (apart from the three other women who had been present) the truth about Anne's horrifying delivery. The event was too fearsome. And I did not want to be blamed in any way for the outcome. Or defiled by it. I believed that in some way I could never explain, the creature Anne had birthed was bewitched.

Yet by keeping silence I felt that I was betraying King Henry's trust in me, and this unnerved me. I wanted to be trustworthy—though trustworthiness was rare at court. But where Anne and her dead baby were concerned, I didn't dare.

"Why do you ask?" I said at length, licking my lips nervously. "The child did not live."

The king paced fretfully.

"Anne refuses to speak about it, and Norfolk says he was told by Bess Holland that there was no child—nothing at all. It was all an imagining in Anne's mind. I know this can sometimes happen, women who desire a child very greatly can sometimes swell, and become ill, and even suffer the pains of birth. Only there is no child. Is that what happened to Anne? I rely on you to tell me the truth."

I shook my head. "I cannot deceive you, sire—but I am

heartily sorry you have asked me. I wish the truth could remain buried at Lornford."

He stopped pacing, reached down and took my face between his two large rough hands, bringing his own face close to mine.

"Jane! This is as urgent a question as you will ever be asked! This is about the succession to the throne of England!"

We looked into each other's eyes, and I felt myself growing warm. I was at once frightened, stirred by his power, and drawn to him, for the first time, both as a man and as my king, who I had known familiarly for years. I was weak as water in his strong hands.

He released me and I cleared my throat.

"If I could have some wine, sire—" He shouted for a servant and in no time a tray with goblet and cups was brought to us. I used the time while we waited to gather my thoughts.

"This is how it was, Your Majesty," I began when I had drunk some of my wine. "We did not know, when it was going on, whether it was a thing of the devil or a mere accident, a mistake of nature that could happen to any woman at any time. We were very frightened. There were only four of us who knew about the child. A midwife was found in Cheam but she was too frightened when she saw Anne's hand with the extra finger and she ran away before the creature was born."

"The creature?" Alarmed, Henry sat down beside me, intent on my face, my words.

"Anne was in terrible pain, you understand—so terrible that she fainted. She never saw her son—if it was a son."

Now the king was incredulous. I went on.

"As I say, there were four of us, myself, Bridget, Bess Holland and a cook's assistant who was very strong and brave. Afterwards we all swore to keep secret what we knew of Anne and the thing she bore."

"But what was it?" the king demanded, a quiver in his voice. "Was it a demon?"

"It was a misshapen lump of flesh," I managed to say, "that did not live."

"Did it have the appearance of a child at least?"

"I can hardly bear to tell you."

"I have seen horses in foal that deliver legless brutes, litters of pups with one pup dead, malformed, dwarfish—"

"This was unlike any living thing I have ever seen."

"So it was living, not dead."

I drank more of the wine, then closed my eyes, trying in vain to remove the memory of the thing from my vision.

"It wriggled. Its ugly head waggled. Its twisted mouth gaped. Then it was still."

I felt ill and hoped I would not disgrace myself by spewing. I went to the window and gulped the fresh air.

"All right, Jane," the king said, his voice low. "That is enough. And you believe it was more male than female."

I nodded.

"Was it baptized before it died?"

"No, sire. It was not—fit for baptism."

In the silence that followed I could not weep, for I had felt no pity for the monstrous thing Anne bore. But the horror of the event affected me deeply nonetheless. It was as if I had come close to a mystery—not a wondrous spiritual mystery, but a thing of enchantment nonetheless. A rarity.

I felt the king's arm around me.

"You must rest now, Jane. You have had a shock."

"I have told no one else about this."

"I believe you." He stood as he was, with his arm encircling me comfortingly, for a few moments, lost in thought.

"You know what this means, don't you, Jane?"

"That the Nun of Kent's final prophecy has been fulfilled. That Anne's firstborn son would die."

"No doubt my people would say that, if they knew the truth. But I refer to something much more immediate. It means that I am married to a woman who cannot give me an heir to my throne. If she had another child—ten more children—they would all be freaks. I am cursed, Jane. God has cursed me for marrying this damnable woman. I must rid myself of her, before His curse falls on everyone in my court and kingdom!"

It was from then on, I believe, that my own destiny began to become clear.

The king had taken me into his confidence, as I had taken him into mine. We had forged a bond. From then on our purposes were joined, and we worked toward a joint outcome. We worked together to ensure the preservation of the throne.

But this happened over time, not all at once.

First King Henry sent me to Kimbolton Castle, where Catherine was lodged.

"She is said to be very ill," the king told me. "She may soon die. I know you are fond of her. You have my permission to visit her. See how you find her. If she knows she has not long to live, she may be willing to forgive me, to do me one last favor."

"And what is that?"

"She may be willing to agree, at last, to enter a convent. The ceremony can be performed quickly, if I so order it. All that is required is that a sister of the order be present, and a priest. Once she has taken the veil, she is no further hindrance to me."

"But your marriage to her was declared null long ago."

"Yes—but when my marriage to Anne is dissolved, as I am determined it will be, there must be no earlier union to hinder me from marrying yet again. I have taken counsel with Cromwell and other legal advisers on this."

I made no effort to sift through these complications. The matter of the king's marriage, that great and cloudy issue that had troubled the court and indeed much of Christendom for so long, was now, it seemed, to be revived. But I had only one task: to visit the ill, beleaguered Catherine in loving friendship and ask for her cooperation.

Catherine's sadly decayed bedchamber at Kimbolton Castle was dark and small, the floor sagging and the old stone walls chinked by gaps that let in the wintry air. The light from the dying fire revealed a low bed, frayed bedcurtains and— the room's single ornament—the former queen's treasured prie-dieu, which she had embroidered herself as a girl and brought from Spain so many years earlier. The sickly smells of lavender and opium mingled with the odor of illness and decay, and as I watched Catherine's gentleman usher Griffith Richards put a log on the fire from a small pile beside the hearth, my heart sank.

I knew then that the princess dowager, once Catherine of Aragon, proud and lovely daughter of the great Queen Isabella of Spain, was indeed in her last days.

I sat down on a bench beside the bed. As the room brightened from the leaping flames I saw that we were not alone. Catherine's long time friend and waiting lady Maria de Salinas, much aged since I had seen her last, was sitting quietly in one corner and a young serving boy stood in another.

"How long has she been this way?" I asked Maria, looking down at the gaunt, ashen face asleep on the lace-trimmed pillow.

"Since All Soul's," came the answer. "It is the dropsy—and her broken heart."

A rustling of the bedclothes drew my attention to the princess dowager's wrinkled, blue-veined hands, which were clutching at a rosary of ivory beads.

I heard her softly say my name.

"Jane."

"Yes, milady princess."

She beckoned to me to come closer.

"Caterina. My mother's name for me." She smiled wanly. "Please."

"Caterina then." She reached for my hand, and pulled it toward her head.

"Brush my hair, Jane."

I looked over at Maria de Salinas, who took a silver-backed brush from a wooden chest and brought it to me. I began to brush Catherine's sparse grey-white hair. She closed her eyes in pleasure.

"You were always a good girl," she said. "A kind girl to me."

I went on brushing. Presently I said, "The king sent me to see you, with a message."

Her grey eyes grew wide. I could tell that, weary as she was, and ill, her mind was spinning.

"He is going to take me back then? He is going to make me queen again?"

Her words were pitiable, but I tried not to let them unnerve me.

"He is concerned for your health. He asks that you do him the great favor of agreeing to enter a convent."

She stiffened, and I drew back the brush at once.

"Never," she said simply.

I could tell by the finality of her tone that it would be useless to try to persuade her.

"He will be disappointed," I said.

She made a faint sound. I realized that she was laughing.

"I'm sure he will," she said. "And how is he?"

I resumed my brushing.

"Bald. Bad-tempered. Hoarse from shouting. His head hurts and his leg hurts. He walks with a golden walking stick."

"Does he still wear that foolish pouch of spiders around his neck?"

I nodded.

"Ah. He fears the sweat."

"And that is not all he fears," I said, incautiously.

Catherine had become much more alert as I spoke of the king. She tried to lift herself up, but then fell back onto her pillows. Her eyes were bright and fixed on me.

"Oh?"

"He is ill at ease—about his marriage to Anne."

"So that's why he wants me out of the way! I am an obstacle to him. He means to put Anne aside and marry again. But I am a hindrance."

Maria de Salinas stood and approached the bed.

"I think, Mistress Seymour, that Her Highness is very tired. You should leave her in peace."

I noticed that the Spaniard continued to speak of Catherine as if she were still queen.

"Of course." I got up from my bench.

"You will come tomorrow, Jane?"

"I will if you wish it, dear Lady Caterina."

Catherine called for her gentleman usher and ordered him to have a room prepared for me.

"And be sure she has enough logs to last her through the night."

"But Your Highness, we have so few," Griffith Richards began.

"Have you no sense of hospitality, old man? We must take care of our guest first, then see to ourselves."

My room was icy cold, my blankets thin. Griffith Richards was apologetic.

"Our supplies are scant," he began. "We are sent very little from the court in London. The king—has not been generous. He says the queen is contrary and will not obey him as she ought. He expects her to provide for her own household, but she has no more money of her own—"

I drew out my purse of coins and gave some to Richards. The silver overflowed in his hands.

"There must be firewood in plenty in the village. And whatever food and wine you need. Go quickly!"

He could barely utter his thanks, he was so overcome. But I hurried him on his way, before calling for a servant to make up my own meager fire and climbing gratefully into bed.

My fire had nearly gone out the following morning, as the grey dawn was breaking. The cold woke me. But I had hardly begun to wash and dress when new logs were brought in and a fresh blazing fire laid. Soon afterward Griffith Richards knocked on my door and told me that the queen would like me to share her bread and tea. His manner was grave, as always, but as he led me to the princess dowager's bedchamber his movements seemed brisk and spry, and a new liveliness shone on his face. A fresh wind of hope was sweeping through Kimbolton, despite the grave illness of its most important inhabitant.

Much to my surprise I found Catherine sitting up in her bed, her hair gathered under a cap and a warm blue woolen shawl wrapped around her bony shoulders. She smiled happily at me as I came into the room, and indicated that I should sit at a table beside her. As we broke our fast, helping ourselves generously to plates of warm bread and butter and honey, I could see that she savored the food, her satisfaction was apparent and the lines of pain and worry that had been etched deeply into her forehead the night before were less visible in the daylight.

"Tell me, Jane," Catherine asked me when she had finished her meal and wiped her mouth on a clean linen napkin, "why is the king going to put away his trollop?"

I thought for a moment.

"They quarrel," I began. "She is vexing to him. And—"

Catherine leaned forward in her eagerness. "And what?"

I paused once again. How much should I reveal about the king's marriage to Anne? Then I thought, what harm would it do to tell this dying woman the truth? Though in fact, just at that moment, she did not look like a dying woman, she looked aged, and worn, but there was a vitality in her that I had not seen since the days when I served her as her maid of honor.

What harm would it do, I thought again, to tell her the truth? Unless it would awaken her old sorrows. In the end I went ahead.

"Anne gave birth to a—a very odd, abnormal babe that died."

Catherine nodded. "The nun's prophecy. The nun said that Anne's firstborn son would die."

"Yes. And the king is certain that she cannot ever bear a healthy male heir to the throne."

There was silence for a time.

"If he means to be rid of her," Catherine said matter-of-factly, "then there is one certain way."

I waited for her to go on, thinking how satisfying it must be to her to contemplate the removal of her rival, the woman who displaced her and brought her to such depths of humiliation and pain. But then, I had to remind myself, Anne was not the cause of Catherine's downfall, only the instrument of it. It was King Henry who had brought all about—and now he was seeking to repeat what he had done, only with Anne as the victim of his displeasure.

"Before the unfortunate Jane Popyngcort left England," Catherine said, "she confided to me that she knew of a certainty that Henry had slept with not only Anne's sister Mary—which all the world knows—but Anne's mother as well. My advisers told me that under canon law, this incest would make any marriage between Henry and Anne invalid. Jane gave me a written statement swearing to all that she saw and heard, which I have shown to no one but Cardinal Campeggio. It would bear weight if my husband chooses to forswear Anne."

"And there is something else," I added. "Something I myself am prepared to swear. Something I have been keeping hidden in my heart for a long time, waiting for the time when Anne would suffer for the evil she has done."

I told Catherine the story of my love for Galyon, and Anne's attempt to bribe him to lie with her so that she would appear to be carrying the king's child. Of how he confided to me everything Anne said and did, how terrified he was. And then—of how he died. Murdered, I felt sure.

We talked on, of the strong rumors that Anne had arranged the death of Jane Popyngcort, and how Anne had connived with a cook to put poison into Henry Fitzroy's food.

"She is desperate," Catherine said. "She will go to any lengths to get what she wants. But she is only making her situation worse. Before long she will be caught, trapped in her own web. That is the way I have always seen her, as an alluring but deadly spider, sitting at the center of her web, waiting for her victims to come to her. Now she herself must be entrapped. And this time she will not escape."

TWENTY-ONE

THAT summer King Henry, in the best of spirits
and feeling better than he had in some time, threw
aside his golden walking stick and went on progress with the
men closest to him.

Anne was left at home to sulk, and even Madge Shelton—
dimpled, plump Madge who was his favorite playmate—did not
come along when the king rode and hunted with the eager fervor
of a much younger man through the thick forest, returning each
evening with fresh game and a lust for more pleasure.

Week after week the royal progress continued, until at Ned's
invitation the king and his companions came to stay at Wulf Hall,
our family home, where the hunting was excellent in our park
and nearby woods. It was there, one evening, that King Henry
surrounded himself with the men closest to him—Charles
Brandon and Thomas Cromwell, my brother and Nicholas
Carew, Archbishop Cranmer and other churchmen and

attorneys who had played prominent roles in the nullity suit and the breach with Rome.

His purpose, apart from enjoying a night of rousing congeniality, was to bring together those best able to help him in his goal of freeing himself from Anne. And partly because Wulf Hall was my home as much as it was Ned's, and because the king often said that he trusted me and treated me with exceptional fondness, I was among that group gathered in the great hall, though I sat alone and apart from the others, keeping a respectful distance and not thrusting myself forward as Anne would have done, had she been present.

Even the mighty duke of Norfolk was there that night, though the king had always disliked and distrusted him. The duke had made it known that he considered Anne to be a disgrace to her family and that he was displeased with her—indeed with all his Boleyn in-laws. It was this fissure within the duke's family, Ned told me, that led the king to bring Norfolk into his inner circle.

Dining at an end, the wine flowed freely and the king offered toast after toast.

"To Coeurdelion!" he cried, honoring his favorite mount who had miraculously survived the killing murrain. "And to many a joust to come!" He drank, and the others joined him. "As you can see, my bad leg is healing—"

"And your third leg too!" came a bawdy voice, making the others laugh loudly. "No matter what some may say!" Anne's taunts about the king's lack of virility were well known, and had often been heard and repeated.

"Madge would know! Ask Madge! Where is Madge?"

As the guffaws and raucous jokes began to fly around the room I shrank back into my niche off to the side of where the king stood. I was only too conscious of being the only woman present—and only present because the king had asked me to stay. Embarrassed, I worried that the men, who had already drunk quite a lot, might call for women to be brought in for their pleasure, and an orgy might begin. But before that could happen, the king called for quiet and reached into an inner pocket of his doublet.

"I have here," he said, "a tragedy. A play I am writing. I have never written a play before. It is about my wife. It is called *Jezebel*. In it my wife carries on with a hundred men."

Uproarious laughter greeted this remark. Henry had been vilifying Anne to his friends and councilors for months, so the content of his play came as no surprise.

"And now let me tell you my other good news. Crum here"—he indicated the stout, round-faced Cromwell, who grinned—"has brought me a prize!"

Wide double doors opened, and through them came soldiers leading a short, bob-haired man, bound hand and foot and gagged. He struggled against his captors. He was red-faced from terror.

"See what we have here! A Frenchman!"

Whoops of laughter from the men in the room.

"And not just any Frenchman, but a French cook!"

"Is this one of the hundred men?" I heard Charles Brandon ask. He had recently been appointed Great Master of the King's Household.

"This miserable wretch is a cook my wife brought from the court of King Francis." Henry advanced menacingly on the trembling man.

"Imagine what this cook told Crum when he was racked, and stretched, and pulled on the wheel until his limbs were near to being torn from their sockets!" The king paused.

"He confessed that my wife paid him to put a vile Italian concoction in my son's soup! A poison mixture that killed three poor beggars at the gate after they ate of the soup and could have killed Henry Fitzroy as well if he hadn't spat out the awful-tasting stuff!"

"Now then, master cook, how say you to dining on your own Italian dish?"

Henry waved his hand and a tureen was brought, steam rising from the hot liquid inside, and while it was held out to him he took a flask from his pocket and poured the contents into the tureen.

The cook's gag was torn from his mouth, and the bowl held to his lips.

"Here!" King Henry shouted. "Eat! Enjoy!"

The poor man squirmed and struggled, keeping his lips shut tight, trying to turn his head away from the poisoned liquid. He fought so hard I thought his eyes would pop out of his head. I had to look away.

"Well, go on," the king taunted, "we're all waiting!"

Finally he struck the man a blow across the face.

"No? You have no appetite for poison? Then I have no choice but to dispatch you by other means." Now his voice rose to its loudest, most fearsome pitch. "Have this man boiled in oil!" he shouted.

On the king's command guardsmen came forward to seize the retching, slobbering man and drag him away, while the other men in the room clapped and whistled their approval.

"My wife," King Henry was murmuring. "My loving, pure, innocent wife! This is what she has done. This and worse things."

In the aftermath of this drama Cromwell stood once again.

"Let it be understood by all here present," Cromwell said, "that we can do nothing to bring Queen Anne to justice while the princess dowager still lives. There must be no unwanted objection to His Majesty's possible remarriage to a suitable partner."

"But the princess dowager is frail and ill, is she not, Jane?" the king interjected. "When you visited her, she was in failing health, was she not?"

I spoke up. "She was. She is."

"She cannot live out the year, would you not agree?"

I shook my head. "I cannot wish her swiftly out of this world, Your Majesty. I can only pray for her, that the Lord's will be done to preserve her life or take her unto Himself."

The king chuckled and walked over to embrace me fondly. "Spoken like a good daughter of the church, little Jane. Ever loyal and true to your former mistress."

To the others he said, "Crum is right, we must wait for the princess dowager to leave this earth—which should be soon."

But as it happened, Catherine lived on into the winter, and while she yet lived, there took place another startling shift in the expectations of the court.

Changes came tumbling at us quickly, from all sides, as that year of 1535 drew to a close. King Henry, in a sudden reversal that left all his advisers stunned—even my canny brother Ned—made a bargain (a cynical bargain, to be sure) with the emperor and allowed his alliance with the French to fray. Anne trumpeted in triumph that she was pregnant once again. The great oak in Severnake Forest, the tree many said had been planted by William the Norman nearly five hundred years before, fell to earth during a thunderstorm. And most startling of all—Madge Shelton became engaged, not to the king as everyone expected, but to Sir John Everthorpe, an aged man of seventy-one who possessed only a modest estate.

During the Advent season a rumor spread rapidly throughout the court that when King Henry summoned Madge's father and mother into his presence and told them that he intended to make Madge his next queen, they cautioned him not to. With the greatest respect, they confided to him that marriage to their daughter would only lead to disappointment. They had consulted midwives, they said, and the midwives had concluded that Madge was not fertile. She would never bear an heir to the throne. Shortly after this interview Madge's betrothal to Sir John was announced. As the elderly Sir John already had five sons and several dozen grandchildren, Madge's infertility was not an impediment to her future marriage.

"It is all a ruse, to be sure," Bridget told me. "What really happened was that with all the plotting and intrigue around Anne, Madge decided she had no stomach for becoming the king's next victim. The way she put it was, if the king could throw away two wives, why not three? Besides, she said, the king stinks of the sores in his leg, and of the medicines he takes. And he wears spiders to bed. So she got her parents to find her another husband."

All this happened while Anne was boasting that there was a prince in her swelling belly, and Henry was sometimes brooding, sometimes laughing with his fellow conspirators and joking about who the real father of Anne's child might be—if indeed she was carrying a child at all. I did not know what to think. Was the king the father of Anne's child, despite his insistence that he was not? Those of us in her household did believe that she was pregnant, but I dreaded that she might give birth to another monstrous child. And I wanted no part in her coming delivery.

To say that that Advent season was an awkward one would

be far too restrained; it was like the ominous lull before the great storm, a storm that ultimately broke over the court with a fury nothing could tame.

But during that lull my life changed, and all, it seemed, in the twinkling of an eye.

I was spending Christmastide with my family at Wulf Hall when, within days after learning that Madge Shelton was not fit to become his queen, King Henry came to visit me, bringing me a gift—a long rope of gleaming pearls.

"Dear Jane, how charming you look," he began as he placed the lovely pearls around my neck. "These bring out the delicate fairness of your skin." He had never before complimented me on my looks, only on my virtues. And he had never before brought me a gift. I was on my guard at once.

"We have often spoken freely to one another, Jane. I must do so now. Tell me, truthfully, if the royal midwives were to examine you, would they say that you were fertile?"

At first I thought his words must be some sort of outlandish jest. I did not know what to say. I straightened my spine. I straightened my skirt.

"Come, Jane. You must know."

"I have no reason to think they would not," I managed to reply, after looking at the king in puzzlement for another minute.

"I need not tell you why I am asking. I must have a son. I imagined Madge as his mother. Now all that has changed. Madge will not be my wife, and I must go in search of another.

"Here is the vision that haunts me," he continued. "That keeps me wakeful during the long nights. May I share it with you?"

I nodded.

"I die," he began.

"What?"

"In this vision, I die. I could, you know, suddenly, at any time. My leg—it could swell and make me very ill, so ill I couldn't breathe. Or I could have an accident while hunting, or I might lead my armies into battle and be killed.

"After I die, Henry Fitzroy reigns," he went on. "But he is weak, he coughs constantly, and besides, everything seems to frighten him. In my vision, he dies soon after I do. Princess Mary then rules—Elizabeth is far too young—with the imperial army keeping her on the throne. And she overturns everything I have worked for these last ten years. She returns England to popish dominion! She damns my memory! My people hate me!"

"But sire, they hate you now!" I heard myself say, surprised at my own boldness. "Especially those who heeded the prophecies of the Nun of Kent. They whisper that you are the Mouldwarp, the evil bane of England foretold in myth. As long as you and I are speaking freely, then I must tell you, your people still obey you, for the most part, but more and more they are longing for—for a different king."

"All the more reason why I need a strong son. To give them hope."

He took my hand in both of his.

"Jane, can you give me a son? Will you?"

Fearful, I quickly took back my hand, and said the first thing that came into my mind—which was that I would need to talk to Ned.

"I can tell you what your brother will say. He will congratulate you on your cleverness in entrapping the king."

"But I have done nothing to entrap you, Your Majesty. The truth is, I am afraid of you. And I have never thought of marrying except out of love."

"Don't you love me a little bit? I find I have become quite fond of you."

"I have only loved two men in my life, Will Dormer and another who I mourn and who will never return to me. I would be untruthful if I told you I could love you as a husband."

"Perhaps fondness can be enough then."

It took me several hours to begin to regain my composure after my conversation with the king. I had never imagined that I would hear him ask me to become his wife. Me. Jane of Wulf Hall. Sensible Jane. Jane who was not a beauty. Jane who was nearly thirty years old.

Jane who King Henry trusted.

I shook my head, as if trying to restore my reasonableness, my sanity.

And after several hours the idea did not, after all, seem so entirely unreasonable. Assuming I was able to have a healthy child, I might indeed make the king a good wife. I had no noble lineage, but I had no overbearing relatives either. I was not shrill or demanding. I knew the king well and we had never clashed. I would be a quiet, reassuring presence in his life, and unlike Anne, I would be trustworthy.

Yet I wondered, should I do what Madge Shelton had done and find a way to say no to the honor the king was offering me? Was she wiser than I?

So many thoughts rose up to alarm me—memories of King Henry shouting at Catherine, treating her rudely. Denying her comforts in her last illness. He could be so vengeful, so fearsome! Anger seemed to rise in him like a sudden storm, and when angry, he could be cruel. I thought of the ghastly scene I had witnessed, when the king tried to make the wretched French cook drink poison, and then had the man dragged off to be boiled alive. I thought of the executions of monks and friars and other holy men, men of conscience, who had defied the royal will.

What if I married King Henry and then the kingdom was invaded? Or the people rebelled? But then I thought, Ned would protect me. He would foresee danger and make certain I stayed safe.

As the king had predicted, when I went to talk to Ned he was full of praise.

"Just think what this will mean for our family, Jane," was his immediate response. "The Seymours will be raised high. The next king, your son, will bring the blood of the Seymours to the throne. Think how proud all our relatives will be—and how the king will enrich them with honors and offices."

"Including you."

"Especially me. Thank you a hundredfold for what this will mean to me."

"Of course I do not love him," I put in, knowing this would have no effect on Ned, who regarded romantic love as an impediment to happiness rather than as a treasure worth all other treasures combined.

He thought a moment. "You already have a partnership of sorts with the king," he said after a pause. "He trusts you, as you often say. Believe me, trust is essential if two people are to live together and enhance one another's lives instead of causing constant irritation and pain—as I know only too well."

I knew that Ned was referring to the old scandal in our family, our late father's seduction of Ned's wife Cat and Ned's own cruel rejection of his wife and children.

"There is one other thing to consider, Jane," Ned said thoughtfully. "The old king, King Henry's father."

"What about him?"

"He grew—very violent, almost a madman, as he got older. People say our king is going to do the same."

"You imagine King Henry is going mad?"

"Like father, like son."

"But you are nothing like our father, Ned. He was immoral, and did not manage his estates well. He cared nothing for his tenants—"

"True enough, but—"

I had a sudden thought. I interrupted my brother.

"Ned," I went on in a serious tone, "you must understand that if I decide to accept the king's proposal and become queen, there can be no lingering scandal attached to the Seymour name. You will have to come to terms with the family you abandoned, with your wife Cat and your remaining son Henry."

Ned looked over at me, startled. "What do you mean, my remaining son? Not that I could ever be certain that Catherine Fillol's children were mine, you understand—"

"Catherine Fillol Seymour's children," I corrected him. "And what I mean, Ned, is that your two boys were stricken with the sweat eight years ago, and only Henry survived it."

I was amazed at the expression that came over my brother's face. I had never before seen him sorrowful, or remorseful. When he spoke his voice was soft.

"He was my favorite, little John," he said.

I waited, remembering John's pitiable death, the children who had crowded around his bed as he died, the unbearable pathos of that scene, that loss.

"I was there, with him. Will was there too. We did our best to see that both boys recovered, but only Henry was strong enough. Henry has grown into a fine boy, a boy who would do honor to any family. And a boy who resembles you, Ned. You are his father. You and no one else. If I decide to marry the king, will you agree to acknowledge him, and love him as your son?"

My brother, usually so full of pride and confidence, now hung his head and nodded.

"You have my word, Jane. Thank you." And he enfolded me in a rare brotherly embrace.

There was one more visit I needed to make before I gave the king my answer. I rode to Kimbolton once again, bitterly cold though it was and along a road bounded on both sides by deep snowdrifts.

I found the princess dowager very weak, but not too weak to receive me with a smile. Her physician, Michael de la Sa, was courteous but cautioned me that his patient tired very easily and that I must make my visit a short one.

"Caterina," I said, bending down to kiss her cheek, "I have come to ask your blessing. The king has asked me to become his wife."

The old woman gave a slight nod.

"Yes, Jane. I will pray—" She paused for breath. I could tell that her every word was an effort. "I will pray that you give him the son I could not."

She beckoned to Maria de Salinas, and spoke a few halting words to her in Spanish. Maria went to where Catherine's embroidered prie-dieu stood against the wall. She lifted the heavy piece and brought it to me.

"She wants you to have this. She asks that you pray for her soul."

I nodded through my tears, and looked back at the bed. But the princess dowager had fallen asleep before I could tell her goodbye.

TWENTY-TWO

J ANE, dear," Henry said as we rode downriver in
the royal barge, a sharp cold wind whipping up waves
and rain beginning to pelt down around us, "now that we are
agreed together, I want you to come and live in that house."
He pointed to an elegant old stone manor rising up on our left,
with lawn and gardens stretching down to the riverside.

"It was built by my grandmother," he went on, "but she never
lived there herself. It was always a place where visitors stayed,
often foreign visitors. Cardinal Campeggio was lodged there when
he came to preside over the legatine court. Come, I want to show
it to you."

We disembarked at the river stairs and went up onto the
lawn. Lights burned brightly inside the house, and servants
came out to greet us formally, kneeling to the king and bowing
to me. I knew that I had to become accustomed to this, but it
seemed strange; I, Jane, was now a person of consequence. I was
the lady who was going to marry the king.

The house was spacious and pleasant, the furnishings much to my taste. Clearly Henry had gone to some trouble to make certain the arrangements would please me.

"I want you to be comfortable and contented here," he said, "and to stay in this refuge, away from court, until we are married." I had left Anne's household at Christmastide, as soon as I accepted the king's proposal, and had been staying at Wulf Hall. But Henry wanted me closer at hand, close enough so that he could visit me whenever he chose. My new dwelling was perfectly situated to allow me quiet and privacy yet allow him to come and go with ease from Whitehall.

The princess dowager had died peacefully only a few days earlier, just at the start of the new year, and I asked Henry if I might invite some of her former servants and officials to join my household. He was agreeable, and so I began by making Griffith Richards my gentleman usher. Others—gardeners, laundry-women, ewerers and musicians, grooms and pastrycooks—were swiftly added.

There was a great deal to do, and my days were full. I had never before had an entire large household of my own, and though I was familiar with how things were run in the palace, the responsibility for overseeing everything had never been mine. I relied on Griffith Richards and others he chose to appoint the necessary servants and arrange each of the house-hold departments so that they would run smoothly.

Almost from the day Catherine died I was besieged with letters, requests, visits from those eager to receive my favor. The ever-flowing undercurrents of power and influence were swift and efficient; it was apparent to all that with the princess dowager dead, Anne would soon be put aside and I would become the king's wife. It was only a matter of time. I became the focus of attention and ambitious hopes on all sides. And while this did not surprise me, it burdened me. I was after all grieving for Catherine, whom I had loved. And part of me dreaded the new role I would soon be called upon to play.

I dreaded, as well, the events that I knew must soon occur, for there was no doubt that my future husband's purpose was to have Anne condemned and dishonored. How much further than that he intended to go I did not know, and did not want to know.

I welcomed my new household tasks as a way to preoccupy myself so that I was not constantly ruminating on the gossip that came from the court; I tried to shield myself from the conversations of my servants as much as I could. But every time a boat came downriver with supplies for the pantry, or bringing a letter or message or gift from the king, the latest news came with it. I could not even take refuge in the garden, as I hoped to do, for the gardeners exchanged news with the wherrymen and mudlarks and the river was the richest gossip stream of all.

I learned that the king had fallen while riding recklessly in the tiltyard, at Greenwich, and that he had lain senseless for hours. That during those terrible hours all his advisers expected him to die, and made a pact that they would support Henry Fitzroy as his successor, and not Anne's unborn child.

I knew that a few days after the king's remarkable recovery from his accident, Anne's pains had begun, even though her baby was not expected for many months, and that the tiny un-formed thing had not lived. I heard what was being said after that stillbirth, that the curse of the Nun of Kent still lay over Anne and would never leave her.

Not long after Anne's sad disappointment the king came to visit me, bringing me jewels and pouches of gold coins and almost an entire bargeload of silks and velvets, lengths of lace and gold and silver trimmings.

"Thank heaven you are well recovered from your fall, sire," I told him after he had kissed and embraced me, smiling happily. "Your recovery is a gift to your people."

He brushed aside my reference to his alarming accident. "As you may have noticed, I'm a tough old bird, and hard to kill. It would take more than a horse falling on top of me to send me out of this world."

"Is that so?" I teased. "I seem to recall you telling me just the opposite not long ago."

I saw that he enjoyed the teasing, though as we walked up to the house across the broad lawn I noticed that he was once again limping on his sore leg, and he seemed a bit unsteady, holding my arm as we went along.

"Let us speak of happier things. Of our wedding, and the life we will share together. It is high time you ordered your wedding dress, and the gowns for your attendants. What say you to a wedding mass in church? Or would you rather a quiet ceremony at Whitehall, in the queen's closet?"

"Whatever would please you, sire."

"That's my good girl." He rubbed his hands together, always a sign that he was in good spirits, and ordered the barge of fine stuffs unloaded. It pleased him to lift the lengths of cloth and trim from their baskets and hold them up to the light so that their colors shone forth and the metallic trims shed tiny sparks of fire.

"How lovely you will look as my bride, Jane," he went on. "I will be very proud to stand beside you when we repeat our vows."

"Henry," I began—but he put his large hand over my lips before I could go on.

"I know what you want to say, my dearest Jane. It troubles you that Anne must soon face her accusers in court and be brought to justice. That our marriage must wait until she has paid for her treasons."

I almost blurted out what I was thinking, which was, at that moment, "This is a marriage that will be made in blood," but I held my peace.

I looked into Henry's eyes, and saw there what I had always seen: high intelligence, slyness, warmth, self-satisfaction, and ruthlessness. We knew one another well enough to guess each other's thoughts.

"Is there no other way?" I finally asked.

He looked down at the roll of silk in his hands.

"No, Jane. There isn't. She must meet her fate. But you need not witness it, or be a part of it. You are blameless. I want no shadows over our marriage."

"Nor do I."

He took both my hands in his, a gesture he often used when we were together.

"Think of me, Jane, not of your former mistress with her many transgressions. Rejoice with me. I feel as if I have been freed from a dark enchantment. As if I have come out from hell into heaven. And you, my dear, are my good angel."

On the morning that Mr. Skut came to measure me for my wedding dress the river was filled with boats and the roads were clogged with people.

"They say she's to die this morning," Mr. Skut remarked. "The queen that was. I never thought ill of her, myself. But then, she liked my designs. She favored me."

I tried to shut out the sounds I was hearing, and did not encourage Mr. Skut to tell me any more. But the many voices, the galloping horses and drums beating, the noise of shouting and cheering that reached us faintly but unmistakably from upriver left me in no doubt about what was happening there, at the Tower. Every time I tried to speak of something other than the fate of Queen Anne Mr. Skut brought our conversation back to the dread topic.

"I hear that many were suspected of having treasonable relations with her," he said. "George Taylor, her receiver, and the sewer of her chamber, Henry Webb, and Thomas Wyatt and Richard Page. Imagine! There were said to be dozens of men, she even hid them in her sweetmeats closet."

I shook my head. "That is only gossip. I do believe she was guilty of crimes, but while I served as her maid of honor there were no men in her sweetmeats closet!"

"None that you knew of, anyway," said Mr. Skut. "They say she was clever. She probably hid them from you."

He held up a length of shimmering cloth.

"What do you say to this pale peach satin for the bodice, and this darker rose damask for the skirt?" he asked after a time. "The king sent me a message to say that he prefers to see you in stuffs of pink or peach."

"I am happy to choose what my husband prefers."

Mr. Skut sighed. "In that you are certainly unlike the queen that was. Whenever I made a gown for her, she always chose the colors the king liked least. Just to spite him, I always thought."

I had nothing to say to that.

"You'd do well not to cross him, you know," the dressmaker added. "He greatly dislikes women who cross him."

"Yes, I know."

He worked on in silence for a time. At length he said, "It was her uncle, you realize. His Grace the Duke of Norfolk, who presided at her trial. They say he shed tears when she was condemned, but I don't believe it. After all, he knew she was guilty. There were even stories from the French court to say she had lovers there too. Do you suppose she did?"

"I can't say." I was thinking of Galyon. She had certainly wanted him—though whether she lusted after him or merely believed he could give her a child who had the same coloring as King Henry I would never know.

Galyon! Surely she deserved to die for what she had done to him. She was paying the price of killing him, or of forcing him to jump to his death. Anne dies this day for killing my beloved, I said to myself. Her death is a just punishment.

"What do you say to gold tassels from Flanders, to trim the hem of the skirt?" Mr. Skut was asking. "I have some very handsome ones, very costly. The king told me I was to spare no expense in the making of this gown."

I nodded. "Then let us have the gold tassels, by all means. After all, this is my one and only wedding day."

Hearing this, Mr. Skut suddenly stopped what he was doing and smiled at me.

"May I say, Mistress Seymour, how very glad I am that your joyous wedding day is coming at last. I could never have imagined, when you asked me to put away the gown I was making for you years ago—the blue and cream one, you remember—I could never have imagined that one day I would be creating a wedding gown for your marriage to the king. It is a very great pleasure for me, as well as an honor."

"Thank you, Mr. Skut. I could never have imagined this either. But let us hope and pray it is for the best. I will certainly have the finest and most beautiful wedding dress ever seen at this court."

The king sent at least a dozen midwives to examine me, and all judged me to be fit to carry the next heir to the throne. He also sent astrologers to cast my horoscope, and they concluded that my future held nothing but favorable events.

There was only one shadow across the sunny slope of our forthcoming marriage, and at the time I thought little of it.

On the night before our wedding the king held a banquet, joking with me that it was in celebration of his "last night of freedom."

I felt a sliver of fear enter my heart at those words.

"What do you mean, my lord?" I asked him as gently as I could. "Are you thinking you are about to be ensnared?" I remembered what he had said when I told him I needed to talk to Ned. He had said that Ned would congratulate me for having ensnared him.

"Only entangled in your golden web, my Jane," was his light answer, but I sensed a faint edge of rancor that troubled me.

"If you like," I went on, "we can wait to marry until the harvest season. You can enjoy your freedom all summer long."

But he only pulled me to him with a friendly hug, holding me so tightly against him that the large jeweled pendant I wore around my neck felt as if it were boring into my flesh.

"I will wed you now," he said with force. "Not later. And I will have no other."

Yet at the banquet, I saw that he singled out two very pretty young girls, sisters, and paid them very marked attention. They were the daughters of Sir Richard Wigmore, blond and dimpled like Madge Shelton, but far younger and more slender, with a shyness that I knew appealed to the king.

He flirted with both girls and danced with them. (I am a poor dancer, as I am quick to admit, and prefer not to display my clumsiness in front of the court; the king spares me this embarrassment.) But he continued to laugh and joke with them, standing not far from me all the while, until I began to feel left out. I had often seen him do this with Anne, deliberately ignoring and snubbing her while he was entirely preoccupied with another woman. I had seen him do the same thing with Catherine when I first came to court. In those instances his purpose was clear: he meant to wound, and to indicate his displeasure.

I wondered, was I mistaken? Was I misinterpreting his attentions to the girls? Was it possible he meant no insult to me at all, but was merely in high spirits and demonstrating his excess of delight by carrying on a mock wooing? Was he eager to show the court how lusty he was, not only with his bride-to-be but with young girls?

Then I overheard a comment that stung.

Ambassador Chapuys was walking past, close enough to me so that his words reached me. He was talking to a younger man, Charles Stansbie, one of the king's new privy chamber gentlemen, a man I did not know, and they were laughing together. He spoke confidingly, in low tones, but there was a lull in the music at that moment and my hearing is keen. I was well able to hear what he was saying.

"She's nothing, raised from nothing," he said. "She was just the first womb to come along."

Of course the ambassador was speaking about me. I was certain of it.

Tears sprang to my eyes, though I swiftly brushed them away. Was this what the court thought of me? And much more important, was it true? Had Henry reached for me, once he was certain that Anne could not bear his son, simply because I was fertile, and safe, and convenient? Because he believed I would be—unlike Anne—submissive and loyal?

The king was approaching, and I hastily dabbed at my eyes once again so that he would not see that I had been crying. Before he reached me he turned back to the two sisters.

"Farewell, girls," he called out cheerily. "I only wish I had met you before I chose Mistress Seymour to wed!" They laughed, and so did he, and I did my best to join in. I told myself he meant only to flatter the girls, not to belittle me. His tone was light and bantering, not at all lascivious.

Yet I felt a pang. Somehow I knew that deep down, my husband-to-be meant what he said. Even now, on the night before our wedding, he was beginning to regret being caught in my web, and wanting to free himself from its choking toils.

TWENTY-THREE

OUR wedding was a quiet one, held in the queen's closet at Whitehall, very early in the morning. It was Maytime, and the small room was full of flowers and greenery, with leafy boughs adorning the walls and tall urns filled with sweet-smelling blossoms. Henry brought me a wreath of peach blossoms to wear in my hair, which I wore long and loose, falling to my waist, the way he liked it best.

My wedding gown was much admired, as I was sure it would be, and the few guests and witnesses who attended the ceremony said kind things about my appearance although I was certain they would have been far more effusive had Madge Shelton been there in my place.

"My sweet, shy girl," was all Henry said as he kissed my cheek. "Now we are one, and we can look forward to having a large family."

Our own family relationship—our blood kinship—had been a last-minute problem before the ceremony. The royal genealogist had discovered that we were cousins, related in the third degree of affinity; had we still been under the authority of the Bishop of Rome we would have needed a papal dispensation in order to be married. But as the Bishop of Rome no longer had any authority in England, Henry dismissed this as a minor hindrance, and it was ignored.

Out of all the women in my new royal household, I chose three to be my wedding attendants: Bridget Wingfield, Anne Cavecant and—after obtaining the king's permission—my former sister-in-law Catherine Fillol Seymour. As it turned out, however, only Bridget was able to attend me, which she did, dutifully, a tight smile on her feral face. She did what I asked of her, loyally, but with misgivings. Anne Cavecant was too ill; the tumor in her side had grown larger and appeared to be sapping her strength and energy. And as for Cat, when I wrote to her asking her to join in my wedding she sent a message back to say that she would be prevented from attending me but needed to see me and hoped I would receive her. I agreed without hesitation.

When she arrived I was surprised by her appearance. She was wearing the gown, wimple and veil of a novice. She was taking her vows at the convent of St. Agnes's.

She knelt and I raised her up and reached out to embrace her.

"Cat, my dear Cat, let me look at you! I always thought you might take the veil. I hope you will be blessed in your vocation."

She kissed me and wished me happiness in my marriage to the king.

"Our abbess has allowed me to leave the convent in order to come here and speak to you, Jane," she said when we had settled ourselves. "I have come to appeal to your piety and goodness." She paused, then went on. "We have learned that the king intends to close St. Agnes's and sell the property. He believes the selling price will be high because of our sainted sister

Elizabeth, known to all as the Nun of Kent, and the holy essence of her life and miracles that resides in the convent. It is truly a blessed place, a holy place. It must not fall into secular hands. It must not be defiled.

"We cherish one special relic of the holy Elizabeth," she went on. "A relic that has worked many miracles and continues to heal and restore the sick and dying even now, even though the blessed nun is no longer among the living. We believe that something of her power continues to reside in this relic. If it is moved or disturbed its powers may be diminished."

"Perhaps any new owner of the convent will respect the relic as you do," I said, knowing full well how unlikely that was.

"If only we could be certain of that," Cat said. "If only we novices and sisters could continue to live in the convent and fulfill our vocations. I appeal to you, Jane, as the king loves you, convince him to keep our house open and not sacrifice it as he has so many others."

Cat's plea struck a chord with me, for though I have no Romish tendencies and am a true daughter of the church in its new form, I regard the mysteries of the divine with awe. And among those mysteries are the miracles performed at sacred shrines.

I was well aware that my husband was ordering the destruction of more and more religious houses and that many were being dismantled or converted to secular manors. Ned had described to me how the sales of these former church lands were enriching the royal treasury a hundredfold. The treasury clerks called the newfound riches "monks' money," Ned said with a smile.

Ned himself had profited when King Henry gave him several former priories with many acres of farmland. My brother was not only richer than ever since my marriage, he had received the title of Viscount Beauchamp. He did not flaunt his newfound dignity, but I knew it made him proud. To his credit, he kept his word where his son Henry was concerned and took the boy into his household as he had promised me he would. In time, I hoped, the Seymour estates, honors and "monks' money" would pass to my nephew.

Though Cat's message and the plight of the religious houses concerned me, I had to confess that I too had profited from the transfer of church lands into the royal coffers. On my marriage to the king he had greatly enriched me by granting me more than a hundred manors plus the wardship of five castles and much forest land as well. Among these properties were former monastic houses and estates. The scope of this gift was too great for me to comprehend at first, but over time I became accustomed to the fact that as queen I was a very wealthy woman and I set my almoners the happy task of distributing alms with lavish abandon.

The beggars that gathered morning and evening at the palace gates, the poor of London that congregated in St. Paul's churchyard, the needy in villages near the capital all came to expect generosity from "good Queen Jane," as they began to call me, and it gladdened my heart to be able to ease their want, if only a little.

But at the same time I knew, and greatly regretted, that more than a little of the wealth the king had bestowed on me was "monks' money" and now I was learning from Cat that the convent of St. Agnes's might soon be turned to profit and torn down along with so many other religious houses.

"Dear Cat, I will do all I can," I assured the anxious woman opposite me. Yet even as I said the words I felt my heart sink. All my instincts told me that to King Henry, St. Agnes's was just another religious house to be closed up and sold to the highest bidder, the profits used to increase the royal treasury.

Henry was drawing up plans for our summer progress. We

would go where the game was abundant, for hunting was the king's chief preoccupation during the summer season. But we would not go far, he assured me, as he did not want me to tire myself and he hoped that I would soon give him the good news that I was expecting a child.

It was, of course, what I hoped as well. I wanted above all things to be able to give Henry a son—two sons, a whole quiverful of children if the Lord favored us. And in the earliest weeks of our marriage, the doubts I had had about the king's ability to sire children began to dissolve. I remembered only too well what Anne had said about Henry's lack of virility, but when he came to my bed he proved to be lusty and energetic in his lovemaking. To use one of his own favorite phrases, he entered the lists of love and conquered.

"How like you this pastime, my shy Jane?" he asked me when he had satisfied himself and reached for his bedside goblet of wine.

I always assured him that his love made me a happy and contented wife—and invariably added that I hoped to be a mother soon. This seemed to be what he needed to hear, and having heard it, he rolled his expanding girth away from me and was soon snoring.

To be sure, I cannot write here all that I truly felt. Having known the beauty and richness of Galyon's love I found King Henry's diligent but uninspired rutting (for that is what it was, pure animal lust) lacking in pleasure. And certainly lacking in wooing, affection, tenderness, the deep connection that makes two loving hearts and bodies one. I had known this—and having known it, no other man could ever offer it to me again. Or so I believed.

The most I hoped for in my marriage to the king was that we could create an heir to the throne together, and then a brother for him, and then—whatever fortune sent us. I hoped the astrologers were right, and we would be favored.

Our departure for the countryside was delayed so that a vital task could be begun: the intricate planning and arrangements for my coronation. Henry told me he wanted my coronation festivities to be the grandest spectacle offered to Londoners for many years.

"Grander than Anne's coronation?" I asked. I remembered Anne's coronation festivities only too vividly, the elaborate pageants, the hundreds of boats on the river, the soldiers and musicians—and the near silent crowds along the roadsides, withholding their cheers of approbation because of their disapproval of Anne.

"Far grander," the king said. "And far more joyful. I want this to be the most splendid coronation of a queen ever, in fact. I will write the music myself. We will have—ten pageants, no, a dozen pageants. I have always wanted to design a grand pageant of the muses. The nine muses." He stroked his chin thoughtfully. "Just imagine! Nine lovely women, each lovelier than the one before—"

For a time he was lost in his imaginings.

"You could be Calliope, Jane. The chief of the muses. Except that she was a singer and you can't sing a note."

He was right, I had no singing voice. I tended rather to croak like a frog.

"Never mind! We will find someone to sit near you and sing for you. And Madge can be Erato, the muse of love poetry—"

"Why Madge? Why not Bridget? Or one of my other matrons of honor?" I did not want Madge Shelton, my husband's former lover, brought to court to be near him again. Even though she was married, I could not be certain he would restrain his lust for her, and I had no illusions about his fidelity to me. We had not married for love, merely out of fondness, and I was all too aware that King Henry had never been faithful to any woman, certainly not his wives.

"Very well then, Bridget. It hardly matters. And Frances, that pretty young daughter of Lord Wycherley, the one that dances so lightly on her feet, she would do very well for Terpsichore." He went on, happily matching each of the muses with an attractive lady of the court, until I urged him to stop.

"But don't you see, this will be the finest display ever offered to the people of London. They will surely love it—and love me. You'll see, Jane. I'll bring in the King's Works to build the nine stages. All my painters and craftsmen will be put to this one task. We'll have children's choirs and acrobats and players—"

He broke off, and looked at me intently. "Jane, what do you think of this idea? Shall I present my play? My *Jezebel*? I haven't finished it, of course. I would have to complete it, rehearse all the players, find the actors to play Anne's hundred lovers—"

I shook my head. "Better not include any reminders of the past."

"Yes, you are right. Of course. I'll just ask Crum what he thinks."

I felt certain Master Cromwell would agree with me that to present a play about the late queen would be distasteful. I hoped the king would not pursue this ghoulish whim.

At last the coronation arrangements were decided upon and set in motion, and toward the end of June we left on our journey, our progress slow because of the hundreds of carts and wagons, our large mounted escort, the heavy trunks and baskets and chests needed to transport and supply the royal household, which was immense—larger than at any time in my years at court. The king's hunting tent alone, with its trappings and furnishings, took twenty carts to move from place to place, though he used it rarely.

We traveled first to Dover Castle where Henry walked over every inch of the massive fortifications, making certain all was in good repair. Dover would be a natural landing point for an invading army, he wanted no fallen masonry or hidden tunnels underground to allow an enemy to seize the fortress and bring foreign soldiers onto English soil. After a few days of hunting we moved on, through pouring rain along flooded roads, to Rochester, then to a series of manor houses whose owners did their best to accommodate us all.

The hunting was poor, and the king was in a sour mood. Yet I approached him in hopes he would divert our journey and allow me to visit St. Agnes's.

"Sire, I would like to ask whether, of your goodness, you would allow me to go to the convent of St. Agnes's, where there is a wonder-working relic of Elizabeth Barton. I should like to make a pilgrimage there to ask the Lord to make me fruitful."

"Elizabeth Barton? The damnable Nun of Kent?"

"Many women who are barren say that after a visit to her shrine they bear fine sons."

Henry looked skeptical. "The Nun of Kent was a creature of the imperialists. She was wicked."

"Nonetheless, if you will grant me this favor, I would also like to take my maid of honor Anne Cavecant, who suffers greatly from the swelling in her side."

His eyes glazed over. He was tired. He started to say no, then gave in to weariness.

"If you must, Jane," he said with a wave of his hand. "But I do not like you paying tribute to this false prophetess. You are queen now, what you do and say is watched and heard. Your every word and deed ought to do honor to the throne, not appear to oppose it. And everyone knows I had the Nun of Kent put to death for her treasons."

I was warned, nevertheless I went ahead, aware that I took pleasure in doing what I chose despite my husband's objection. Aided by my servants I bundled Anne Cavecant into a wagon and made the short journey to the convent.

I found the courtyard of St. Agnes's crowded with pilgrims, all hoping to touch the golden reliquary that held a bloody rag torn from the linen shift worn by the nun on the day she was executed. In that rag, I was assured, lay a wondrous divine power.

My arrival caused a commotion. People swarmed around me, calling out "Good Queen Jane!" and wanting favors, asking for alms, or begging me to speak to the king on their behalf. I was becoming accustomed to these pleas and requests, and to having people thrust written petitions in front of me. I acknowledged the petitioners as graciously as I could, but tried not to let myself be distracted. I had come to the convent to see Cat—and also in hopes that my maid of honor would benefit from the healing power of the shrine.

I entered the convent and made my way to the room that held the golden reliquary, ordering my servants to bring Anne in after me and put her down on a pallet beside the shrine. She was pale and still, her eyes closed, her breathing shallow. For weeks I had had the feeling that she did not have long to live, though the royal physician, when he examined her, would say only that she was dropsical and that he had no medicine to give her.

A peaceful, serene feeling came over me as I sat in the small room. I felt my muscles relax and my worries fall away. A sweet sense of repose and a stirring of hope began to envelop me. Around me, others came and went—a young mother with a crying baby, a woman leading a blind man, couples leaning on each other, one poor soul who crawled on his knees slowly and painfully up to the reliquary—but I remained quietly undisturbed. Only when I heard my name whispered and saw Cat, her grey nun's habit enveloping her, kneeling respectfully beside me did I awaken from my welcome restfulness.

I was quick to embrace her.

"Dearest Jane—I mean Your Highness—"

"Please, Cat, let us be sisters, as in the past, with no formalities between us."

She smiled. "Then, sister dear, will you come with me to the arbor, where we can talk?"

She led me into a small garden where the quietude was interrupted only by the coming and going of other nuns. I told her about her son Henry, how Ned had taken him into his household and was doing his best to be a benevolent guardian to him.

"We owe you a great deal, Jane," Cat said. "If it weren't for you, I would still be locked in a cell, and who knows what sort of life Henry would have had?" Neither of us mentioned John, but I felt sure we were both thinking of him.

Cat paused a moment, then took a deep breath.

"Jane," she said earnestly, "can you save our convent? Can you save St. Agnes's?"

"I don't know. I haven't yet spoken to the king about it. I must tread carefully, and choose the right time to approach him. He has convinced himself that all monasteries and convents are dens of vice, and deserve to be destroyed. That he profits from their destruction seems to him almost a virtue." I sighed. "He is clever at logic. He can argue that a sunny day is a thunderstorm, and be convincing."

"And he is not entirely wrong," Cat admitted. "There has been wrongdoing and vice among the monks and nuns, assuredly. But the religious houses have always done much good as well. I have seen it, and am now part of a community of sisters that carry out their charitable mission with great diligence. The convent of St. Agnes's has been a refuge for hungry villagers when crops failed. A shelter for frightened serfs when their overlords were fighting. This house has stood, a bastion of mercy, a symbol of God's love amid human want and cruelty, for nearly three centuries. And a miracle-working shrine. If the king orders it sold, and the new owners tear it down—as they surely will— what will take its place? Where will the villagers go for help and shelter? And for healing? For there is healing within these walls, Jane. I have witnessed it."

"I will try to be as eloquent with my husband as you have been," I told Cat. "I will do my best."

We returned to the room where Anne Cavecant lay inert on her pallet. We knelt together to say our prayers, and afterward Cat left and I stayed on, lost in quiet meditation, savoring once again the atmosphere in the room, the serenity and absence of worldly concerns. When evening came I was offered hospitality for the night and slept on a hard bed under a light blanket, though the night air held a chill.

On the following morning I went to Anne and saw, to my delight, that she had a faint hint of color in her cheeks. She opened her eyes and seemed to welcome the ministrations of my servants who bathed and dressed her and offered her food. Hour by hour she seemed to grow stronger before my eyes as she was laid once again on her pallet before the reliquary and I resumed my vigil nearby. I was all but unaware of the passage of time, so happily intent was I on watching her grow stronger, her eyes brighter, her body beginning to quiver with renewed animation.

On the following day she sat up and tried to walk, no longer hampered by severe pain, and I saw a strength in her halting movements that I had not seen in a very long time. And beyond this—wonder of wonders—when she let me touch her side, I could feel that the tumor was no longer as large as it had been, nor as tender. In the privacy of my sleeping room she opened her bodice and showed me, quite unashamedly, the place where the large swelling had been. All that was left was a reddened pustule the size of a walnut.

"Thanks be to God!" I cried out, disturbing the nuns' silence. But I was happily forgiven and Cat brought her sisters in to witness the remarkable healing Anne had undergone.

The following morning we left to rejoin the royal party on progress, feeling what I can only describe as a holy joy. I was certain that the power of the divine had enveloped us, a power that resided in the place where the Nun of Kent had lived, and seemed still to reside there. I prayed for the fortitude to convince the king to preserve that holy place, so that others might honor it and receive the blessings of healing in generations to come.

When, shortly afterward, we rejoined the traveling court I lost no time in taking Anne Cavecant to see the king. I found him sitting by a window surrounded by his dogs and his fewterers, watching the rain pour down and spoil his day's hunting. Anne was full of smiles and glowing with health. The contrast between her former torpor and her present vigor could not have been more startling, and the king had to acknowledge it.

"I am truly glad to see you looking so well," he said to Anne, doing his best to adopt a courteous tone, "and I hope your recovery continues. I only wish there was a cure for my damnable leg!" he added darkly.

"You must go to St. Agnes's, sire," Anne blurted out. "The shrine will do you good."

The look he gave her was full of irritation.

"Faith needs no shrine, girl," he said sharply. "It is your faith that has restored you. The Lord and your faith. Not some dead nun."

Anne left us then, at a signal from me, and slipped quietly out of the room. I should probably have left with her, given my husband's frame of mind and the nervous edginess he always displayed when his leg pained him, but I was still overflowing with amazement and happiness at Anne's healing. I felt an urgency to open my heart and mind to Henry about it. I allowed my exuberance to overcome my good sense.

"With your permission, sire," I said to my husband, indicating that I wanted to sit opposite him. He gave a slight nod.

Though it was not easy to contain myself, I was silent for a time, waiting for the right moment to speak. Henry sat looking out at the rain, his hand idly stroking the heads of his big dogs, who came up to be petted, tongues lolling.

"Does it really matter, sire, how Anne's cure came about?" I said quietly. "All I know is that she was put before the shrine, near death, and now she is thriving. Who can say what divine alchemy was at work? Do you not believe that holy relics gather spiritual force?"

"So do demons. So do witches." He was gruff. He did not look at me, but continued to scratch the dogs' ears and glare out at the rain. Suddenly he stood, shakily, and wincing from pain. He began to walk out of the room, then turned back to me.

"It matters not, in any case," he snapped. "St. Agnes's has been sold to Sir Henry Bedingfield. It will be torn down within the month."

"No! It must not be!" I rose to my feet and quickly knelt before Henry, my hands clasped in supplication.

"The convent is a holy place. Unlike any other. Hundreds of people have been cured there. I have felt the healing power of the Lord there. I saw with my own eyes how Anne was restored. It is wondrous. It is—like a resurrection. A holy resurrection. A miracle—you must not destroy the miracle—" I was beginning to babble in my earnestness.

"No more!" the king roared. "Do not provoke me, Jane! I have no stomach for an argument!" His color rising, he looked around the room. "Where is my damned walking stick?"

One of the grooms ran out of the room.

"Get up!"

I got to my feet. My face was wet with tears, my heart pounding. I could feel that my headdress was askew.

"You and your prie-dieu! You and your pious prayers!" He spat, and the dogs, alarmed, scattered. "Don't you know anything? Have you lived at court all these years and been so blind? Can't you understand that the money that comes into my treasury from the sale of these criminous houses, these fonts of evil, where sin and lechery have gone on unchecked for centuries— can't you understand that this wealth is keeping the armies of the emperor from overrunning our realm? How do you imagine our soldiers are equipped and our fortresses repaired? Do you think the coins just fall from the sky, like manna from heaven?

"If you must pray, Jane, then get down on your knees and pray for guns, and ships, and arms for the trained bands, and mercenaries from over the sea! That's the only kind of miracle

England requires! The monks and nuns with their precious relics can go to the bottom of the ocean for all I care!"

The groom who had run out came rushing back, short of breath, carrying the king's gold walking stick and handing it to his master, who grasped it roughly.

I moved aside to let my furious husband pass, thrusting his stick into the rushes as if the imperial enemy were underfoot.

"Damned meddling!" I heard him mutter as he went out the door. "You can forget about a coronation. I have no taste for it now!"

TWENTY-FOUR

IN the middle of a dark night that summer, while we were staying at the manor of Colehill, we heard the creaking and trundling of a cart being pulled into the courtyard.

Henry awakened me, full of apprehension. We heard the voices of guardsmen in the courtyard, went to the window and saw torches being lit and the household being roused. The crescent moon hung low in the sky and I could tell it would not be dawn for some hours.

One of the privy chamber gentlemen knocked quietly on our chamber door and told the king he was needed urgently in the stables. Waving away the other servants, the king in his night-shirt and I in my robe, bedclothes wrapped around us for warmth, we made our way outside and across the courtyard to where the rough-looking cart, filled with straw, lay half hidden under the eaves.

As we watched, the straw was lifted to reveal a long leaden cylinder, unadorned and unmarked.

"It is the prince," the chamber gentleman said in a low voice. "Your instructions have been followed. The body will be taken to Thetford and buried there."

"Was there a priest with him, at the end?"

"I do not know, sire. He was very ill. I was told there was almost nothing left of him."

I saw my husband's shoulders droop at those somber words.

"Get on then," he said after a time. "No ceremony, no headstone. Put him in the crypt. It is consecrated ground." He turned aside, without pausing to watch, as the straw was replaced atop the plain leaden form and the cart was driven away.

The sickly Henry Fitzroy had finally died, his sudden death casting a pall over our traveling household. My husband had given orders that there be no official acknowledgment of his passing; it would not do, he said, to alert his enemies to the fact that he had no male heir, legitimate or otherwise, and that both twenty-year-old Mary and three-year-old Elizabeth had been declared bastards by Parliament.

All eyes were turned to me. Why wasn't I carrying the king's child? Was there something wrong with me? Were the sovereign and the realm to be disappointed yet again?

We had been married only a short time, I wanted to say to those who cast furtive looks at my belly. Soon. It will happen soon. I knelt on Catherine's prie-dieu and prayed for the grace to give my husband a son.

For he was suddenly full of dread. The death of Henry Fitzroy had quickened his everpresent superstitious fears, making him believe that the curse of the Nun of Kent had not been lifted by her execution, even as the blessing of her healing power continued to flow through her relics.

"I should never have sold it, should I Jane," he said as we dined together. On the previous night Henry Fitzroy's body had been brought to the manor where we were staying, and although we had been prepared to move on to our next destination Henry had decided not to go. He needed to rest, he said. He needed to recover for a day or two from hearing the grave news of his son's passing. So we stayed on, and at midday we sat down to eat.

"I am right, am I not? It was a terrible mistake to sell that convent."

I saw that the food set before my husband on silver platters had hardly been touched, the meat still in a juicy mound, the loaf of fine white manchet still whole, the goblet of wine nearly full. His usually rosy face was grey, as grey as the skies that had remained cloudy for many days on end during our lengthy progress. The lines around his eyes and mouth seemed to have deepened in the wake of his bereavement, his whole face sagged with the weight of his grief and loss.

"Are you listening to me, Jane?" he snapped. "How can you eat? Why aren't you in mourning for the lost prince? Why aren't you dressed in black?"

I put down my knife and my morsel of bread. I wiped my hands and mouth with my napkin, then smoothed the skirt of my tawny gown.

"Forgive me, Your Majesty, but you said you did not want any of us to wear mourning for the prince, or hold any funeral or even say prayers over his grave at Thetford."

"I know what I said! Put on a black gown at once! That tawny one offends me."

I did as he asked, hoping that in the time it took me to dress he might recover his composure. But when I returned to the table clothed in black velvet and resumed my seat, it was evident that his foul mood persisted. He glared at me.

"Well? Have you nothing to say?"

"I have done as you asked, sire. As you see. I have put on mourning."

"But have you nothing to say about the convent?"

"Only that I wish it had not been sold."

The king rose from the heavy oak table, grasping it by the edges as he did so and making the table shake. My wine goblet tipped over.

"Why didn't you say so before!" It was a demand, not a question. Knowing that no matter what I said or did, my husband's anger would not abate, I rose to go.

"If Your Majesty will give me leave," I began.

"Sit down, Jane, and answer me."

Praying inwardly for patience, I sat down again. To my relief, the king did too.

"I did try to convince you that St. Agnes's should not be sold. But you paid no attention. In fact you were angry with me, as you are now."

"You should have tried harder," he grumbled—but his tone was less harsh. He filled a goblet with wine and drank it off. "Don't you see what you have done? By failing to convince me you have allowed the very thing to happen that I most feared. You have caused the wrath of the nun to fall on me. You may have caused the royal line of the house of Tudor to come to an end."

This was more than I could endure. More than any wife should have had to endure. I stiffened.

"I failed! I allowed your son to die! I think, sire, that you are the one who has failed! You failed to listen to my pleas. You failed to heed the warnings of the Nun of Kent! Or to respect the divine power she possessed. I did nothing but be your loving and obedient wife. You cannot blame me!"

As I spoke the king looked at me, at first quizzically, then with growing surprise and interest.

"Jane! Such fire! I have never seen you so aroused. But it matters not whether you are tart or meek; all that matters now is that I have disturbed the shrine of that vengeful, hateful woman Elizabeth Barton, and she has punished me by cursing my son and killing him."

He thought a moment. "And no doubt she has cast one of her spells on you, Jane, to make you barren."

"I am not barren!" I insisted loudly. "The midwives have assured me that I can have children. Surely it is only a matter of time. We have been married only a few months."

"Prize cows are in calf as soon as they are bred."

"And prize bulls do not breed sickly heifers who die before their time!"

I spoke without thinking. As soon as I heard the words come from my mouth I clamped my hand over my lips. I could feel my face growing hot. How could I have allowed such bitter words to pass my lips? And with the king in pain and mourning his son.

"Never mind, Jane," Henry said presently, his tone bleak. "I am being punished. What are a few unkind words compared to my grieving—and my dread of our future?"

Sad as the prince's death was, and alarming as my own failure to conceive seemed, there was worse to come, and darker threats to follow. For in the fall, after we had returned to the capital and the weather began to turn cold, messengers arrived with the alarming news that Lincolnshire had risen in revolt, and the nearby counties were smoldering into rebellion as well.

There were protests and marches, armed assaults and angry demonstrations by those who called themselves pilgrims but were no better, the king said angrily, than rebels and traitors who deserved to be hanged. Day after day the reports came in, of banner-carrying pilgrims—their protests encouraged by Ambassador Chapuys and his sinister ally Father Bartolome—who condemned the destruction of the monasteries and wanted a return to the old religious ways. Mythic prophecies about the end of time, stories about King Henry and his wickedness were spread, along with tales of new taxes and harsher laws. And as the unrest grew, there were assaults, tax collectors and royal officials were murdered, towns and villages laid under siege.

It was feared that the entire north of England, and possibly Scotland too, would soon become a lawless wilderness where the king's authority had no weight and misrule prevailed.

Henry fumed and shouted and even threatened to go to the north himself at the head of an army, but the rebellion continued to grow—and to grow increasingly dangerous to the security of the realm. Ned warned that the peril was greater than Henry realized, cautioning him that an imperial army was gathering in Flanders and that the Scots might soon come down in force to join the rebels.

Meanwhile there was no legitimate heir to the throne, and I could feel the eyes watching me, waiting for the grace of motherhood to descend on me—or, as the more vulgar among my husband's subjects said, for the king himself to descend on me and make me pregnant.

As the deep snows arrived to blanket the north and make the roads impassable, the rebels retreated, placated by false assurances that Parliament would settle their grievances. I was by this time beside myself with worry. I was all but convinced that my husband, for all his efforts in bed—efforts which left him winded and red-faced, panting from his exertions, while I still did not conceive—was lacking in virility. Anne had been right all along in saying that he had no force or strength. Either that, or the curse of the nun fell across our bed and made it impossible for me to bear a child.

Ice began to form along the edges of the Thames, and day by day its thin crust spread inward toward the onrushing center of the river, the ice thickening faster than the tides could sweep it away. Vendors set up booths on the frozen waterway, and Londoners, diverted by the rare sight, forgot the danger of the cold to ears, toes and fingers and slid and danced across the slick cold surface.

For weeks there was no fresh fish to be had and the capital's grain stores were depleted. Beggars froze in the streets and the crowds at the palace gates, waiting to receive my abundant alms plus bread and bones, the outscourings of pots from the kitchens and the scrapings from plates, had never been larger. Still, there was a sense of merrymaking in that Christmas season, and I rejoiced most of all, for it was then that my prayers were answered at last and I conceived a child.

A child! A growing life within me, the hope of the realm, as Bridget said happily. ("And about time too," as Ned remarked, though I saw a hint of a smile at the corners of his thin lips.) All my ladies were happy for me, the astrologers were greatly relieved. The birth chamber was made ready and the midwives prepared to move into the palace as soon as my quickening was confirmed.

To say that I was greatly relieved, after months of barrenness— a harsh word that I had heard all too often since our marriage the previous spring—would be to say far too little. I was overjoyed, and not only because I had finally accomplished the thing for which the king had married me, but because I was to have a child of my very own at last. A dear, loving, child of my very own. Even to write the words warms me and gives me great pleasure.

I hardly let myself imagine all that could arise to spoil this lovely prospect. Yet I knew only too well that many babies died, that some never quickened and were lost, and that my own child might possibly turn out to be, not the son Henry avidly sought, but another princess. I tried not to imagine any of these things, and especially not to imagine that my infant might scarcely be a child at all, but a monstrous misshapen thing like Anne's misbegotten son.

With my ladies and maids of honor I sewed and embroidered bed linens and pillows for the baby, listening while we worked to readings from uplifting books and lives of the saints. Month by month I watched my belly swell, slightly at first and then more and more obviously, proud of the signs that I would soon be a mother, proud when the official announcement of my quickening was made to the whole court and the happy news was sent to foreign courts to still the rumors that King Henry was no longer able to father a child.

That my pregnancy was advancing amid hangings and beheadings—the gruesome harvest of the dangerous northern rebellion—saddened me but did not taint my own joyful hopes. My son would rule, in time, as a merciful king, a godly king who would not reign amid rebellion but would preside over a peaceable and prosperous realm. And I would look on in pride and thankfulness.

Such were my daydreams in those months of waiting.

Joining me in my hopeful time was dear Will, whose ever expanding duties and responsibilities now included overseeing the ordering of my household. My faithful Griffith Richards was aging, and ailing; although he remained my devoted gentleman usher he often had to rest and any exertion made him short of breath. He needed help in carrying out his many tasks and Will was appointed to help him.

Obedient to his parents' wishes Will had married a proud, unsmiling woman with a fine figure and handsome features who made no secret of her aversion to me. The marriage was not a happy or harmonious one; Will suffered, and spoke often of what he called his "chafing yoke." When his wife galled him he fled to my apartments and I was always delighted to see him. Even when he was heavy-spirited I was glad to have him nearby, especially when the king was in one of his foul moods or when, as in the aftermath of the rebellion, we quarreled.

Our quarrels were in essence the same quarrel, often repeated. Though I felt certain that my husband's happiness and relief at my pregnancy meant that he valued me greatly, and would never put me aside as he had Catherine and Anne (at least not until my child was born), still there was a strong difference between us that continued to cause strain and anger again and again.

For I, like the northern rebels, clung to the old ways of the church—the religious houses, the time-honored forms of worship, the prayers and deep beliefs that had endured for centuries. I was in no way a daughter of the pope, and I knew only too well that popery meant political danger. Yet I wanted the old ways to continue, while Henry felt smothered by them.

Out with the old! he often said. Old authorities, old customs, outworn superstitious beliefs!

When I so much as hinted that the rebellion might have been sent by God as a warning, as a sign that the destruction of the convents and monasteries was contrary to His will, my husband grew furious.

"Get on with your sewing, Jane, and leave these matters to your betters! Have a care, lest your meddling bring you to grief, as it did Anne!"

When Henry shouted at me, and Will, hearing his shouting, grew grim-faced and resentful, I was comforted. I imagined that I had a champion in Will, a defender. If I should ever need rescue, Will would be at my side.

I confided to Will what Ned had told me about my husband's sharp and at times vicious temper. How Ned had cautioned me that my husband's late father King Henry VII had become so violently angry at times that he had seemed like a madman—that indeed some at his court did think him mad.

"It is a disease, this fury," Ned had said. "It gets worse with age. No doubt your son will inherit it in his turn."

"Never mind," Will reassured me. "I promise you, Jane, I will always be nearby to protect you, should you need me."

This fancy that I might need rescue was, I felt sure, only one of many fancies that came over me as a result of my pregnancy. Nearly all the mothers I knew nodded in agreement when I said this, and shared odd fancies of their own. I became prey to sudden shifts in mood—now lighthearted, now tearful. I had a craving for quinces. I could not abide cats, where before I had always loved them. Most striking of all, I was hungry for quails, and had a fresh supply sent from the countryside every week and stored in the royal larders.

By the middle of September it was time for me to take my chamber, and I withdrew with my ladies to the queen's apartments at Hampton Court, which my husband had ordered refurbished for my delivery.

I would not be honest if I did not admit that I was fearful. Fearful of the pain to come, or that something could go wrong. I sought to clear my mind of fear, to think only of the happy culmination of my hopes. I prayed daily for divine favor.

All was in readiness. My child kicked vigorously and the midwives felt my belly and smiled.

"The people pray daily for a prince," they told me. "The Lord's favor is upon you."

I rested, I dined on my quails, and waited for the pains to come.

When at last I felt a clutching in my belly and an ache in my back it was nothing like what I had expected. I hurt, but not too badly. It was no worse than when I had lifted something too heavy or ridden for too long on an unmanageable horse with an ill-fitting saddle.

I thought, I can endure this.

But within an hour the clutching had turned to a hard clamping pain that left me gasping and the ache in my back was like no other ache I had ever felt. The midwives brought me a posset to soothe me, and put a charm under the bed to draw out the pain, but nothing gave me ease, and I lay suffering all night and into the next day. I grew weak and very weary.

I had thought that Henry, knowing of my suffering, would come to give me strength and comfort but when I sent him a message I was told he had gone to Esher to escape the plague, and that a great many of the household servants had gone as well.

I was terrified then. What if I should become ill with the plague while I was trying so hard to give birth to my child? What if he was born with the plague? What if the midwives deserted me?

I heard men's voices, shouting, insistent voices, coming from another part of the palace.

"Has the king come back from Esher?"

"No, it is Master Dormer."

"Summon him."

"Your Highness knows that no men are allowed in the birth chamber."

"Summon him at once."

The voices grew louder, and I recognized Will's resonant bass. He was causing a commotion.

Dear Will! How overjoyed I was to see him when he all but forced his way in among us, saying he had been sent by the king to see how the queen's pains were progressing.

"Jane!" He came toward me, hearty and smiling, arms outstretched.

His smiling concern gave me renewed vigor. He assured me he would stay with me until the baby arrived, if that was what I wanted.

"All the royal physicians have gone with the king," he told me. "They fear the plague. Cowards!"

I lacked the energy to condemn the physicians. All I wanted was for my ordeal to end. I drowsed between the assaults of pain, and overheard Will talking in low tones to the principal midwife. I could tell that they were talking very seriously, but their words were indistinct. After a time I slept, or so it seemed later, when once again I heard Will's voice.

"Jane, dear, I must talk to you. It can't wait."

I opened my eyes and did my best to attend to what he was saying. "The king is not here to decide what must be done, so you and I must decide together. Shall we?" He took my hand and held it in both of his. I felt his warmth and strength. But I had to fight against the weariness that tugged at me, beclouding my understanding.

I nodded.

"The midwives say they can reach in with their instruments and bring the baby out. They will give you an opiate to help you bear the pain."

Through the fog of my increasing drowsiness I had a vivid memory. I remembered going in to Catherine's birth chamber early in my days at court, and finding her in bed, with an empty cradle beside her. There were no faint cries, no lusty newborn wailing. The baby was nowhere to be seen. Then I remembered catching sight of a bloody bedlinen, and realizing, with horror, that the child had not lived. That dark room with its telltale signs of death had reeked of opium. The opium Catherine had been given for pain. The opium that had killed her child.

If I drank it now, my son would not live. I was certain of it.

"No," I managed to say. "No. I will try again."

"The midwives tell me that you may bleed, Jane. You may bleed until you have no more blood."

I nodded. "Save my child," I whispered. "Save my son."

Will bent down and kissed my cheek.

"Dearest, dearest Jane," he murmured. "Good Queen Jane."

Mercifully, I cannot remember the next few hours, but Will has assured me that my struggle to give birth was a heroic one, and one whose outcome was never certain, right up until the end. He saw to it that I was given no opium and that throughout the evening and the early part of the night there were torchlit vigils in the courtyards of the palace and processions of the faithful praying for me. The scourge of plague lay over the countryside and this, combined with the scant harvest, made everyone expect the worst. Nearly all the midwives, Will told me, had given me up for dead by the time I groaned and strained one last time against the hands that pressed down on my belly and—at last—pushed my child out into the world.

My son.

I wish I could remember that moment, but I cannot. All I

know is that the world had dissolved into a blur of pain and exhaustion and I was lost in a delirium of bad dreams.

When I awoke, hungry and terribly thirsty, daylight had come. My husband was there in the room, looking immensely pleased, and my boy was in his golden cradle beside the bed, and Will stood with Master Cromwell and Ned and a crowd of others, all rosy-faced and full of satisfaction.

"Edward," everyone was repeating. "Prince Edward. Edward the Sixth of that Name that shall be." For it was St. Edward's day, the 12th of October in that year of 1537, and through the goodness of the Lord, England had a prince.

TWENTY-FIVE

I had thought I might end my account when my son was born, and it has taken me four days to feel well enough again to continue my story. But tired though I am, and feeling unwell—the midwives say it will be a month or two before I am fully restored to strength and health—I want to write of my Edward, and of the great delight he has brought me, and of the king's satisfaction and the merrymaking and the rejoicings he has ordered.

First I must say that though my son is quite small, and the physicians peer down into his cradle and murmur to each other that they wish he had more color in his cheeks, he is a sturdy baby and his cries fill my chamber. The wetnurse assures me that he sucks lustily. Already I hear Cromwell telling the men in the outer chamber that there must be another boy, as soon as possible. In case the worst happens, and Edward does not survive. I shudder to hear this. Of course Edward will survive, and I trust there will be a brother for him, in time. Several brothers, and sisters too. But not right away. My ordeal was so painful—and Will says I nearly died. No more babies for a while.

Besides, my Edward is perfect. I love looking at him while he sleeps. His round white cheeks, his sparse tufts of red-brown hair. His long eyelashes. His small rosebud mouth. He has the narrow face and wide-set, slanting eyes of the Seymours. I hope that in time he will have his father's broad-shouldered, muscular athlete's body, though to look at him now you would not imagine he would ever be sturdy enough to joust or run or ride to hounds.

I hope he will be musical, like his father. I try singing to him and I imagine that his eyelids flutter just a little when I begin my lullabies. He slept soundly through the clamor of bells, the shouting of the crowds that greeted the news of his birth, even the great guns that were fired again and again, hour after hour. There are not many guns here at Hampton Court; Ned told me that in London, as soon as word reached the Tower that my son had been born, the great culverins were fired hundreds of times, all through the day and into the following night. Such a salute, he said, had not been heard for a hundred years. Ned is proud indeed of his small nephew, to exaggerate so much.

Yesterday was Edward's christening. I was not present of course, not having been churched and still keeping my chamber. But I heard in great detail from Bridget and Will and Anne Cavecant and others how my little prince remained quiet and composed throughout the long ceremony in the chapel, with his half-sister Mary beside him as his godmother and his other half-sister Elizabeth, just turned four years old, carrying the baptismal cloth. The astrologers were present as well, wearing new gowns presented to them by the king, their smiles of satisfaction very wide—or so I was assured.

How I would have liked to hear my son's titles proclaimed: "Edward, son and heir to the king of England, Duke of Cornwall and Earl of Chester," on and on through a dozen titles and honorifics. It would have given me such pleasure to hear the choir sing and the prayers repeated. And then, as trumpets blew a fanfare and the guns once again boomed forth, to see Edward sanctified and brought into the faith of Our Lord and under His merciful protection and care.

After the christening he was carried back into my chamber in his christening gown and purple robe and laid in my husband's arms, while one by one the officers and other members of our households gave us greetings. Henry had not wanted to allow this small ceremony, as there was still plague at Esher and even in the kitchens and stables, some dozens of our servants had died or been taken ill. But in the end he agreed, and the procession of our faithful servants went on, while the baby slept. Before long I slept too.

When I awoke I found that the preparations for my churching had begun. Mr. Skut had sent baskets of satins in many shades of blue for me to admire and choose from. He is already sewing my churching gown. All my ladies are to have new gowns as well, and new kirtles and headdresses and satin slippers to match. While I drowse, and continue writing this account, my maids are amusing themselves by going through Mr. Skut's baskets and talking of light things, of how the gowns from France are being made narrower now than in past years, and of the jewels the king has ordered for me to wear at my coronation (for now there is talk once again of a coronation, perhaps in a few months).

Ned is to be made Earl of Hertford, a great honor. My husband has already made him a rich man, but now his wealth will be far greater, with lands and manors in nine counties and income from hundreds of tenant farms. He is very grand in his fine new robes and feathered hats. But he does not give himself airs, and I believe he gives my husband good counsel.

Tomorrow morning I must allow my maids to dress me in a gown of fine red velvet trimmed in miniver and accompany me to the presence chamber where I will receive the congratulations of all the dignitaries and ambassadors, the nobles and townspeople, even the children from the surrounding villages bringing sheaves of wheat to honor me and my son. I hope I have the strength to receive their good wishes, for there will be a great many people and it will take a long time to acknowledge them all. Will has promised to stay nearby, and Griffith Richards as well. My husband has been so busy ordering banquets and jousts, feasting for the Londoners and a grand pageant of welcome for baby Edward that I have seen little of him. I do not expect him to be with me tomorrow. He must show himself in all the villages from here to Richmond, for there is a rumor that he has died and in order to squelch it he must let the people see him.

In truth I feel relief that he will not be present with me, for he can be trying at times, and I am feeling queasy today and have had a discharge. The physicians say this is good, that I am purging the bad humors from my blood. I began feeling ill after eating a plate of quails and drinking malmsey wine. The wine was strong, and the quails, I must admit, had a curious sour taste, they did not taste the way good quails normally do when prepared correctly and eaten soon after being killed and cleaned.

I said nothing at the time, to be sure. I did not want to offend Lady Lisle who had sent the quails all the way from Calais. I remember wondering whether the ship that brought them had been delayed, by bad weather or a need to wait for some important passenger to reach the harbor. Ships are often delayed in making their crossings. And if they had food aboard, the food spoils.

I cannot help clutching at my stomach as I write these words. I am surely ill, and it is because of the quails. I must purge myself . . .

Queen Jane ceased writing her account on the night she suffered a bloody flux and had to be put to bed. She asked me to keep writing in her book, recording all that was happening in those first days after the prince was born. She said I should write just until she was well enough to resume writing herself. She trusted me to put down everything that happened. To tell the truth. Which is what I will do.

The truth was, my dear Jane was not well cared for. She overtaxed herself, and there was no one to restrain her. I did my best, but I was not her husband. (Lord forgive me, I wish I had been!) All I could do was stay nearby and make everything as easy for her as I was able.

I knew she should never have spent that long, endless day receiving the well wishers, sitting until she was stiff and exhausted in the high-backed chair with no cushions to ease her. I could tell how tiring it was for her, smiling and returning everyone's greetings with her kind welcoming smile for hours on end. She hid her exhaustion well, and her hunger also, though she told me later that she had felt not only a pain in her stomach but a sharp clutching in her bowels. She said she felt as if an iron hand gripped her, and squeezed her without mercy, and would not let her go.

She was ill, and no one physicked her. That night she hardly slept, she was so ill. A messenger was sent to the king but he did not come right away. He could not, for the false story that he had died of plague was spreading and he had to make certain his people saw him and knew the rumor was not true. He feared that if his subjects in the north country believed he was dead, they might rebel once again.

It was two whole days before King Henry came to Jane's side, and then he did not stay long. He saw that she was weak and hot with fever, and I saw him turn his face away and call for the prince. He took Edward in his arms and showed him off to us all. He delighted in the boy. But he could not bear to look at Jane, for he saw death in her eyes. I am sure he did. And having seen it, he handed the prince to the wetnurse and hurried away to the hunt.

I shouted at the midwives but all they did was to give poor Jane a posset of opium. "It will bring on the sweat trance," they said. But I knew the posset did no good. Nor did the charms they brought to put under her pillow, or the sprigs of dried lavender they hung over the bed to soothe her spirits.

If prayers could have saved her, then she would surely have survived, for not only was everyone in her household praying but there were prayers and processions every day by the local people for the healing of Good Queen Jane. Her confessor was near at hand, and he heard her confess her sins and ask for forgiveness. But she was deluded, confused in mind. The fever was making her imagine things. She thought that she had committed fearful sins, and wept from guilt. I did my best to console her, but she gripped my hand tightly and I saw such terror in her eyes that I was beside myself with concern. I did not want her to suffer in mind as she was suffering in her thin, shivering body.

The only thing that seemed to bring her comfort was the sight of the prince, who was laid in her arms for a few minutes at a time. Her face grew soft at the sight of him, and her worries and terrors seemed to lift.

I will not write much of the last days, when her body leaked its discharges freely and her sweet face was creased with deep lines of pain. The king stomped in and out of the room, saying he would go to Esher to hunt, whether the queen was improved or not. His blustering was meant to hide his fear. In truth he did not want to watch Jane die. And he knew that I would stay with her to the end. We did not speak of this, but I am sure he knew.

We heard the royal hunting party ride off very early in the morning, long before dawn, on the twelfth day after Edward was born. Within the hour Jane's confessor was once again at her bedside, anointing her with the oil meant to sanctify the dying. I could not bear to watch. I was too weary and too filled with sorrow. When I came back into the room later, I saw that she was alone. The priest, the confessor and even the midwives had gone. She was asking for water and I held a cup to her dry lips.

Through my tears I looked down at her, her white face glowing faintly in the candlelight, and despite all, I thought her lovely. I told her so, and saw the merest smile on her pale lips.

"Galyon," she said. "My Galyon. My love."

"Jane! It is Will, Jane!"

But she looked past me, her eyes fixed on something or someone I could not see. Her poor mind was full of fancies.

I knew I could no longer reach her with my words, but I imagined that the sound of my voice might soothe her. So I talked to her a little, of how different our lives would have been had we gone aboard the *Eglantine,* and sailed off to the Spice Islands, and lived in a paradise far from everything we had ever known.

"How much easier it would all have been, dearest Jane," I said, holding her hand and kissing it. She gripped my hand, and I thought, for a moment, that I saw recognition in her eyes. But then her fingers grew limp, and her eyes were closed, and I knew that she had gone on alone.

* * *

My Jane, Good Queen Jane, died on the twenty-fifth of October in the year of Our Lord 1537, a year of dearth but many wildflowers, a year of great sadness for me. I suppose it must have been a year of sadness for our sovereign King Henry also, but he wore no mourning for Jane, and hid his grieving well. And before even a week had passed he was sending out his ambassadors to France and the Low Countries and even to faroff Cleves, searching for a new wife, and boasting that he knew of at least nine ladies who would be honored to share his bed and his throne.

It was left to me to keep my vigil by her tomb, and do honor to her memory as best I can, and to vow that as her son grows, I will tell him the story of his mother as I know it. I will not fail you, Jane. I promise. I will do my best.

NOTE TO THE READER

Once again, dear reader, a caution and a reminder: *The Favored Queen* is a historical entertainment, in which the authentic past and imaginative invention intertwine. Fictional events and circumstances, fictional characters and whimsical alterations of events and personalities are blended. Fresh interpretations of historical figures and their circumstances are offered, and traditional ones laid aside. I hope you have enjoyed this re-imagining of the past.

1. What do you think it was that drew King Henry to Jane Seymour and led him to make her his third wife? Was it simply a desire for a wife less temperamental and imperious than Anne Boleyn, and likely to give him a healthy son?

2. King Henry came to believe, when married to Anne Boleyn, that she had cast a spell on him to induce him to marry her. Doesn't infatuation always cast its own spell?

3. Some of Jane Seymour's contemporaries described her as "full of goodness." In your own reading, have you found novels about "good" women of the past to be less compelling than those about disreputable women or villainesses?

4. From what you know of Tudor history, do you imagine that King Henry's marriage to Jane Seymour was the happiest of his six marriages? Do you think it is significant that when Henry died, his remains were placed in a single tomb with Jane's so that they would be united in death?

5. What do you think Jane would have thought of Henry VIII's image in popular culture as a royal Bluebeard who bullied and mistreated his wives and ordered the executions of two of them? Would you agree with the sardonic Victorian writer who suggested that the plainness of Henry's queens was, "if not a justification," at least a credible reason for his willingness to discard them?

6. How would the course of English history have changed if Anne Boleyn had died of the sweating sickness in 1528 instead of surviving to marry the king? Or would it have made little difference?

7. Many of Jane Seymour's contemporaries believed that the end of the world was at hand. Why do you imagine that each generation seems to find so much destruction, confusion, and hazardous mayhem in human society that a future of any sort appears unlikely? Why are prophecies of doom so compelling?

8. In *The Favored Queen*, Jane Seymour idolizes King Henry's first wife, Catherine of Aragon, as "a model of courtesy and charity," who had "played her thankless role with uncommon grace." Yet it was rumored that Catherine was poisoned by her enemies at court. What was your opinion of Catherine?

9. Have you thought of writing a historical novel or entertainment about any person from the past? If so, who?

Turn the page for a sneak peek at
Carolly Erickson's new novel

THE UNFAITHFUL QUEEN

Available September 2012

ONE

Tower Green
May 1536

THE new-mown grass smelled sweet as we took our places along the verge on that grey dawn, all of us together, waiting for my cousin Anne to be brought out to die.

Though the spring was well advanced there was a chill in the air, and I shivered under my thin Spanish cloak. I drew nearer to my aunts and my grandmother Agnes, sidling up against her long bony body swathed in a gown of watchet blue under her warm woolen ermine-trimmed mantle. She did not look at me, but stood very still, her back very straight, her crimsoned cheeks wrinkled, her lips widened in a half smile. My grandma had once been handsome, so it was said, but her youth was long past and no finery, no amount of paint on her sallow cheeks, could disguise the marks of age. She was said to be the richest woman in England, and one of the most fearsome.

I drew nearer to her now, as the sun began to rise and the first crimson streaks blazed along the horizon. The hour was nearly at hand. The faces of the relatives all around me were growing tighter, aunts and uncles and cousins, ancient great-aunts whose names I barely knew, aged great-uncles who, I had been told, had fought alongside my late grandfather in the long wars that had brought him fame.

At the center of the crowded nest of relatives was my uncle Thomas, third Duke of Norfolk, the head of our family. He stood slightly apart from the rest of us, feet planted firmly, his dark face with its hooded eyes grim, his mouth set in a firm line. His elaborate padded and slashed doublet of quilted yellow silk made him stand out from among the growing number of spectators gathering to watch the dread spectacle to come.

"Get on with it then," we who were closest to him heard him mutter. "Kill the big whore!"

Birds began twittering and chirping as the sky lightened. They swooped in and out of chinks and crannies in the great blocks of grey stone in the ancient tower walls. I watched them, fluttering and flapping their small wings, glad for a chance to be distracted by something other than the grisly business to come. I tried to forget that my cousin Anne, many years older than I and Queen of England, was to die this morning.

I had never seen anyone die by the sword. I did not want to watch. I shrank back among the others, glad for once that I was so small (at fifteen years old, I was a full head shorter than other girls my age), that I could not see over the heads of those in front of me. I could barely glimpse the raised platform, draped in black, with its thick block of wood, the guardsmen in royal livery who stood around it, the tall halberdiers with their sharp-bladed, long-handled hatchets that glinted in the sunlight.

For what seemed an hour or more we stood, weary of waiting, while the crowd grew larger and larger and the sun rose higher.

"Remember, she is not one of us!" my grandmother hissed. "She has betrayed the family! She has betrayed the Howard name! Take warning from her fate!"

Her words unleashed more accusations. Terrible accusations, from those standing near me. I heard someone say that Anne had had many lovers, that every night when she went to bed she had men lined up, ready to do her bidding. Even her brother George!

How could such things be said, I wondered. How could my cousin have so dishonored our Howard lineage? Unless she was mad, or possessed by a demon.

"Do you think she was possessed by a demon?" I whispered to my cousin Charyn, who stood near me, looking remarkably calm and self-possessed, not a single blond hair out of place under her dark headdress, her cloak lifting in the slight breeze, her gloved hands folded in front of her.

"The demon of lust, most likely," was Charyn's prompt reply.

Charyn was seventeen, much taller than I was and much prettier. Her hair curled naturally and seemed to flow without tangles, even on the windiest day. Her grey eyes were never troubled or filled with confusion, as mine so often were. When she spoke, her words were few and crisp and telling, and she always seemed to know just what to say. She would not believe in demons. She was sensible and practical, not easily led astray by gossip.

"He might have burned her, like a heretic," another soft female voice reached me. "But he couldn't. He still loves her."

There was more hushed talk—of the swordsman brought from Calais many weeks before our cousin Anne's trial and condemnation. The swordsman whose sole purpose was to carry out executions.

"He was planning it all along," I heard a man say. "He wanted to be rid of her. He had tired of her. And she was cursed—she couldn't give him a son. So he hired the French executioner. He hired him months ago. He paid him twenty-three pounds!" There were exclamations at this. Twenty-three pounds was a great deal of money, enough to buy several estates.

"Is it true she sent her gold bracelets to her old nurse and rocker, as a last keepsake?"

"She promised to marry Norris, her favorite lover," one daring voice murmured. "She was going to kill the king and then marry him."

"Don't say such a thing—or you will die too!"

The babble of voices, the tramp of soldiers' boots—then the gasps when Anne was brought out and helped to go up the steps to where the block was waiting.

Her step was brisk, lively. There was no heaviness about her. Once again I thought, she is mad, she has gone mad. She does not feel the pangs of her approaching death. Or is she relieved that she is not to suffer the agonies of death by fire?

I felt Charyn take my hand. She had taken off her glove. Her hand was cold in my warmer one.

Some in the crowd were kneeling. I heard sighs. People were drying their eyes. My uncle the duke was frowning.

"She deserves to die!" he was saying through clenched teeth. "She must suffer for her treasons!" We all knew that he had been the one to preside over the group of peers that had condemned Anne. Anne—the favorite child of his favorite sister Elizabeth.

I could see her clearly now, my view was no longer blocked by the capes and mantles of those in front of me. So many of those around me had begun to kneel—though my grandmother continued to stand rigidly in place, and as far as I could tell, none of my Howard relations appeared to be preparing to kneel. Not a knee was buckling. Charyn was trembling, but she stood.

The Lord Mayor and aldermen, solemn-faced in their black robes, watched impassively as the tall, brawny dark-haired Frenchman, his heavy broadsword drawn from its wide leather scabbard, climbed the steps to stand behind Anne. Compared to him, she looked very small. She kept turning her head to see him, to see what he was doing.

I felt Charyn squeeze my hand, her nails biting into my palm, and for the first time my stomach lurched with fear. I lowered my head. I did not want to see this.

Anne stepped forward. Her voice was strong as she asked for prayers. She did not confess her guilt. Rather she swore, on the host, that she was innocent. I was certain I saw her smile. Was she thinking of her daughter, I wondered, in those last few moments of life left to her? Her one child, Elizabeth, the child who the king had hoped would be a prince. Her legacy.

Once again she looked behind her. The swordsman was waiting. The women in attendance on her unfastened her ermine mantle and waited while she took off her headdress and covered her hair with a linen cap.

Did I only imagine that at that moment a cloud covered the sun and the sky darkened? Afterwards I could not remember clearly. I know that I looked in vain for a chaplain. Was there to be no chaplain, to say a prayer with Anne, or read words of forgiveness from the Bible? Was Anne to be denied these final comforts?

She murmured a few words to each of her attendants, no doubt wishing them well, and all but one received her last words with tearful thanks. Then she knelt. She knelt upright. She had no need to put her head on the block, for the swordsman's blade slashed sideways, not downward.

Charyn fainted. I looked down at her. And at that moment I heard the horrible sound: a swishing in the air, a crunching, cries of fright and alarm. Looking up, I saw Anne's twitching body, a rush of blood staining her grey gown deep red, her attendants wrapping something in a reddening cloth.

I could hardly breathe. I staggered. For a brief time everything around me seemed to blur, then my vision cleared and I began to catch my breath again. I saw that Charyn was being helped to her feet. The sky was lightening—or had it ever really gone dark?

The high grey stone walls still loomed, the birds, heedless of the drama below them, continued to soar and plunge, and then to rise, wings flapping, up into the sunny sky.

*   *   *

I never knew what I might find when I went upstairs, into the room we called the Paradise Chamber, the cold, drafty, barnlike room with the lofty ceiling where we girls spent our days and nights when not attending to our duties or our lessons.

When I first arrived at Horsham it was all I could do not to think of the Paradise Chamber as not a paradise at all but rather a sort of dungeon, a place of no escape where we girls were locked in at night and watched by our jailers. We each had a small bed, with a thin mattress and a blanket, but bedwarmers were few, and my feet were always cold at night. The Paradise Chamber was drafty, and the beds farthest from the single hearth got little heat. At the foot of each bed was a trunk that held our clothing and other possessions. Some of the girls hid things underneath their mattresses but as the mattresses were full of fleas nothing of value could be kept there, except coins, and no one dared to put coins under their mattress because everyone knew that was where they were likely to be hidden.

Nights in the Paradise Chamber were full of discomforts. We were awakened by the barking of the watchdogs in the courtyard, or by the moans and coughs of the sick girls among us, or by the cries of others awakened by nightmares.

Some girls wept. One night not long after I arrived at Horsham I was awakened by the sound of sobbing from a bed near mine. The fire in the hearth had burned low and the few candles in the room gave little light, but when I sat up and looked for the source of the sobbing I quickly realized that it was coming from the bed directly across the room from mine. The bed where Alice Restvold slept. Like nearly all the girls in the room, Alice was a distant relation of mine, a few years older than I was, a red-headed girl with a pinched face and large staring blue eyes.

The noise of her sobbing and sniffing annoyed me, I did not like being awakened. But at the same time I was curious to know what was causing her such distress. I got out of bed and, taking a candle, went to her.

"Alice!" I whispered. "What is it, Alice?"

"He—has—gone away," she managed to say.

"Who has gone away?"

"My John."

"He is—your betrothed?

"No!"

"Then who is he?"

"My—beloved!"

Her beloved, I thought. But not her betrothed. I had never known love, but I had seen it, often. I had seen lovers walking hand in hand, lying together in the warm wet grass on May Day, exchanging glances in church or at table—even embracing in darkened hallways. Father Dawes lectured us sternly about lust, the devil's temptation of the flesh, but young as I was, I knew that love was a thing apart, nobler far than lust. A treasure to be cherished. I did not yet understand how the two can be entangled, how confusing the urges and pleasures of the body can be.

"Why would your beloved ever leave you?" I whispered to Alice.

But my question only made her sob more freely and more loudly. Several of the other girls tossed irritably in their beds and tried to shush her.

"She's at it again!" I heard one of them say. "Why can't she just forget him! He's gone!"

Presently I heard a disturbance behind me and in a moment another girl had come up to Alice's bed. A girl I didn't recognize. In the dim light I could tell only that she had long dark hair, loosely braided, and that she wore around her shoulders a thick woolen shawl embroidered in a pattern of deep blue and sparkling silver.

"Stop that noise, foolish chit!" the newcomer said tartly. "You're keeping us all awake!" She did not bother to keep her own voice low, but barked out her words as she reached swiftly under the blanket and took Alice by the hand.

"Come with me!" she said. "I'll give you something to put you to sleep, so we can all sleep through the night." And pulling the weeping Alice out of bed she fairly dragged her to a door at the opposite end of the long room and, taking a key that she wore around her neck, unlocked the door.

"You may as well come along," she said to me as she pulled Alice through the door after her.

We were in a small chamber furnished with two beds, a chest and a low table. It had a sloping roof and a little barred window, beneath which was a brazier full of red coals. The room smelled of smoke and of something else, something heavy and sweet. A scent I had never smelled before.

"You are both new to this house," the girl with the braid said. "You are Catherine, whose mother no one mentions because she was the king's whore. And you are the sniveling Alice, whose lover has married another."

"What?" The shock of the girl's words made Alice stop crying. "What did you say?"

"I said your lover, John Brockley, the gentleman usher, has married another woman. He never told you he was betrothed, did he."

Alice, her eyes wide, shook her head.

"What other woman?"

The girl with the braid went to the wardrobe and began pouring what looked like wine into a goblet. To this she added powder from a jar and stirred the concoction.

"It matters not. When next you see him, he will have a wife."

She handed the goblet to Alice.

"Here. Drink this."

Alice sniffed the liquid, made a sour face, then looked at us. She flinched, but obeyed and drank the liquid in a single gulp. When she finished she wiped her mouth with the back of her hand—something we were admonished never to do—and handed the goblet back.

I stood watching, somewhat dazed.

"Who are you?" I asked the girl with the braid. "And how dare you speak ill of my mother?"

She regarded me coolly. "I am Joan. My father is William Bulmer, Lord Mannering. And everyone in this household knows about your mother, the ill-famed Lady Jocasta."

Alice was staring at me.

"My mother was beautiful. Others were envious of her beauty, and so they defamed her."

Joan smiled. "If you like," she said. "The truth is known, whatever you may say. And besides, she is long dead."

I needed no reminder that my mother had been laid to rest long before, when I was a very small child, barely old enough to remember her. My memory of her was of a great sadness, of something warm and loving that had suddenly vanished from my life, leaving only sorrow behind.

"You guard your tongue about my mother, Joan Bulmer! Or I will whip you!"

"Indeed? I would not advise it. The last girl who struck me was found much bruised and broken, beside the malt-house door."

The menace in her tone made me wary. I knew little of the

workings of my grandmother's large household, but I was aware that every large noble household had its share of ruffians, its cliques, its back-stairs brawls. It had been that way in my father's much smaller establishment. Things went on behind the backs of the stewards—deeds that were never brought to light. Sometimes quite violent deeds. Until I knew more about the ways of my grandmother's establishment I would not provoke this brazen girl further.

But before I could decide how to reply, or what to do, I saw that Alice was slipping down in a faint. To my surprise, Joan reached down and tried to pick her up.

"Help me," she said, and together we lifted Alice onto one of the small room's two beds. She lay there, still and pale, her eyes closed. Frowning, Joan picked up a candle and held it close to Alice's white face.

"Has she been spewing?" she asked me.

"I don't know."

She set the candle back down and felt Alice's stomach and belly, making her moan.

I heard Joan swear under her breath.

"By the bones of Christ, not another one!"

I looked at Joan questioningly, our quarrel and clashing words for the moment forgotten.

"These girls! These rich, protected girls, who know nothing of the world, who come here to this lustpit of a house, and get themselves with child, and then—"

"She's carrying a child? Are you sure?"

Joan gave me a withering look, then slapped Alice's cheek. "Wake up girl!"

Alice protested, pushing Joan away feebly with one hand.

"Don't hurt her!" I objected.

"Hurt her? I'm helping her! I'm going to help her get rid of this unwanted encumbrance! Before we all are whipped till our backs are raw!"

What I was seeing and hearing confused me. This forceful, unsparing girl Joan, with her threats and her slaps and her insult to my mother's memory, seemed to be saying that Alice's disgrace reflected on us all. That we were living in what she called a pit of lust, not a noble household—my grandmother's noble household. How could she say such a thing? And how could she be certain that Alice was carrying a child?

As the night wore on, my confusion lessened. At Joan's insistence ("Do you really want the wrath of the old duchess to come down on all our heads?" she demanded) I stayed on in the small room while Joan administered another drink to the drowsy Alice. This one took longer to make, and smelled so foul that I thought I would retch. The stench of it filled the room.

Poor Alice admitted that she had not had her monthly flux for many weeks and that she had often been sick, that whatever she ate would not stay in her stomach.

"Did no one ever tell you that if you let a man have his pleasure with you there would be a child? Did no one ever show you what to do to make sure no child would be born?"

Alice shook her head.

"Then I will tell you." With a sigh Joan went to the wardrobe and brought out a lemon, which she cut in half.

"Here," she said, handing one of the halves to Alice. "Take this and put it inside you."

Alice, groggy from the drinks she had been given, stared at Joan, incomprehending.

"Stupid girl!" Joan spat out. Then, taking the other half of the lemon, she lifted her skirts, spread her legs, and packed the dripping fruit up into her honeypot.

So quickly did she do this that I hardly had time to be surprised. Alice, after fumbling a bit, managed to imitate her.

"Do this whenever you are with a lover. If you have no lemons, use a bit of sponge. Dip it in vinegar first. Or if you have no vinegar, dip it in sour milk."

"How do you know this? How can you be sure it will work?" I wanted to know. "You are no midwife or wise woman."

"I know," Joan responded, "because I have lain with boys and men since I was younger than you, and I am eighteen now, and I have never yet been with child. I learned what I know from other girls, of course. Older girls. How else?"

She looked over at Alice, who was holding her stomach with both hands.

"She's going to need the chamber pot," Joan told me. "Don't be alarmed. The drink I gave her—the second one—was very strong. The juice of tansy and pennyroyal. It will cause her to expel her child. The pain will be great, but it will not last long."

Alice was doubled over, grimacing and moaning. She squatted over the chamber pot to relieve herself but could only grunt and emit little shrieks. Her forehead shone with perspiration. She reached for my hand, and when I offered it, she squeezed it so hard it hurt.

"Help me," she whispered, then let out a piteous moan.

What happened over the next hour is best left unrecorded, except to write that when Alice's pain was finally past, she was no longer carrying her lover's child. And I, having witnessed her suffering, and done my best to help her through it with soothing words and encouragement, was left exhausted and in need of rest.

But the lessons of that long night stayed with me. If, as Joan Bulmer said, we were living in a lustpit, then I was determined to avoid its pitfalls. I had no lover, but I vowed that, should a lover come to me, I would keep plenty of lemons nearby, and would be wary and prudent in making use of them. I did not yet know how perilous the ways of love could be, and how even the most prudent of girls could fall prey to its perplexing tangles.